Stories of the Sky-God

Spider's Web of Fiction and Drama

Stories of the Sky-God

robert reid

Spider's Web
of Fiction and Drama

Red Hen Press
2007

Stories of the Sky-God: Spider's Web of Fiction and Drama

Copyright © 2007 by Robert Reid

ALL RIGHTS RESERVED

No part of this book may be used or reproduced in any manner whatsoever without the prior written permission of both the publisher and the copyright owner.

Cover art: "Untitled" (aka "Philosopher's Study") by Jerry Uelsmann

Cover design: Olga Vaynkof

ISBN: 1-59709-003-4
ISBN-13: 978-1-59709-003-2
Library of Congress Catalog Card Number: 2005929665

Published by Red Hen Press

The City of Los Angeles Cultural Affairs Department, California Arts Council, Los Angeles County Arts Commission and National Endowment for the Arts partially support Red Hen Press.

First edition

Contents

THE STORIES

Thaddeus	3
Rock Garden	8
Liberation	12
Independence Day	16
Self-Service	27
The Contract	33
Wheels and Miracles	38
The Gate	46
Princess of Darkness	49
The Black Orchid	52
Stainless Steel	55
Cat and Garbage	61
Thread of Light	67
China Doll	76
The Bedraggled Dead	88
Fairy Tales	92
Flight 801 in the Heart of Guam USA	97

THE PLAYS

The Recommendation: A Play in One Act	105
In the Stillness of the Midnight: A Play in One Act	116
Hellas and Death: A Morality Play	126
The Compound	134

Thaddeus

THE TITLE COMES FROM AFRICAN and Native American folktales, the Spider-Ananse cycle of the Ashanti, "How Spider Obtained the Sky-God's Stories," and Spider Woman in Pueblo Indian mythology. Spider Woman and her sisters, thinking, create the World from the human perspective. Spider-Ananse obtains the stories that create the human world via a wager with the Sky-God. Money cannot buy the stories. Human power cannot buy the stories; but Spider, a masterless man, beguiles dangerous animals and, with his imagination, wins possession of the stories that are symbolic of the imaginative power of the gods and creates the humane world.

The stories and plays of *Stories of the Sky-God* occur in the past, present and future of the human world. These stories and plays have a blues theme and the tellers of the tales are 'trickster transformers,' transforming an unacceptable reality of death and separation into tragedy and comedy.

The stories start in the future with "Thaddeus." "The Rock Garden" goes further into the future. "Liberation" takes us back in time in order to go forward. "The Contract" starts our trip forward; and "Wheels and Miracles" continues our journey from past to present and on into future.

The plays take us full circle, starting with the events of the recent past with the absurd tragicomedy of "The Recommendation," and ending with the bizarre tragicomedy of "The Compound" which takes us back into the future and the beginning of this anthology.

Stories of the Sky-God

Spider's Web of Fiction and Drama

The Stories

Thaddeus

THE SUN IS WARM on the back of my neck. Taylor sits, without moving, on the porch. He's been sitting there since this morning, and now the afternoon sun soaks into his black hat. He doesn't notice that the shade left that side of the house two hours ago. The only sign his body gives of the heat is the wet fringe of hair where the hat band ends. From inside the house, I hear Zelma moaning. They're digging the grave in the front yard behind me.

I wonder what people will think a hundred years from now when they pass this yard and see that grave. Foster says some day we'll be able to come and go as we want. The border guards won't be here any more to kill us; and Kansas City, Kansas will just be another part of a much bigger place, the way it used to be. When I go with him up Wyandotte Street to get the granite for the grave markers, he tells me about how they lived in the old days. Foster's hair is white and his face is the color of the granite that he chips to make the grave markers. He runs his fingers through his wiry hair as we stand inside the barn that used to be a warehouse. The sun, seeping through a crack next to the one boarded-up window, marks the air and the floor. Dust floats lazily in the ray of light, making the illusion of peaceful life and movement. A chicken cackles, and the pig, just now noticing us, squeals and comes loping from behind a stack of hay bales. "The people used to work in the factories over in Lenexa," he says. "They'd go there days and work as assemblers. We even used to have some tool and die makers over there. We had old cars and some of the skilled workers even had new trucks. Back then, the people went over into Missouri and the other counties in Kansas to work. The trouble started in Kansas. Those were the wealthiest Howlies. First, they made sure we left their towns as soon as the factories closed. Then, we began to get on their nerves just passing through. The town fathers said it didn't look good for visitors to see our old cars junking up the freeways, and sometimes when one would break down, a policeman would see it before we could get our friend and his car off the freeway. Our friend would be arrested, his old car impounded and turned to junk to pay for their trouble. In the jail, the police always beat the people and sometimes killed us." He studies the pieces of granite, looking for one that he can turn into a grave marker. "You can imagine how the people felt about that, and the Howlies began to talk about how we didn't appreciate the work they provided for us. Said we were not only bad workers, but had become a threat. They closed the factories and moved them to other places. Like now, everything started coming into their airports by plane, and if we were caught in their towns things became even worse for us." Foster picks a piece of granite and rubs the shiny side. It had been honed and polished some time in the distant past. The name "Lillian Washington 1995–" is carved on it with the date of her death left off. Washington is Foster's name. I can see his eyes fill up and he wipes them with the rag. "She disappeared during the time that the Howlies were still coming into Kansas City. They would come down here in the daytime at first, to get things that they couldn't have in their towns. Then they started kidnapping little girls between the ages of eleven and fifteen. Someone came and took pictures of them on their way home from school, and later, thugs would come and kidnap them. The people began to kill any Howlies that crossed into our section of town. Life was over then. That was when the helicopters started flying over and soldiers strafed the streets." He picks up the two hundred pound block of granite, his arms bulging, and rests it on his shoulder. "Check the door, Henry," he says. I push back the bolts on the warehouse door and crack it open. I look up and down the street to make sure nobody sees us and will know that we have stuff in here.

It's almost dark now and Taylor hasn't moved. I can see two coal oil lamps lit at each end of the coolin' board, inside the house. Thaddeus is wrapped in a winding cloth. I can see the imprints of the parts of his body, and I see his face looming into view as if yesterday was now.

Thaddeus is tall and blond. Zelma found him seven years before I was born. She said he was four years old, walking down 52nd Street as if he was on a mission. He walked past her and instinctively, she realized that he was alone and had been for some time. His curly blond hair was dirty and he was barefoot in October. "Thaddeus," she said, naming him the most obscure of the twelve disciples.

Thaddeus is dressed in the border guard uniform that Taylor brought home late one night. It fits him, and Thaddeus is the only one of us that can pass for a border guard. He's over six feet tall with blond hair and blue eyes, and unlike the rest of us, he's not missing any parts, like fingers, teeth, or an arm, that would identify him as one of the people. Zelma took good care of him when he was a kid, and he's quick. In a fight, he never gets hurt and he's made more trips across the border than were ever made before he started.

"Henry," he says, and I put down my book. "Go get dressed. I need somebody to go with me this time." He smiles. Damn! He's been teaching me to fight with my hands and feet. I can even fight with a gun and a knife. Now I get to go over into Lenexa, maybe even Mission. There may be a library over there where I can get more books. I've read the last one he brought me five times already.

Thaddeus is going over the maps that Foster makes from memory and that Thaddeus updates when he returns from his trips across the border. Taylor hands Thaddeus the new border guard ID's that he makes up each trip. "Be careful," he says and grips Thaddeus' shoulder.

"How can we lose?" Thaddeus says; and he turns to me, smiling. I smile back, trying not to be too enthusiastic, imitating his smile. "What I miss, little brother will see."

I ride behind him on the Harley Davidson motorcycle that came with the border guard uniform, my hand just above the Smith and Wesson .38 on Thaddeus' hip. The further south we go, the more houses are still standing, but they're empty. I'm watching for other border guards and thinking of Thaddeus and myself as the police class, because that's important. Thaddeus says that people think about you exactly what you think about yourself. Our survival depends on our imagination and our ability to act. "Lie and believe your own lies," he says, and I can tell by the way Thaddeus straddles the Harley like the power between his legs is alive and invincible that he *is* a border guard. He doesn't even appear to be looking around. He'd better be one if anybody sees us.

I'm amazed at the difference as we enter Lenexa. There are crowds of people everywhere. The streets and the shop windows are alive and noisy. Electricity isn't historical here. I notice as we cross 95th Street on Kenwood Avenue that the lights have pictures on them, telling us when to wait and when to walk. Thaddeus tells me that the Howlies don't read like we do, that they've become so accustomed to pictures that their language is a kind of pictograph. He says they respond to the sights, smells, sounds, and tastes that they've been programmed with. "That's important to know," he says. We are standing in an electronics store, watching a movie on a giant screen. Gigantic blond border guards are subduing and killing a rabid crowd of the people. A particularly ugly and deformed leader of the people is trying to kidnap the wife of the captain of the guards, but the guards and the captain overcome the mob, first with laser guns and then hand-to-hand combat when the numbers are almost equal. Of course, the snarling demon from hell fights dirty, and surprises everyone by snatching the eleven year old daughter of the captain. They cannot conceive of such evil. The daughter puts up a superhuman struggle, frees herself and the next thirty minutes is devoted to the bloody battle to rid the world of these demons from hell.

From here we go to the library. Our last stop will be the gun shop. Thaddeus tells me that there used to be bookstores, but no one reads anymore. The libraries are museums where a few aging media professors still go to read about propaganda, marketing and formula drama before laser disk.

The white haired ancient at the guard station recognizes his superior in uniform and salutes without requesting identification. Thaddeus casually returns the salute; and we enter the STACKS. That's where the books are shelved. Thaddeus goes immediately to fiction. I pick out McNickle who writes about the people in the early days. Thaddeus uses his ID to check out the book, casually mentioning to the flirting young Howlie behind the desk that the book is for the guard researcher, and telling her that it's about ancient warfare. She smiles warmly and says, "I didn't think someone as handsome as you would be reading." They both laugh at the idea. She punches the picture of a book on her computer key, then she scans the bar code on the spine of the book, and we're on our way to the gun shop.

I'm a bit worried about being both related to him and carrying a book. He just laughs, saying they've probably never even seen one. Then it happens. We've both relaxed into the situation. He's a handsome guard and I'm his nephew. What could be simpler? We aren't even to the gun shop when a Howlie pulls up beside us, riding in a limousine, and asks Thaddeus to get in. Thaddeus explains that he's on duty, and when the Howlie shouts, "Do you know who you're talking to?" Thaddeus turns to me and says, "Take the Harley and go home." I did.

That was the last time I saw Thaddeus alive. Taylor heard the car in the night, and looked out in time to see the limousine driver dump Thaddeus' body onto the front lawn. He won't tell me how they killed him.

Taylor is kneeling by the body. Zelma kneels at the feet, and Foster kneels by the other side. I stand at the head of the coolin' board, telling Thaddeus goodbye. I keep thinking he might have gotten away if it hadn't been for me, and Taylor reminds me that I have the talent to take his place. One of us must live.

We pick up the body on the board, carry it into the front yard and lower it into the grave with ropes. Foster puts a tin box at his feet. I put his journal in the box, his obituary and some life history that I have written. Zelma puts in the few pieces of jewelry, his watch, a toy train and the picture of his first girlfriend, now buried somewhere else. We promise that someone will come back and get him one day. Taylor lays his own black hat on top of Thaddeus; and we shovel in the dirt.

Early Sunday morning, we catch the southbound train at Union Station. I change my name to Thaddeus and carry in my mind all our conversations and our stories.

The Rock Garden

Fargo watched them come through the gates of the walled city. The large black motor wagon that his grandfather had called a hearse led a long parade of black motor cars. They would take the box covered with flowers to what he called the rock garden, bury it and cry, as his small sister cried when she was hungry. They wore black and wept incessantly. He wondered if they were hungry.

The guards that would kill children who came too close to the parade must not have been hungry. They did not cry. Last year, he had seen a small boy, attracted by the flowers, break through the bushes and run toward the large motor wagon. He turned red, almost immediately, from the machines that the guards carried. That angered Fargo. He felt that mothers should watch their children.

Fargo's father, angered by Fargo's disgust with the mother, called him a fool and told him to mind his own business. Saying it was a good lesson for all of them. Something about "curiosity killed the cat." These phrases, often tossed out by Fargo's father, came from the Holy works written, apparently, as messages from God. Nobody could remember, though, anyone they knew having said them.

Every month, as a group, they all gathered in a clearing not far from the rock garden and sacrificed a dog or a cat, something valuable only to the children, on a large limestone slab to President. A priest spoke of how

President provided the herbs in the forest and the bits of food in the large metal containers outside the walled city, and how kind it was for President to do this. Then the choir would sing, "What a friend we have in President. All our sins and griefs to bear." And chant bits of phrases like "we the people, to preserve freedom, what's good for business, our inalienable rights, we go now to a better place, and boots are made for walking if you don't like it here."

After this ceremony, a Holy man would speak of his call to express thanks to President who made bits of food rain into the large containers from above and deplore selfish people who allowed children to cry from hunger, saying that the youth who cried today did not understand the sufferings and death of President to give them bits of food and freedom. He would speak of how it rained fire and President ran into the rain, sacrificing himself for us to go to prepare the place in the sky, called corporation, where the bits of food were much larger and made you sick less often. He even spoke of happiness from drinking a liquid in corporation and orgies like those before fire rained from heaven. Saying in those orgies in corporation, everybody loved everybody else and drank the liquid all day long. At times, he became very emotional and Fargo knew that if he would subdue his earthly anger, he too would one day go to corporation.

In the end, the people would break into song, singing, "How beautiful corporation must be. Sweet home of the loving and filled."

Once a month, Fargo's elders sacrificed a small male child rather than the pets of the children. This pleased President, who understood that they gave their all, subduing their emotions and living as he would want them to live.

Fargo asked his father why they never sacrificed any adults and his father told him to shut up unless he wanted to be sacrificed. That was the way they'd always done it and that was the way President wanted it.

Fargo seldom asked questions. He watched and listened. He watched the walls behind the metal cans and when the gates opened he tried to see behind them. Once his father caught him watching from the edge of the forest and beat him severely. Fargo understood this. Children seen by the uniformed men on the walls were killed on sight. Fargo thought that President must love the uniformed men. They never cried from hunger. Fargo always hid when they forged into the forest. They would beat and drag the larger, less malformed of the forest people behind the gates. More than once, while rummaging for bits of food in the metal cans, Fargo had found pieces of girls and boys that he had known among the bits of food. The city people seemed particularly fond of cutting the sex organs of the forest people and "disemboweling" them.

Fargo himself was better formed than most. His belly was not distended and he limped only slightly. President had been good to him in this way and Fargo learned that when President was good to a forest person, he was likely to be butchered. The Holy Man said that the butchered were taken up past the skies to live in corporation with the beloved President, but Fargo doubted. He doubted many things, so he watched the walls more than anyone he knew and he had escaped capture, although his father beat him regularly. Fargo believed that the beatings were better than the dripping groins and holes that he found in the bellies of some of the other children, so he continued to watch from the edge of the forest and only took bits of food from the metal cans in the darkest hours of the night. He never ventured out with the groups to feed from the cans. For this, his father beat him, saying, "He who does not trust President to protect him is damned. All things are ordained by President. His will be done."

Fargo hated his father and remained in the tent because he felt much sadness for his mother. He knew that this was not natural. He often cried when he thought of the time that she would grow sick and die as all forest people did. At times, he believed that he hated President and worried that this would bring some catastrophe on his mother. If one cared for anyone, President was likely to make that person die. Fargo tried very hard not to care and was afraid that President, who read all thoughts, knew that he, Fargo, hated President.

Fargo knew that his mother was less malformed than other forest women and feared for her safety when the uniformed men, who were favored by President, came into the forest to collect people. He would run quickly when he saw the guards leave the walled city and watch her dig collard greens or roots from a hidden position. He watched her blonde hair flowing across her dark face and was aware that her firm tan body, flat belly and voluptuous hips sloping into unusually well formed thighs and long legs made her attractive to all men, especially his hideous father and the forest men. He had seen their loin sacks bulge as they watched her work and he hated them. He knew this care for his mother was no more natural than his hate for President, so he protected her quietly from his hidden position. He feared President knowing and reading his mind, but he continued to care. The horrors he'd seen in the metal cans frightened him more than President.

Today as he watched from the underbrush at the edge of the forest, he saw the gates open for another parade to the stone garden. He was now seventeen and could tell the difference in the costumes worn by those who rode or marched in the parade to the stone garden and whether it was a man or a woman in the box. A man wearing a guard's uniform decorated with ropes and bits of metal wailed horribly over the flower covered box at the grave and had to be pulled away when he lurched forward, jerked the box open and violently pulled a woman dressed in purple and white cloth from the box. He screamed and fought when they held him and took her from his arms, then fell on his knees in fresh mud heaving tortuous sounds and begging his captors to let him take her home.

That night, in the darkest part of the night, as rain soaked the muddy grave, Fargo took a tool and violated the most stringent of President's taboos. He feared, but he did not fear for himself. He had discerned by watching the parades that the costumes of the city people were what made them valuable even to each other. He cautiously, without soiling them in spite of the mud, took the woman's clothes from her body. He even removed the silk garments underneath and, protecting the clothes from the rain with his body, stashed them carefully in a well hidden earthen pot before returning to push the mud back over the nude body lying in the ivory box.

Liberation

THE BOY ALWAYS KNEW they were out there, hovering. He imagined them watching the people with empty eyes from under the short cap bills of the flat topped, round caps. Their bayonets and sabers glinted in his imagination. When he was old enough to talk, the first word he said after "Mama" and "Papa" was "cap." He thought that was what the big people were saying. They grinned, thinking of the image in the boy's mind. Later he would learn that the caps called themselves the Royal Japanese Imperial Army.

When his parents got wind that caps were in the area, the boy thought the people smelled them and he knew his puppy did. His mother got really nervous and began to rush about the house hiding things: Strange things like the pictures of smiling Americans that sat on end tables and little mementos that she displayed and didn't want spoiled. The boy was always told that he was an American, so he believed that the pictures were of his dead aunts, uncles and cousins that had left or been killed when the caps came. The young men in uniform were his dead uncles.

His Papa smiled at him and said very softly, the permanent laugh lines coming alive around his shining dark eyes, "Get Boots and hide, son."

He took Boots, the puppy his father found at the edge of the jungle, and ran across the backyard into the jungle to wait behind a net of brush and thick grass. He would wait, holding the puppy, for his mother to come and get him. She knew where he waited and she always came.

Liberation

The boy loved the puppy, and he knew that the caps would eat Boots. His father said they had to bottle feed Boots because the caps ate the puppy's mother. He hunched in the brush arbor and the puppy helped him watch. He imagined the caps threatening with grunts, pushing people and eating everything in the house, especially any meat, hot spicy chicken or beef that they gambled on saving for special occasions.

He collected pictures of dogs from old magazines that his mother kept hidden in a closet. They were American magazines, *National Geographic, Look* and *The Saturday Evening Post*. They had always been there and she let him take them out and went through them with him every day. The only dog he didn't like was the bedraggled, dirty spotted thing he saw in *National Geographic*. It was always either cowering, eating the dead meat of other animals or ganging up on helpless small animals. His mother said it was a hyena. He thought it must be related to dogs the way the caps were related to people. The caps, also, would eat anything, and he knew that they were afraid of Americans like himself and his father. He worried about his father not being afraid of them. The caps, like the hyenas, bullied in groups. He often dreamed about the time when the other Americans, the soldiers, returned and he saw these hyenas cringing at the sight of their clinched fists. He would hit the door of the closet, saying: "There. Take that you ugly cap! Take that! You won't eat any more puppies!"

Mrs. Hanna Chance Torres had, on her bureau, a hat like the Americans wore. It was her brother's American Army hat. It had a round brim with four tapered indentations that formed the top. He always wanted to touch it, but he knew that the hat was special and only to be viewed. Her brother had been shot when the hyena caps had come. Some day, he would join the Army and have a hat like that. It was an American soldier's hat. He would never even touch a hyena's cap. He told his father that Mrs. Hanna would probably let him hold it but Geraldine, the baby, would put the brim in her mouth and slobber on it like she did everything else. He wouldn't let her play with Boots. She pulled Boots' hair and ears. Her fingers locked and she pulled. He knew it hurt Boots and the baby really wanted to stick Boots in her mouth to love him. She was always in the way.

Then, the planes came. The people became ecstatic, laughing and crying, "They're back!" The boy and his parents ran happily to their dugouts. Even Boots ran, nipping at the boy's trousers and barking. But when the best was about to happen, the worst happened.

He was between his mother and father, holding onto Boots. Boots even knew to be quiet and not try to get away. They were on the dirt road when it started to rain. The boy could not see the end of the parade of people in front and behind the four of them. The caps were on both sides, hurrying up and down the road. A cap clubbed a man between the shoulder blades. The man stumbled into a young lady in front of him. She jumped quickly out of the way. Another cap slapped her.

Then it happened. Mrs. Hanna fell to her knees, holding baby Geraldine, and crying. The boy didn't see why until he realized that her uncle lay in front of her, blood coming out his nose and ears. The rain poured and the bombs flashed like lightning. He heard the bones crunch as the cap slammed the butt of his rifle again and again into Mrs. Hanna's skull. The boy watched the screaming Geraldine. He willed the motions of Auntie Marie as her hands reached in slow motion for the baby.

The bombs flashed, and as the people moved, the boy saw the soldier's hat lying on Mrs. Hannah's chest beside the road. He watched Geraldine all through the night and he cried for her and himself. She could play with the puppy.

The first day in the camp, a cap reached quickly, scruffed Boots and jerked him from the boy's arms. He stabbed Boots with his free hand, and the boy watched as the hyena, holding Boots by his hind legs, chopped and broke Boots' neck with the edge of his hand. He lunged, screaming and pounding at the legs of the hyena. He wanted to hear the cap's skull crunch the way he heard Mrs. Hanna die. The boy never knew that the cap made his mother clean and butcher Boots.

Days passed and there was no part of the camp that the boy didn't understand. All his life the smells, sounds and sights of the camp would trigger the dreams that motivated him and were always with him.

He could tell the difference between Geraldine's cry and any other baby's cry. When she cried he saw the still sad face of Mrs. Hannah beside the road with the sacred hat on her chest, her hands folded over the brim; and he heard the crunch of the hyena's rifle butt into her head. He checked instantly for Auntie Marie, crying: "Auntie Marie! The baby!"

He felt the pain on the orphan baby's sad face as she sat alone, her hand holding Raggedy Ann by the edge of the doll's checkered dress. "Raggedy Ann is always dirty," he thought. Every edge of the doll must have been in the baby's mouth. He smiled.

Once he walked up to her. She put up her hands with the doll dangling from the pudgy little fingers, offering it to him. "Boots," she said. "Where's Boots?"

He said he didn't know and then he couldn't think of anything else to do. Not any more. Sometimes he thought the Americans would never come and his mother would disappear like his father. Now, the caps came more often and the picture of the hyena came to mind as he watched them fondle their swords and knives and caress their rifles. From the edge of the jungle, where he waited behind the dense foliage, he watched their rifle butts while they looked like hungry hyena's at his mother. He worried. Maybe they ate the women that they killed, but his mother told him to wait, and he always waited. If she had to go with them he waited, not even sleeping through the night, until he saw her familiar long hair, petite body and unmistakable walk from a great distance. When she approached his hiding place he would jump out laughing and happy for the moment.

Then one day she didn't come back. He waited, thinking, "She will come to get me." All the next day, he waited. Throughout the night he kept seeing her movement in the dark or hearing her step, but the sound or sight always faded. The day the caps left, hurrying into the jungle dragging a few young girls with them, he thought: *She'll be back now.* He waited.

The soldier pushed his helmet back, reached in his pocket for a package of Camel cigarettes, and looked around the edge of the jungle. The boy sat perfectly still. In all those days he had learned something from the animals. His only protection was to sit perfectly still. If this was really an American and not a cap he would know. Americans, like himself, knew everything, like he knew where Geraldine was all the time and like he knew when his mother was coming. The soldier shook his head at the tattered remains of the absent campers, looked around the edge of the clearing and started to leave. Then he fixed on the spot where the boy waited.

The boy knew. He came out of the jungle and, looking up at the big smiling face, he reached for the Marine's extended hand. "I'm an American," the boy said and took hold of the Marine's finger.

Independence Day

July 4, 1944

> *Beneath the cement foundations*
> *of the motel, the ancient spirits*
> *of the people conspire sacred tricks.*
> *They tell stories and jokes and laugh and laugh.*
> Simon Ortiz, *"Washyuma* Motor Hotel"

MATT AND PAUL FELL ASLEEP that night, their beds side by side, talking about freedom in English. They heard an occasional explosion, and Paul said he hoped the Japanese weren't killing people.

"I don't understand what's keeping the Americans," Matt said. "Don't they know what's happening to us?"

"They know," Paul said. "They've seen the Philippines."

"I miss the movies," Matt said. Through the window he saw the stars still gleaming in the clear night sky over Guam.

"And the radio," Paul said. "If we could only have a radio when we wanted it."

"If I could be in two places," Matt said, "I'd be up there and down here with Mom and you kids." Matt was watching the stars. "It's funny how you can see into the sparkling darkness and you can't get away."

In the other room he heard his little sister, Josephine, say "Good night, Mother" for the first time and his mother answer "Good night, Josie. Sleep tight." Josey had been afraid of the dark since the first time the Japanese came at night and took their father away. Now, she often called out far into the night and sometimes had nightmares, screaming in her sleep.

Matt knew the little kids were hungry and often scared. He told them the stories about the old days when they had plenty to eat and

Independence Day: July 4, 1944

they didn't have to be afraid. There were fourteen children. There might have been sixteen, or at least fifteen, if it hadn't been for the war. Little Franklin Delano hadn't had a chance. He was born into the hunger. Matt wondered if President Roosevelt knew how much the people loved him and prayed for the Americans that were not condemned to die slowly this way.

"I can't imagine being free to live," Matt said. He heard Fred tell his mother that he thought he saw an American plane earlier in the afternoon.

"Maybe," Josephine said. "Go to sleep now, and tomorrow we will go see Auntie Rita."

In the darkness, Matt dreamed. He was in a camp where fear ruled. The fence was high but he was outside the latticed wire. First, he heard the people talking.

"If we kill ourselves, the cowards won't hurt us anymore," one voice said. Then Matt stood, holding hands with a shadowy lady and looking over the cliff at Two Lover's Point. They looked down to the deep water below as the surf disappeared beneath the cliff. The height made him dizzy; but for the first time he was not afraid. He leaned into the wind and her soft hand held him in its firm grasp.

Suddenly, over loud speakers came, "The Hawaiian Wedding Song," and another voice saying, "Did you hear what happened in Merizo? If there were only somewhere to hide."

Then, Matt rode a large white horse like one he had seen in a movie and he was singing "You'll never walk alone" to the beautiful girl with long flowing hair. She rode behind him on the horse now, her hands on his waist. There was no saddle and the horse came dangerously close to the cliff.

Matt saw the Japanese. First, they were in his dream going over the cliff, and he thought *We have escaped them. They are sheep, tumbling off the cliff, men, women and children. Some of them are driving the camouflaged vehicles off the cliff.*

Then, they stood in the doorway to his and Paul's room; and Matt realized he was awake and soldiers had come like before. They stood, weapons in their hands with bayonets fixed. One of them held a lantern that lighted their mask like faces in the darkness. Matt's fear made him see their pale faces float like evil spirits, independent of their bodies, their eyes showing as black holes.

"Get dressed. Now!" one of them said, pointing his bayonet in their direction.

Paul stood up too quickly, exclaiming in English, "Oh shit!" without thinking. Matt winced at the blow from the rifle butt that smacked Paul's face like a bat hitting a softball, and knocked him backwards over the bed.

The four Japanese soldiers shoved Matt and Paul, handcuffed, to the front of the raised desk at the police station. From the room behind the desk, Matt heard Japanese voices angrily demanding something, and punctuating the demands with blows to the furniture or to the bodies of their victims. He heard something break and then a man's voice cry out in pain. The room was quiet for a minute. Matt's imagination filled in the silence until a grunt turned into a blood curdling scream that ended abruptly with what Matt thought must have been loss of consciousness. Matt remembered a neighbor telling him about the bruises around the anus of another neighbor's corpse that they saw while they were cleaning the corpse for burial. He knew they used their batons in imaginative ways.

The corporal behind the desk was watching Matt. *It's as if he were watching a trapped animal, annoyed at the animal's existence,* Matt thought. Paul's face was far too swollen on the left side, a huge bump growing out of his left eye and temple, for Paul to reveal any expression.

"Your turn now, American bastard." The soldier next to Paul spoke the words in Japanese. Matt stood up, moving toward the soldier. The soldier pulled Paul to his feet.

"No." Matt said. "He's hurt and he's just a kid."

"Shut up and sit back down," the corporal behind the desk said. Two soldiers came out of the back room carrying the unconscious body of their prisoner on a stretcher.

They always spoke in Japanese. You would learn Japanese or pay for every failure to hear; and Matt understood the language. He learned quickly and only pretended not to hear when the response was dangerous. He did not respond now. He simply prayed, without moving his lips, that Paul would be left alone, and he hoped that Paul's eye, now swelled shut, was OK.

He was not so lucky. The two soldiers hustled Paul into the room on their return trip.

Matt vomited on the wooden floor when he heard that endless scream that the torture built to coming from Paul in the room behind the desk. Something hard hit him in the back of the head, and he woke up outside as daylight came to the knurled tree that rested his head. He touched the tree and whispered to the Taotaomona that the Chamorros believed lived in these ancient trees. Surely the ancient spirits would kill the evil things behind the masks. They were dead already and stank of eating disgusting things. Matt supposed they looked human to people who didn't know what they did. Matt saw their faces as masks, made from skin, pulled from the faces of dead Chamorros. Matt could hear his grandmother saying, "Even booney dogs know to stay away from dead things."

"I didn't come to them," Matt whispered to the Taotaomona in the tree. "Do something!"

Independence Day: July 4, 1944

Then Matt saw the booney dog, its radiator ears alert to the two soldiers coming out of the police station. It was tied to the tree beside him.

The triangle shaped soldier handed him the talan tangan branch. The one wearing glasses pointed his bayonet toward the tree. "Kill the dog," he said. "You have three strikes, like in your ball games. If it isn't dead, you will be."

The triangle shaped one raised his rifle and feinted the butt toward Matt. Matt had seen them club a woman to death, and he saw and heard, again, the rifle butt smashing into the black hair, matted with blood. Nausea started to well, but he moved, taking the branch and talked to the dog, a stray breed like the coyote in American. "I'm sorry," he said as the dog, realizing the threat, snapped his mouth shut then jumped back, struggling against the rope and yelping. Matt hoped the Taotaomonas would strike the soldiers dead before they struck him.

He swung the stick. It bounced into Coyote's skull as Coyote jerked, yelping and tangled himself around the tree in the roots and trunk. The squat triangle shaped soldier poked Matt's back with the point of his bayonet. Matt swung the talan tangan with all his strength. The club cracked against the dogs skull. Matt knew himself as the instrument of their favorite sport, clubbing life to death. The howling dog's eyes clamped shut and he fell as Matt slammed the third blow into the side of the dog's head.

The one wearing the glasses handed him his unfixed bayonet. "Clean it." he commanded. *They eat dogs,* Matt thought. *The filthy dead keep their corpses moving by eating dogs. They eat the best of what we have and take the rest.*

Matt cut into the carcass of Coyote, and as he did he saw the puppies, all of them dying now like their mother. His hands covered with blood, he picked the puppies out and lay them on the ground. He cried, thinking of his mother and little Franklin Delano not having enough to eat as he skinned the dog for the well fed scavengers.

Matt watched Josephine cleaning the blood from Paul's face. Her thin brown face was pinched, and her forehead was lined by worry, hunger and anger. "They are like mad dogs," she said. "Stay out of their way. That's all you can do."

"They smell," Matt said. "And they eat dogs."

"Did they eat the puppies?" His mother asked, wiping the blood from the corners of Paul's mouth. Paul appeared to be asleep, his eyes blackened and swelled shut.

"Probably," Matt said. "The Taotaomonas must kill them, they eat the dead."

"They eat the living," Josephine said, and Matt knew she was thinking of Franklin Delano buried next to his grandmother, and he worried about his mother eating less than any of them. She was so thin.

August 1945

Matt stood looking into the casket. The lines imposed by hunger, worry and fear for her children had disappeared from his mother's face. Her head that he had seldom seen resting, lay stiff against the satin pillow. The flickering candles around the casket softened the harsh tones of death that escaped the undertaker's abilities with make-up. Matt kept thinking of his mother wiping the blood from Paul's face. The hands, folded at the point where the silken blanket turned down over the edge of the coffin lid, were spotted with bruises. Matt wondered how that happened. He put his hand on hers and stood with her throughout the night.

December 24, 1946

Matt focused on the red lamps at each end of the ironwood wreath behind the rows of bottles. Ironwood branches could almost pass for pine or cedar. The bartender reached back, picked up the bottle of Jack Daniels in front of the wreath and poured a shot for the sailor in front of the bar. The lamps reminded Matt of the flickering candles encased in red and decorated by saints and angels on the tombs in Umatic, just under the hill at Fort Soledad.

Bing Crosby sang that he was dreaming of a white Christmas, and a sailor asked Juan Muna, who sat next to Matt at the table, where to find those beautiful island girls he had heard about. Juan Muna was directing him to Roberto Marquez' pig sty in Jona. "They're so pretty," Juan said. "You will never forget them. Very light complected and they squeal with joy when you pet them."

Matt laughed. The sailor set his glass down on their table and left the Quonset hut.

Juan smiled. It was the first time Matt had seen Juan smile in a long time. "What are you laughing about?" Juan asked, still grinning. "He'll have more fun tonight than you will." Juan looked toward the ocean and Matt followed his gaze. The back door of the Quonset hut opened onto the beach and a breeze cooled the bar.

"Sometimes I think women are all mermaids," Matt said. "I dream of them with long flowing hair, playing harps and beckoning me into the bay. When I get there they fade. I wake up thinking about the dead and the dying."

"Think about the stars," Juan said. Pinup pictures decorated one side of the hut.

"They're even more out of reach," Matt said. He looked up into the clear night sky of perpetual summer. Christmas lights decorated the trees in the park across the street. From a distance the brilliant colors in the darkness caused Matt to think about the toy Chevrolet truck he found under their ironwood tree one Christmas morning. It was blue with real tiny head lamps lit by a battery. He still felt the magic, tinged with sadness, when he remembered the truck. It had been a long time since anyone or anything had shone with a halo of magic like those tiny head lamps on the toy truck.

"Maybe that's the Star of Bethlehem," he said to Juan and pointed toward a particularly brilliant star that sparkled between the black vault of the sky and the crawling ocean.

"Yeah," Juan laughed, "and we're the wise men from the East. Saddle up your caribou and we will ride, ride, ride." Matt laughed with the image of a bull cart headed to Bethlehem down a narrow dirt road in Inarajan. He and Juan yelled "giddy up!" carrying caskets of incense and myrrh.

"At least it's up," Juan Said. He sipped his beer. "The American should be arriving at the Marquez farm by now."

Matt laughed. "I've seen them so drunk they'd go for a street sign. Marquez had better watch out for his hogs," Matt said. They both started laughing and couldn't stop. Juan finally sobered the conversation with, "Anyway, I suppose it's good to see them back."

"I keep thinking about when they weren't here, and I find it hard to believe that they're doing us any favors now," Matt said.

Christmas day Matt went with Juan, driving the jeep, up through the mountains following the winding road to the top and down into Merizo. All the roads in Guam went in a circle, but this way of going around the island was particularly pleasant. You could see everything from these heights. As you started South you saw the remnants of the war, disabled trucks sitting around smashed buildings. Engineer Corpsmen bulldozed piles of metal trash and debris that was strewn about the islands by the occupations and the invasion. The higher you went, the cleaner the land under you became, and as you reached the top, you looked down into ravines and valleys that were a brilliant green. At the higher altitudes, natural springs flowed from caves down the sides of the mountain. The water was cold and tasted of watercress. Driving along the beach past Merizo, cool air blew off the ocean as the surf rolled up on the sandy beach.

They parked the jeep at the bottom of the hills. Juan took his bag and they began threading their way, first through the sword grass, and then through the dense brush and teeming plant life of the jungle.

"I call it my bag of tricks," Juan said as he stooped to pick the leaves off a particular plant and put them in his bag. "I followed my Uncle Joaquin up this path years ago. We were looking for devil's weed and gaurana root. I always wanted to be a Surahanu like him, and he taught me what he knew of the medicine," Juan said. The path followed a stream as they continued around the base of the hill, past the wooden crosses where the people died in the Faha massacre. A caribou stamped through the brush and into the stream to their right.

"Do you believe in magic?" Matt asked.

"Why?" Juan said.

"I think it will take magic to get the blood out of this ground," Matt said.

Juan pulled off his broad brimmed straw hat and looked toward the crosses. "It's already gone," he said. "The red dirt you see is the blood in your mind."

"And in my dreams," Matt said. "In my dreams they are still here. The Japanese threaten. The Americans greet and smile, and the Chamorros suffer and die. Slowly."

"There is no magic," Juan said. "As Surahanu I know that, but they are always here." The path became steeper, and in the coolness of the height and the encroaching darkness they approached Juan's house. It was set into the side of the mountain, and the rock and masonry front was overgrown with vines. The tangle of brush opened into a rock patio. Juan went past the thatched patio into the darkened house while Matt stood just outside the door. A kerosene lamp flickered and a warm light came alive as Juan placed the globe over the flame. He went to the wall and lit two more kerosene lamps at each end of a gallery of pictures in black and white. The faces in the flickering light were of the dead and surviving. Matt could tell the difference. The dead wore happier masks, posing for the pictures. The surviving, in the black and white pictures, stared into the emptiness of vacant homes, their hair and lives in disarray. Some of the children clutched blankets to their chins. Their faces were passive and sad, their long hair pulled tight to the backs of their heads and parted in the middle. The dresses were woven in bright Chamorro colors and designs. Matt knew that by the shades of gray, white and black. The blankets were of a dull color, probably olive drab.

"The Americans come and go," Matt said. "If it were not for them maybe the Japanese would not have killed us."

Juan, kneeling in front of the wall, lit the lamps. Replacing the globe on the second lamp, he crossed himself, stood up and turned toward Matt. "We are not dead," he said. "We are here in the land, in the trees, in the soil and in this room."

Matt pointed to one of the pictures. "Rosa Perez is dead now," he said. "I always thought she was very pretty." Matt remembered her kind brown eyes when they didn't have that vacant look. He saw her full lips, smiling, in his mind's eye. They were not closed and turned down at the corners as they were in the picture.

"I saw her the day she died," Matt said. "She was outside what was left

Independence Day: July 4, 1944

of the old post office in Hagåtña. She was skin and bone. Her hair hung dead and lifeless."

"The soldiers came too late for some of the people," Juan Muna said. He pounded a root from the shelf across the room on his medicine stone. Then he rolled the pestle back and forth over the mortar, grinding the root to powder. He moved his lamp to the small table beside the large flat medicine stone, illuminating the shelf covered with roots, labeled sacks of herbs, newspapers, stacks of magazines and other documents. His books were along the opposite wall above his desk made of oak boards. Matt wondered where he got the boards, lumber from trees that didn't grow on Guam, but he never asked questions. He knew Juan would tell him what he wanted him to know.

"They didn't care," Matt said. "One of them killed her." He pointed toward the sad picture of Rosa. The picture brought her starving image into the present. It was always there in his mind, and when something conjured up his memories of her he wished he could physically go back and take her with him as he left the shell damaged post office. He would imagine himself calling her name. She turned, her face still striking with high cheek bones, full lips and eyes that lit up, seeing him. He took her hand and they walked across the park to safety, away from the hyenas. He held her as he had when they were teen-agers. She giggled, broke loose, and ran toward the Taotaomona tree with its knurled roots, most of which were above ground, in the back yard of the old high school. She was well as he imagined her – soft, warm and taut in all the right places.

"They didn't care," Matt said. "One of them killed her."

"They were making love," Juan said. "Her bones were fragile from malnutrition. Her heart was broken by her ribs."

"He could see she was sick," Matt said. "He was an animal."

"He was lonely maybe," Juan said.

"They don't feel," Matt said. His memories of Rosa always ended with this fury. He saw her weakened body – lifeless and raped, and he tried to recapture the aura that surrounded her in his teenage life. For a long time she was all he could think about. The first time he kissed her and she returned the kiss, he thought *so this is what the songs are about*. He wandered for hours of days in a dream where fantasy becomes reality for the first time in an adolescent's mind. She was really there and he could touch everything beautiful and she touched him.

Matt looked out the door. Far down toward the valley in Merizo, a candle, encased in red glass, flickered. Matt thought someone had put the candle before one of the crosses that very evening. Maybe they were kneeling there still. Those crosses commemorated the dead all over the island, and along the path of the Mannengon death march. Sixteen people were left entombed in the cave at Tinta. The Japanese herded the bravest and best into that cave, fearing their patriotism as the Americans delayed their invasion day after day. They threw in hand grenades and finished the job with the butts of their weapons. Matt still winced when he felt the crunch of gun butts against the heads and faces of his friends and family.

"Maybe they don't dream," Juan said. "Perhaps we should help them. They also, have killed and been killed."

"Not in their homes, not their lovers, mothers and children," Matt said. "They treat us like animal property to be salvaged. They roam the streets, fornicating and writing letters to their fiancées back home."

He looked again at the sad, surviving picture of Rosa, and he realized that Juan had cut those pictures from the newspapers.

"It's the way I keep our history," Juan said, "the picture's in the newspapers and I write down the stories. If we don't preserve our stories there will only be photographs with rescuing soldiers in them of a people overjoyed to be delivered. The stories of the desertion of our island when the Americans left, and of our grief, death and separation will only be told by the people if we keep them in our hearts and minds; and we will."

"Rosa was beautiful before the Japanese came," Matt said. "I remember those days and that body when both were full, alive and magnetic. I remember her in a red dress, bordered in yellow patterns, wearing shell earrings that bounced in the energy of her face. My parents loved her. My mother always pointed her out to me from the time I was a child, and I would try to talk to her at fiestas. She was so pretty and I was so awkward. Her hair flowed like tall grass in the wind, and at night I would lie in my bed and dream of her.

I cried when I saw her outside the post office in Hagåtña. I smashed the butt of my M-1 rifle against a tree when I heard about her death. My first thought was to hunt down the soldier. Stalk him and kill him.

The Colonel, Holgrave, gave the weapon to my father during the ceremonies at Mannengon. My father was a council member during the war and the Colonel said he had fought the good fight. My father passed the rifle on to me. I am the oldest son."

Juan studied the face of Rosa, and then Matt's face. "It's like a typhoon," Juan said. "The destruction itself can't have a meaning. If it does, nothing means anything. Remember, you know the people are here with you and they have always been here with you. Their spirits are in your mind and in the land. Their stories are on our tongues and in our minds."

"They are under the land, stiff and cold in decaying silk and cotton dresses," Matt said. "And people, who never cared, expect us to thank them for leaving us to die. The Japanese soldiers killed us for being Americans. We starved and our women and children died."

Independence Day: July 4, 1944

Juan ground the root to a powder and scraped it into an iron pot. Turning to a fireplace against the back wall, he set the pot on the stone hearth and reached for the gourd on the mantel. He sprinkled ground herbs from the gourd into the pot, added water from the galvanized steel bucket and hung the bucket above the kindling wood on an iron hook.

"They act as if we are the spoils of war to be used and left at their convenience, regardless of the consequences," Matt said.

"Do you think that's the way they treat their own?" Juan said.

"They will pay," Matt said.

"You are paying," Juan said. "You are paying because you trusted them and they hurt our people. Your mother died and Rosa was killed. You think these things happened because you, your father and the council trusted the Americans enough to be born Americans."

"If you are born into something, how can you be blamed for the betrayal?" Juan stirred the mixture in the pot and reached for a box of wooden matches. The spurt of sulphur flame lit his weather beaten, wrinkled face. The furrows were deep, but the laugh lines were still visible as Juan lit the kindling.

"You are not the first to blame yourself and you are not alone," Juan said. "Pedro Cruz blamed himself and his own men for not being able to fight off the entire Japanese army as they came into Hagåtña. He blamed himself because some of his men deserted, and the bravest, Vince Chargaulauf, was sacrificed. That's what you're doing. You blame yourself because you lived, and the Americans didn't care whether we lived or died and we were wearing their uniforms and fighting their war. We *believed* it was ours. It was, and it still is. Think how those must live, treating their own with disrespect. Disregard them. You don't hate typhoons. You know it's there and protect yourself as well as you know how."

"Every minute they waited to come back after they deserted us more people died," Matt said. The kerosene lamps in the darkness gave the pictures of the surviving women and children an eerie three dimensional quality. "Where are the men in that picture?" Matt said to Juan.

"Dead," Juan said. "They were herded into caves and into trench mass graves by the Japanese. They were killed. When we found the survivors there were only some of the women and children. Grandmothers without sons, mothers without sons and families with no future."

"The olive blankets? Are those the gifts of the soldiers?"

"No. Those were the blankets of the Chamorro American soldiers already dead. That is the difficulty. You see, we're not all dead."

"Why should we be?" Matt said.

"I didn't say we should, but you think so. That's why you hate the people you trusted to save us. They didn't save Josephine, your mother, and Rosa, your intended."

"Then they should pay."

"No. They won't. You will sacrifice yourself for them."

Matt laughed, and Juan joined him. It was the bizarre laugh of the ancient spirits that comes with the first thread of light. Matt realized, as he heard the irony, that Juan was telling the truth. It was a recurring cycle that started with Magellan on the beach in Umatic and did not end with the thirty men grenaded and machine gunned in the Faha trench.

"You and I are like the survivors of Faha and Tinta," Juan said. "Felipe and Ignacio Cruz, and these faces, tell the story of how we died. You and I, we tell the story of how all of us pass through these deaths to live forever."

As the red light cracked the darkness of the bay below them, Juan Muna handed Matt the fruits of the red-tinted ground of the people. Matt sipped the liquid and said, "Fort Soledad is buried."

"All of us are still here," Juan said, gesturing north, south, east and west.

Self-Service

I WAS EATING BREAKFAST before going down the hill to open up the store when I saw a letter lying on the table. It was from my older brother Jeremy. It was open so I guessed Dad had read it. It was just like the letter Jeremy'd sent six months ago, all about how much he missed seeing Dad and how he'd come home the first chance he got. I put the letter back in the envelope and finished eating my bacon.

When I got to the store and stepped up on the cement porch, I noticed that the oiled wooden floor was clean. Clifford, who works with me in the store, was standing on a small stepladder behind the counter putting baking powder cans on the shelf.

"You must have gotten up early," I said as I pushed against the Colonial Bread sign on the screen door.

"I woke up at three and couldn't go back to sleep," he said.

"From up at the house it looked like there was a car down here before."

Clifford dusted off one of the cans with a rag from his hip pocket. "It was the man from Leed's Wholesale Grocery. I gave him the list we made up yesterday. The truck will be here Friday."

"Did Dad put tenpenny nails on the list?" I walked around the counter picking up an empty match folder and threw it in the trash can.

"No," he said.

"I reminded him yesterday just before I left. I guess he forgot."

I rang up *no-sale* on the cash register and checked to see if there was enough change left from yesterday. There were only five one-dollar bills so I opened the safe and took out ten more.

A green '41 Ford rattled up the gravel road from the direction of the cemetery and jerked to a stop parallel with the front door. Bill Tate got out of the car stiffly and guided his protruding stomach through the door.

"What can I do for you, Bill?" I asked.

"Just throw a couple blocks of salt in that Cadillac out there," he said.

Clifford said he would load the salt and headed toward the side of the store where the dairy supplies were. Tate took a bottle of Coke out of the cooler and handed me a nickel. I rang up five cents on the register and dropped the coin into the drawer. Then I took the pad marked "Tate" from its place in the drawer under the cash register and wrote down two blocks of salt and the price.

The heavy screen door slammed and Dad came in. He was scratching his full head of white hair cropped short in a flattop. He didn't look seventy.

"How's farmin' Bill?" he asked Tate.

"Dry, Chuck, awful dry." Tate reached in his shirt pocket for a cigar. "If we don't get some rain soon my alfalfa's gonna' dry up and blow away. How's business?"

"If we have another depression we're going to be in one hell of a shape," Dad said. "The boys up north, working in the factories, were all out of work last time." He leaned back against the counter on the other side of the room. It was covered with straw hats, all kinds, from the dressy Texas to blue and red cowboy hats.

"That boy of yours works up there somewhere, don't he Chuck?" Tate stuck the cigar in his mouth. I'd never seen him light one. He used them for chewing tobacco.

"You mean Jeremy?" Dad fumbled with the drawstring on one of the bright red straw hats. "Yeah, he's workin' in a car plant in Detroit. He makes good wages, that boy does."

"I ain't seen him since he was a kid, I don't guess," Tate said.

"He don't come home very often, his work keeps him busy most of the time. He always was a hard worker you know," Dad said.

"I reckon he took after his old man some then." Tate laughed. He rocked one of the wicker chairs with the palms of his hands on the chair back.

"Many a day we got up at daylight and worked 'till dark plowin' fields and haulin' hay down on the farm before we moved up here, and when we moved up here I remember we painted this whole store in one day, except for the sign. We had a sign painter from Blue Springs do that, and me and Jeremy lifted it up there above the awning by ourselves, just the two of us. He always was a strong one. He comes home every time he gets a chance. Probably be coming home again soon."

I stocked candy bars in the glass show case on top of the counter and pretended I wasn't listening. I glanced out the front window and saw a car approaching from the north, trailing a cloud of dust. Tate was right about it being dry. I could almost taste the dust in the air. The car ground to a stop in front of the gas pumps so I put the candy bars down and went outside.

"Yes sir?" I said, walking around the rear fender of the car.

"A dollar's worth." The man handed me the key to the gas cap and went into the store.

While the cents whirled off on the gas pump, I could hear Dad inside talking to Tate and the stranger with the angler's hat about somebody I thought must have been dead for twenty years or more because I didn't recognize the name.

"You know Luther Thomas don't you Tate?" Dad asked.

"I remember him," the stranger said.

"He was in here a while back," Dad said. "Hell of a nice fellow. What that son-of-a-gun wouldn't do when we were younger wasn't worth doin'. I ever tell you about the time we got drunk over in Little Rock and busted up a whorehouse?"

"I don't reckon," Tate said.

Then I quit paying attention and his voice just kind of droned on into how the head matron of the whorehouse had told this Luther Thomas what a sorry specimen of a man he was and how both of them got mad, beat up the bouncer, and smashed up the furniture. It was a very childish story.

I checked the oil and went back inside. "Did the Tindle Feed salesman come by while I was gone?" I asked Clifford, who was behind the counter finishing with the candy bars.

"I didn't see him," Clifford said.

"The next time he comes, if I'm not here, tell him I don't think we'll buy any more of his feed. We've got enough to last six months even if people hadn't rather use Lathrops. I already talked to Dad about it."

Then I heard Dad's voice again: "Sometimes I'd like to go back to farmin' myself Bill. It don't seem long since Milly and me brought Jeremy and the baby up here and took over the store." Tate looked at me and then shifted his eyes quickly.

"That Jeremy was a lotta help to me though. He would've made a first-rate grocer. It makes a man proud to have kids like that that look up to him and respect what he does."

Tate looked down at his brogans like he was trying to decide whether or not they needed a shine, and the stranger took off his hat and started picking at one of the plugs. I started into the back stockroom. Then I heard Dad asking me to wait a minute. I hesitated a second, not wanting to look at Tate and the other man, wishing Dad could keep his mouth shut part of the time.

"Yes, Dad," I said, stopping in the door and turning around. He was walking toward me.

"I noticed you started buying bread from that new bakery in Little Rock." Tate and the stranger were behind him arguing about what kind of bait a largemouth bass would strike at this time of year. "I think we better go ahead and get our bread from Colonial."

"I meant to talk to you about that Dad," I lied. "But you were busy with something else. The other bakery's salesman stopped by and offered me a pretty good deal, so I thought I'd better take it."

"We've been buying Colonial ever since I can remember," he said.

"This is cheaper, Dad," I said. "You always said to watch the prices."

"Well, I guess it's okay," he said. "I kinda hate to see us change though. The guy that drives the Colonial truck has given us real good service for years, but I don't suppose a fellow can afford to lose money." He turned around and went back to join Tate and the stranger in their conversation about largemouth bass.

"Minnows, that's the only thing to use," Dad said. "These new plugs ain't no good. One Sunday on Wilson Creek, down below the dam, Jeremy and me caught twelve big ones apiece in no time at all on minnows about an inch or so long."

In the stock room, I took as long as possible getting a carton of Camels. When I got back out front the men were gone and Dad was standing behind the counter.

"Son, I don't think that idea of yours about self-service would be of much use to us in a store this small," he said. He reached into the trash can for a leaky pen that I'd thrown away.

"Why not?" I asked. "We're going to have to modernize to keep what business we've got, and it's certainly the only way to increase it."

"I don't see it that way," he said. His opinion was fixed. If he didn't see it that way from the beginning there was no possibility of him ever seeing it that way. I didn't say any more.

"I got a letter from Jeremy yesterday," he said. "Now there's a son a man can be proud of. I remember when we first bought this store. He was sixteen then, and he worked right along with me fixin' up the store and buildin' up the business. We worked hard buildin' those shelves and painting the place the way it is. We did all this work by ourselves. We even had to build a partition between this front part of the store and the stock room. After the bus brought him home from school he'd be right down here helpin' me until closin' time. He says he'll come home for a visit as soon as he gets a chance."

I wondered if Dad even knew what the hell self-service was. He didn't seem to notice anything else. Here we were standing on an oiled wooden floor. Every other store in the country looked white, clean, and bright, with new fluorescent fixtures and white metal frozen food cases. He seemed almost afraid I'd tear down the drab brown shelves behind the counter and put in a few lights. I left him behind the counter and went out front. He was beginning to get on my nerves again.

The Tindle Milling Company truck was backed up to the cement porch, and the driver was unloading sacks of feed. I hurried over to the truck.

"What the devil are you doing?" I asked.

The driver dropped another sack off the truck bed. "You ordered fifty hundred pound sacks of feed."

"The hell I did."

"I have a signed requisition," he said, handing it to me. "Signed by Charles Vincent."

"You'll have to load 'em again," I said. "That's Dad's. You know he doesn't order things around here anymore."

"What?" He looked at the requisition again. "Well, I'll be damned. I guess that's not your signature. It keeps me busy just fixin' what those salesmen mess up."

"I'm sorry," I said.

"You could help me with these sacks," he said.

I started throwing the sacks of feed up on the truck and wondered what the hell possessed Dad to order feed that he'd been told we didn't use any more.

By the time we'd finished, we'd both worked up a pretty good sweat, and the dust from the road didn't help matters any. The truck driver thanked me and drove off. I went back into the store, slamming the screen.

"Why did you order feed from Tindle?" I asked Dad. He had a blank look on his face like he didn't know what I was talking about.

"Wasn't that what you said to do? The Tindle man came and I remembered that you said get something. I thought it was dairy feed."

"It was tenpenny nails, and you weren't supposed to order them. Clifford was supposed to order them. You couldn't even remember to put them on the list. How could I trust you to order anything?"

"You trust me?" He started to get mad and I was glad, because I was already sorry for what I'd said. But he didn't say any more. I waited a minute and then I went on back to the stock room, hoping he'd forget. I picked up a case of Carnation milk and took it up front to start filling up the empty shelf.

I turned around to see what he was doing once, and he was puttering around toward the back of the store with some old plowshares that people didn't use any more because everyone used tractors instead of horses. I'd tried to get rid of them once or twice, but he wouldn't let me. He looked awfully stoop shouldered back there among those dusty plowshares.

"Dad," I said, "maybe we should keep buying Colonial bread. After all, a fellow never can tell what kind of service he's going to get from a new outfit."

He quit fiddling with the plowshares and wiped his forehead off with his dirty old handkerchief. Then he shuffled on up toward the front of the store not even looking at me.

"I guess you'll be throwing those out," he said.

"What?" I asked.

"The plowshares," he said.

"What about the bread, Dad?" I said, hoping he'd answer me, but knowing he wouldn't.

"It sure is hot," he said. "It was hot when Jeremy and me hauled that sign up here from Blue Springs. It ain't the same any more. It's faded. Maybe you'll put up a new sign too," he said. He went on out the heavy screen door, letting it slam shut behind him.

"Dad?" I said. And then it seemed kind of silly to ask about the bread again. I couldn't think of anything else.

The Contract

To Donne, a thought was a rose or maybe a rose was a thought. Oh hell, I never could keep it straight anyway. And him standing there with his piece of chalk, scraping on the board again and "sp" "sp" all over my paper that he'd handed back a week ago. I'd like to know what the hell "sp" was supposed to mean. Why didn't it say "Isp" or something, and in the rest room on the wall was the word "pevert" and over it was written "sp." The chalk was scraping again and time was passing. An hour and forty-five minutes, an hour and forty-five minutes and the test was over. Why didn't he just write it all over the board? Or why didn't I just write it all over my blank piece of paper? Donne was a what? I could feel the sweat on my forehead and my clammy hands. I needed about two pages of what Donne was and all I could think about was "an hour and forty-five minutes" and to Donne a thought was a rose or a rose was a thought and I wasn't sure which.

I walked out of the hot sun into the cool hall and up the cool stone steps to his office on the third floor. Inside I could hear a typewriter going tap—taptatap clickita clickita clickita. I had the letter in my hand. In the left hand corner it said Milton W. Riley, Dean of Students.

A secretary sitting in front of a desk with the telephone receiver up to her ear said, "Just a minute, Marge." She looked up at me. "Can I help you?" she said. It was obvious she didn't want to.

"Is Mr. Riley in?" I picked at the letter in my hand.

"Who may I say is calling?" she said, putting down the receiver.

"David Clark," I said. She got up and went into the office directly behind her from which came the sounds of the typewriter I had heard.

She came back and, picking up the receiver, she said: "He'll see you now." I went into the office.

"Mr. Riley," I said. He looked up from his desk.

"Yes, Mr. Clark?"

"I have a letter here about my grade average. I signed the contract."

"According to that contract you must have a C+ average," he said. "A C+ or you can't petition the committee. Is that clear?" And behind him the typewriter was going tap, tap, taptaptap.

"I'll try sir," I said, handing him the contract. He was shuffling through some letters that had just been typed.

"Would you please not put the addresses so far to the right," he said to his secretary, running his fingers through his thinning hair. He turned back around.

"I'm sorry Mr. Clark," he said. "I realize it's difficult, but you know we're not running a diploma factory here."

"Thank you for your time, sir," I said, turning to leave.

I walked down the stone steps and outside. Why in the hell did it have to be so hot. The sun beat down and my head hurt. The sun hurt my eyes. Upstairs in the room, the typewriter was still going tap, tap, taptaptap.

Then I thought of the box houses, the dump trucks and the nuts and bolts. You could drive a dump truck or you could put nuts on bolts. Wasn't that what they did? And at night you could watch television. The black and white pictures on the square little screen and the sun making my head ache. Then you get old and tired and all your life you've put nuts on bolts and watched television because you couldn't afford to get drunk, or maybe you went to church three times a week because you couldn't afford to believe this was the only life you had. And the kids were crying. You couldn't watch your television in peace because the kids were crying. You only got to watch it five hours a day and the kids were crying.

"The examinations, why be so nervous about the examinations?" he said. "I take dexadrine myself. Been on it for years. Gives me more time to study."

"Yes, but what about essay questions? You've got to organize," I said. The band pounded away behind us.

"Don't worry about it, Clark old boy. It ain't no big thing. What's a C+ average? Another round," he said to the bar maid. She went back to the other side of the bar.

"I haven't made it since I started. Why should I make it now?" I said, setting the bottle down, and wondering why the hell she brought a glass instead of a mug. Schlitz was on tap. I didn't like Schlitz.

"I'll help you," he said. "I'll get you the pills. They'll make everything different." He put down his mug and lit a cigarette with his shaky hand.

The sleeping pill hadn't worked. The clock's luminous dial said 12 p.m., and the little red hand crept around the face.

"But honey I can't go out this late at night," a voice upstairs kept saying. Why the hell couldn't she shut up. I'd heard the whole thing since the phone rang, and the little red hand still crawled around the luminous dial.

Revival of classicism with Roger Ascham, Jonson was a classicist, Donne was a metaphysical. To him, a rose was a thought. Eliot said that. Who the hell cares if a rose is a thought. "You're not mad are you honey?" Honey, honey, honey, it looked like she'd at least find a word that wasn't cliche. A faucet was dripping in the kitchen, that damn landlord. Two hundred dollars a month and he couldn't fix the damn faucet. And the garbage, sitting on the cabinet next to the sink in a wax carton, I should have emptied it. The luminous hands said 1:45. I lay, perfectly still. I almost fell asleep, and then I moved again. And Dad, what would Dad say?

The sun was hot and my head hurt. Dad was sitting on the wagon tongue, his thin gray hair running back in wisps from the center of his head and getting thicker toward the back.

"That's a hell of a job," he said. The horses moved and the wagon tongue creaked. "Whoa," he said, "Whoa!" I could taste the dust in my mouth, and I could feel the prickly pieces of hay under my shirt.

"I'd rather do just about anything," I said, feeling my head ache from the effort of talking.

"We better get this in the barn before we eat." He threw his pitch fork up on the load of hay, and reached in his pocket for his handkerchief. "A thousand dollars for tuition is a lot of money," he said. He wiped his face with the handkerchief. "I guess we can't waste no time restin'."

"I don't have to go," I said. He was so damn tight he had to make me feel like he was working himself to death for it. "I could stay here the rest of my life, now couldn't I?"

I stepped up on the side of the wagon and jumped up on the load of hay. Then I went to the back of the wagon and climbed up to open the double doors of the loft. He started pitching it up to me and I stacked it in the loft

The faucet was dripping again. The two little luminous green hands said 2:30. I could hear the mouse in the trash box, rustling among the paper and tin cans. What was it? Somebody said if you lie still it's as good as sleep. I don't think so. I think they said that so you wouldn't worry about going to sleep and would go to sleep. He'd flunk me.

"Clark, you failed the midterm," he said, rubbing the palms of his hands to wipe off the chalk dust. He had chalk dust on the back of his coat. "The paper was unacceptable. Don't you have a dictionary?"

"The Dean said a C+ average, Dr. Pope. I've got to have half B's and half C's or I don't come back."

"You've got the final left, Clark," he said. He had the chalk in his hand and he was scraping on the board again: "First year composition will meet in room 213, 2 p.m."

"If I make a B on the final will I get a C?" I leaned against the scarred wooden desk in the front of the room.

"You did better than this in first year composition." He put the chalk back into the tray. "You surprised me, Clark." He brushed his hands on his coat.

"I can't seem to think anymore," I said. I flicked the ashes off into a jar lid that was on top of the desk. I wondered where it came from.

"At least you could have looked up the words in the dictionary. Then maybe the paper would have been acceptable." Outside the window, a lawnmower roared. It seemed like they mowed that grass twice a day. "I'm afraid I can't help you much Clark," he said. "But, like I said, you have the final. I hope it's in your favor."

Upstairs the woman was pacing the floor. I guess she couldn't sleep. Why didn't she at least stay quiet? The clock said four a.m. I got out of bed and picked up my notebook.

I'd taken the pills and I felt like I could do it when he got there and started passing the examinations around the room. Outside the sun was glaring. I wished it was raining. The rules said no smoking, but I took out a cigarette anyway. I finally got the shaking match up to the cigarette. I wiped my hands on my trousers and took hold of the pencil. Outside, that damned lawnmower was going again.

John Donne, Ben Jonson, and William Shakespeare, there were three questions. They covered the metaphysicals, classicism, and the sonnet sequences. The chalk was scraping again. Corrections, he scraped on the board, and then beneath it he wrote some words and where to find them.

I started writing but it didn't make much sense and then I remembered that I'd have to organize. My wet hand was slipping down on the pencil. I wiped it on my trousers again. Ben Jonson was a classicist. He believed in a classical adherence to form. I wrote feverishly on the paper and then I couldn't think about anything but the next question and John Donne.

The chalk was scraping "an hour and forty-five minutes" on the board. That meant at least an hour and fifteen minutes had passed. I started to write quickly but it was a jumble and the lawnmower was rumbling in my aching head.

I left my test and went out into the hall. "You can't petition the committee," Mr. Riley would say. I felt in my pocket for my bus ticket. Dad would say: "A thousand dollars! A thousand dollars, mind you, and he comes back and says: 'Well, I guess I didn't make it.' Now maybe he'll learn that a thousand dollars don't come easy enough to throw away on nothin'."

Wheels and Miracles

"I got the gift of God in my fingers and the power of the Lord in my brain," Harry laughed. He reached out from under the '41 Chevrolet truck we were rebuilding. "Give me a 1/2 inch box end to put the finishin' touches on the Lord's work."

I slapped the wrench into his grease covered palm and said, "Didn't your ma ever tell you? The Lord don't have dirty hands."

The dirty light bulb, hanging from its thick, snake skin cord, spotlighted the truck. It cast a magic blue spell in the dim light, making the grease black floor and the cluttered, grime covered work tables in the background feel warm.

We honed and polished six layers of blue paint. That way, we saw the beauty of it while we worked.

Harry and I worked at Walker's Garage. Walker let us use the garage at night after I realized what the old '41 junker in my mom's back yard could look like.

"My ma never told me nothin'." Harry laughed from under the truck. "She left me a poor victim of pleasure," he laughed.

"And we gonna' find it, ain't we Harry," I said.

"You got it, boy. We're gonna haul our asses to it in this blue chariot." Then, "Goddamn!" And he pushed himself from under the truck, the wheels of the coaster he lay on grated against the cement floor. He shook his head and looked at his hand to calculate the damage to his knuckles. His freckled face looked angry. His thick red hair was flecked with grease from running his fingers through it while he solved a problem. You could always tell when he was about to say or do something. And it wouldn't be a guess. He was almost always right. He would look or listen for awhile, and tell you the truth, whether it was a person or a car engine. He was always looking at his hands and saying, "Jack, my brains are in my fingers. I don't have the advantage of that head room you got. You better watch so we don't fuck up."

Blood oozed from the knuckle of his right index finger. Harry, wiping the blood and dirt on his jeans, laughed. "See what the Lord does to blasphemers. He makes their wrenches slip."

Harry and I never talked about religion much, except to joke. Harry's mother went to church though. It must have been good for her. Harry and I had to run out from under a hail of fire and brimstone every time we stopped by his house. Mine wasn't much better.

I can still remember those days when Harry and I were putting that piece of junk together just good enough to roll it down to the garage. Ma'd be giving some man she lived with hell about his not being worth a damn and her being cursed by the baby and some worthless man to feed. Harry'd look up from the motor of that '41 Chevy, one hand on a wrench, and wipe the sweat that was coming down into his slightly faded blue eyes. He'd look at the cracked white paint on the clapboard house. Then he'd look at me and grin, "You can't say it's borin' around your house." I'd laugh and Harry would laugh too.

"Hell, if I didn't know better I'd, think it was the same man she was yellin' at all the time," I'd say. Then we'd both stop laughing.

"Hand me a 1/4 inch nut," Harry'd say. "We gotta' get outta' here."

But where to? Right now it was to get that '41 Chevy truck down to Walker's garage where we could work on it nights and Sundays. We'd seen it in movies, where guys like us started out and ended up finding some beautiful girl like Sally Struthers in some dreamland where the magic was always right there, to touch and to love you with all that blonde softness and all that understanding feeling in her face. Her eyes filled with the beautiful tears of the tragedy that almost separated them and the happiness of their being together now. Right now, Harry was asking for a 1/4 inch nut and trying to get that pickup moving away from the sound of reality coming from the house.

We watched the girls in our classes and in the lunch room at school; but Harry, who had this habit of reading novels through his classes about poor boys finding a pot of gold and beautiful rainbows, hit the truth one day when I was calling his attention to one of the cutest butts and prettiest faces I'd ever seen. Running the fingers of his left hand through his hair.

He said, "but they seem so out of reach." There was even a touch of hopelessness in his face.

After changing a tire or the oil in somebody else's car, I'd be scrubbing my hands with industrial strength detergent and I'd look up at the yearning face on the calendar of some girl who didn't really have an address. She stood there like an hallucination in the middle of all that dirt and grease in a bikini, asking me to love her. I'd get that same feeling Harry had on his face when he said that thing about their being out of reach.

Harry and I were going to join the Navy and see the world until one day Harry looked thoughtfully out at Charleston Bay, kicked the sand that was everywhere in Charleston with his work boot, ran his fingers through his thick red hair and said, "This ain't it, Jack." When I asked him why, he said, "You realize how big that ocean is? You join that thing them posters advertise and you're gonna' see a hell of a lot more water than anything else."

We both laughed. I thought it was really clever of Harry to figure that out and he had a funny way of putting things. I sometimes thought he'd have been one hell of a stand-up comedian if he'd been born somewhere else.

Don't get me wrong. Harry believed in himself. And I believed in Harry. Most of the time I believed in myself. One of us was always believing that there was no way the two of us could lose.

Harry kept reading those books. He got kicked out of English class and school for two weeks and we both devoted full time to the pickup. Harry's last name was Adams and the teacher had a system. His was the first seat and he never looked up from his novel. Harry said that was all she had, just a whole lot of systems. And he ought to know about systems. I've seen him take a watch apart and put it back together. And I saw it run with my own eyes. He laughed and said, "With these hands, Jack," he held them up in front of me, "we're gonna' work miracles."

"You mean we're gonna' get out of this dump?" I asked.

"More than that, Jack," he said, pushing back the painted white pine chair he was sitting on and getting up from the dingy white table that his mother threw dinner on.

I believed him. That was the only thing that wasn't a joke to Harry.

Harry read this book, *Moll Flanders*, while Ms. Brigham, our English teacher, preached. Harry sat right in front of her, running his left hand through his rumpled hair with his mind over in England somewhere with this whore.

After telling me Moll was a whore, he delivered his opinion on that, "Whores ain't bad, Jack," he said. "Not like some of the fellows think. They're just tryin' to buy something the only way they know how."

"Do they ever get it?" I asked.

"Only in the movies, Jack," he said. "And that's what worries me. What if them movies and books are lyin' about some other things?"

"They can't be, Harry," I said. "Look at it this way, the guy that wrote them books had to see it somewhere."

He just laughed and said, "Hell, man, if it can be done we can do it. Can't we?"

And I said, "You're right, Harry." But I'd also read this book, *Tess of the D'urbervilles*, that Harry had passed on to me. I was still a little worried about us being born in the wrong place.

But Harry was back up, telling me about this place in Washington that everybody was always talking about where there were still wagon tracks that have been there for a hundred years and how we'd have that pickup riding on tires that would take us down those wagon tracks.

"The girls there ain't like these," he said. "It's like those old movies. They're beautiful and honest. They can be soft like a woman, sometimes and they can fix a car another time. And they don't need all that makeup to hide behind."

"We could have a garage," I said. "Like an old blacksmith shop."

"That's right," Harry said. "If that's what we're lookin' for."

"Now," I said, "we've got to get that truck out of Ma's back yard."

We cut across a sandy lot between two crumbling buildings. The weather beaten walls advertised MFA and Sunshine flour in white paint. The clay colored brick intruded through the worn paint. I was walking with my Pa through this same lot when he said, "Boy, don't buy no pig in a poke. That's why I gotta' leave you."

"We aren't going to buy nothin' we haven't seen," I said.

"For sure," Harry said. "We're gonna' see it without the makeup." He looked out across Charleston Bay. "Just look at all that water." We both started laughing. "And we were goin' to join the navy. You ever seen two dumber guys?"

"We got a two week vacation from school, didn't we?" I said. "That's not too dumb. We can have that truck out of Ma's back yard." We laughed even harder.

I always thought of it as Ma's house. A lot of the kids, when they got out of school, said they were going home. Harry and I never said that. We could always hear our mothers saying, "Not in my house. While you're in my house, you'll do what I say in my house."

That was about the time this girl named Lisa, who was a class behind us at Palmetto High School, started hanging around the garage at night while we worked on the pickup.

Her brown hair hung halfway down her back and the thick waves of hair flowed down the sides of a face that, without makeup, looked too pale. Whether we knew it or not, Harry and I were still looking for kewpie dolls. Harry's Ma called the pretty, little grownup dolls she still saved from her childhood, kewpie dolls. So, we called all those out of reach girls at school kewpie dolls or doll faces.

Lisa always wore the same jeans and the same t-shirt that said, "ASK AND YOU SHALL RECEIVE." She'd had it printed on there. I'd never seen another one like it. when I told her I'd never seen that on a t-shirt before, she said, "That's why it's on mine."

When I asked her what the saying meant, she said, "Try askin'."

Harry laughed and rolled out from under the truck. He sat slouched on the coaster and ran the fingers of his left hand through his thick red hair. Harry liked wit like that and she stood there with the same mischievous look on her face that Harry always wore.

"You're O.K. for a kid your size," Harry said.

Lisa looked serious for a moment, and then she said, "No, I mean it. What do you really want?"

Harry and I both stopped laughing. Whatever we really wanted we couldn't put into words. But we really believed that the truck could carry us to the answer.

Harry turned and looked at the ripped and worn through interior of the pickup.

Lisa studied Harry's face and followed his glance with her two bright green eyes that could see and understand anything she looked at. Then she said, "I got sumpthin' to trade." She put one hand on each hip that anybody ought to know could sell a million pairs of jeans.

"I'll fix the inside of your truck," she said.

"For what?" Harry asked. He looked a little troubled and ran his fingers through his hair, trying to figure this girl out. We hadn't let anybody else in on our dreams yet, but I guess she overheard enough to know.

"A ride outta' this dump on the seats I fix when you guys go," she said.

"O.K." I said. "Ain't that O.K., Harry?" I asked.

"Yeah," Harry said, lying back down on the coaster. "Anything you want little sister. But we have to go with you when you shop for leather. This is going to be one quality vehicle."

At first, we didn't cuss or nothing around her. After all, she was a girl and things were awkward until one day Harry bumped his head on the cramped quarters under the differential and he yelled, "Dammit Sis, your ass just weights down that seat too much."

"It looks a hell of a lot better than your face," she said. Then we all started laughing again. It's days like those that you dream about after you've driven yourself somewhere else.

The three of us were walking down the hall at school and this fellow bumped into Lisa, causing him to drop all his books. When he picked them up he mumbled, "Bitch."

Harry beat the hell out of him and we all took Harry's vacation with him. I could understand Harry doing it, but I never really understood how much he liked her until I saw how mad he was. I'd seen him fight before. Harry never got mad. Said getting mad was a weakness. "Get the other guy mad, and he can't calculate," he said. When I asked him about it, Harry didn't say anything. I began to notice him and Lisa leave the garage the same direction every night. When I asked him about that he just said, "I don't sleep as much as you do Jack. I don't like to be in the dark by myself."

"Get yourself a night light," I said and we both laughed. From then on they didn't hide it from me. And we all began to study maps together. Lisa and Harry wanted to go West through the Smokey Mountains. I wanted to go West and North through North Carolina and West Virginia. We kept following little red and back lines with our fingers and Harry occasionally reached up and touched Lisa's face while he watched her electric green eyes. She was beautiful. I almost felt what it must have felt like when Harry reached out, brushed her long hair back from her neck and pulled all those waves that were her body to his own. Freeing herself, Lisa would turn like a child ordering toys to the towns of the map and we'd daydream about how great it was going to be just to be where life was.

Outside, the spring rains pounded the tin roof over our heads and would turn the coming heat to the hot, boring summer that Charleston was to all of us.

Harry said that we should plot our course over the back roads. Said that way we could get to know the towns better. We weren't going anywhere in particular, anyway, and the interstates were always the same place with their tourist traps and gas stations. Lisa said she thought they must have all used the same pattern for miniature towns and truck stops.

We would all live together, as mobile as the truck, and we'd never get separated. Lisa said that together we could make it, and both Harry and I would turn and think about how great it was that Lisa was one of us. She always brought that electricity of hers into the garage with her, and Harry and I would both be looking at our watches to see how much longer we had to wait to see her face. We even stopped talking about how pretty the car was and talked about the day when Lisa first started with us.

All she had to do was to shake her head one way or the other over one of those lines on the map and Harry and I would change to her black or red line and daydream about this or that small town or mountain. And that's the way it was right up until the time that Lisa left us. Lisa would always pick the state, whether it was Oregon or Tennessee, and we would begin to describe things we'd heard but never seen.

I would watch her as her body moved, upholstering the seats and sanding the dashboard. Harry laughed one day when I handed him a screwdriver instead of a wrench. He looked out from under the truck, still laughing, and said, "Jack, that had better not have been a Freudian slip."

We thought we'd found it once in Santa Fe, New Mexico. Lisa worked as a waitress in a Pizza Hut. Harry worked at Tom's garage and I was a cook at Cowboy Bill's Bar and Grill. We rented a small apartment. Lisa picked the furniture that we bought at Good Will and Harry and I painted the walls and put up the curtains. We were even there long enough for Harry to fix up an antique radio while Lisa and I braided these outlandish throw rugs that looked like maps of all the states we'd seen.

When we left work now, we always said we were going home. Lisa and I had changing schedules so it was usually Harry who waited at home with some surprise plans that he worked out in detail.

At first, we couldn't see enough of the geography of the place. If there was ever a rainbow of colors and, to us, unique creations of rock, cactus and thick walled houses that looked as cool as a cave from the outside, this was it.

And then we met this fellow from New York. Harry and I both liked him and he could always think of things to do around people. Everybody liked him. Especially Lisa. Harry didn't notice.

She even began to sound a bit like him. You know, the phrases he used, the little mannerisms and all that. Once I saw her leave work six hours before she told Harry and I she got off. I didn't follow her. Anyway, it was really nobody's business. I couldn't prepare Harry. I hoped he'd never have to notice. Nobody can own anyone else. But I'd sure gotten fond of having her around and Harry'd been happier than he'd ever been since the three of us worked in Walker's garage on that truck.

It happened while I was gone. When I got home he had both our suitcases packed and was sitting on one of the braided rugs, running his fingers through his rumpled, red hair. This wasn't a mechanical problem. He just couldn't work miracles.

"You knew?" he asked.

"Yeah," I said. I sat down on the rug beside him and put my arm around him.

Out on the highway he didn't say a word for five hundred miles. I knew he was talking to one image or another of Lisa all the time. He felt her presence and the tragedy of her never being there at the same time. He'd have to go a long way to escape that.

"Turn around!" he said.

"It won't do any good, Harry," I said.

"What won't?" he asked.

"To go back and beg her," I said. "It'll just hurt like hell."

He laughed that laugh that is more hysterical than real, "Hell," he said, "I'm not going back there. We got to get to the Smokey Mountains before they move 'em. It's hills like that. That's where it is and you can raise stuff on 'em."

Then he began, with the excitement of a man who can't sleep, and doesn't want to think about the thing that's most important to him, to tell me about the mountain folk, and how there weren't no phonies among them.

The Gate

I SAT THERE ON THE GATE, the one that swayed in the middle, and threw sticks at the stupid cow. Ma was sick again, Ma was always sick, and I couldn't go off and leave her just because Bill Nettles' silly old cat had three black kittens and one white one. Bill said I could have the white one if I wanted it, but I reckoned I wasn't gonna' git it 'cause Ma was allergic to cats, and if it weren't cats, it'd be somethin' else just as bad she was allergic to.

"Darrel! Come here a minute." I heard Ma's voice from 'cross the road up at the house.

"What do you want, Ma?" I yelled back, knowin' I wouldn't get no answer. I climbed off the gate and threw one last rock at the hind end of the stupid cow. Then I headed toward the house. As I went in the back door I saw that the screen door was ripped. Pa should have fixed that before he left. But since that was all he was good for, I don't reckon he was much of a loss. Ma was always yellin' at him, but I didn't care. I guess he deserved it if anybody did.

"Ma," I said, "screen door's got a hole in it. Ain't the flies gonna' get in?"

"I guess it ain't no matter now," she said.

I sure wasn't expectin' that, because as soon as I said it I could hear her yellin' at Pa and he wasn't even here.

"Damn you, Jake, you and that boy ain't never been anything but a nuisance to me, what with you sleepin' and eatin' and him trackin' in dirt and always whinin' about goin' some place, and to cap it all off neither one of you fools have even got the sense to fix the screen door"

"What did you say Ma?"

"I guess it don't matter now."

Boy, you can bet your life I wasn't gonna argue with that.

"Ma," I says, "seeing as how you're so sick, maybe I could go to Bill Nettles' house so I could use his phone to call the doctor for you." I thought she would tell me to shut up, git the aspirins, and stay in the house. But Ma didn't say that this time. She just thought a minute.

"Yeah I guess you'd better," she said.

I was kinda' tickled when I heard that. "I'll do that, Ma," I said, "and I won't be gone too long neither."

I left pretty quick. I passed the creek and was headed toward Bill's house. It was kind of hot and dry, and the hot sand sure felt good on my feet. I was already thinkin' about those kittens so I guess that's partly why I forgot all about Ma.

Well anyway, it wasn't too far to Bill Nettles' house, and Bill he saw me comin' right near as soon as I reached his turn off road, and I heard him.

"Ma! It's Darrel them dogs is barkin' at," he yelled.

Bill met me about half way up the road by the chicken house and asked me if maybe I wouldn't like to see the kittens, and he said he had a new baseball glove he'd like for me to see, too. Well, I never had anything like that so I sure did want to see it. Bill always had nice things and he wasn't stingy neither.

Well, forgettin' why I came over, we played with that ball glove awhile. You sure could catch with that a lot better than with your bare hands, and then we went up and looked at the kittens. Them kittens sure was cute, and Bill guessed they might be registered or somethin' like that if anybody knew who their Pa was.

Time seemed to pass mighty fast till it started gettin' dark, and then all of a sudden I felt a kind of a lonesome feelin'.

"Say Bill," I said, "I guess I better get on back home." I tried hard to keep the shakiness out of my voice because Bill wouldn't understand how it was, and I headed for home without even waitin' for him to say anything.

By the time I reached the road above Bill's house, it was dark and some clouds were kinda' shiftin' around like it might rain, but it always looked like that and it never did rain. I passed the creek and hurried on up toward the house, and was almost halfway there before I realized that there weren't no lights in the house.

I ran as fast as I could the rest of the way, and as I came up on the porch I held my breath, but I couldn't hear anything inside.

"Ma!" I says, "Ma, you in there?" But she didn't answer. I hoped maybe she'd already gone to sleep, but when I opened the door and saw what was there I couldn't even breathe. She was layin' there in the floor all gray and clammy lookin' with her eyes wide open.

All of a sudden, I didn't know what to do. I just stood there feelin' terrible all over, and then I began to realize how come she died, and I wished to God I could die too. I don't know how long I stood there, but pretty soon somebody came up behind me. I ain't been back there since.

It was a nice funeral, everybody said she looked natural and all. They sung some nice songs all about how heaven was nearer since ma was there, and "No Tears in Heaven" and almost everybody cried or tried to. But me, I couldn't be any closer to hell. I sat there the whole time shakin' and feelin' sick all over. The doctor he said it wasn't my fault, but I know better.

When I came out of the church, the whole sky was cloudy like it might storm. I followed the people up the dirt road from the church about a quarter of a mile to the graveyard. Then they took Ma out of the hearse and the preacher said somethin' about her leadin' a good life and somethin' else about givin' her soul up to God, and then they put her in the hole between two others. Then I heard some shovels clang and a dull thud that left kind of an empty feeling as the dirt hit the coffin. For some reason, I couldn't help thinkin' about the mud and all seepin' between the cracks in that wine colored box. Ma always did hate dirt. She was always bitchin' at me about how I might just as well live in the pigpen with the rest of the hogs. Now here she was, all covered up with dirt and maybe even a few worms.

It would've been better if Pa had been there, but we never could find him. The folks over in South Hampton said he had left there over two weeks back, and nobody knew where he went to. The day he left he just kind of wandered off, and Ma never bothered to ask him where he was goin'. I asked Ma if he was comin' back and she said he was like the rest of the animals around here, he'd come back when he got hungry. But he never did.

I didn't notice that almost everybody had gone until one of the men that filled up the hole said he guessed I'd better come with him, but I just headed on across the road towards home. I looked back once and I thought I was gonna' bust out cryin' again, but I didn't. I turned around and ran as fast as I could until the graveyard was out of sight.

The sun came out again as I crossed the creek. I went on up the road and passed the gate that swayed in the middle. Nothing looked the same. Everything seemed quieter somehow and the cow even looked lonesomer. A chicken cackled up next to the house with a kind of dull quietness. I passed the gate again on my way to Bill Nettles' place.

Princess of Darkness

IT'S AN OVERCAST DAY. Inside these walls it can be any season, any day, any place on Earth; and then again, it can be no place. That's the worst, when I don't have a choice of places to be and I know I'll never see her again. I'll never see anybody again. I'll never be able to lose consciousness or dream again. I sit on the edge of my bed and look four feet across to the white wall, my window on the world. I hear her say, "Your houses always look occupied. They don't look lived in . . ."

Across the bare, hardwood floor I see her oxblood leather jacket over the arm of my one other piece of furniture. I smell her perfume as she bends to kiss me. I'm just waking up, and her warmth feels good, her face comes into focus. She is smiling, but something is wrong. "I have to go now," she says. "I don't want to, but I must." She fades. I call to her. I want to hurry to the door before the car starts to move and she disappears; but I'm paralyzed. I can't get off the couch. The last thing I hear is the car engine.

"Shut that damn thing off!" An engine is running somewhere, an engine without an exhaust system, and from one of these cages, a lunatic yells. He wants his peace and quiet. I laugh.

She smiles from my cluttered desk. I remember now what was wrong before. I got the body right in my mirage. It is soft and smells alive. It was the face. The face wasn't alive. The last time I saw her she gave me the picture. In the picture she smiles for a photographer who is telling her to say cheese. Her dark hair and bangs make her look like an Egyptian in the tombs. It's the only picture I have of her. Scratched across her shoulder and onto her neck like graffiti are the words, *In Loving Memory*.

It's growing darker outside. It must be. I can hardly see to read the *In Loving Memory*, and the frozen face could be anybody. I reach across the desk and turn on the desk lamp. The light conjures the feeling of other cold rooms in winter. She's back.

I'm at my desk in the basement apartment. Outside, snow is piled against the one, high window above my desk, blocking my view. The electric heater by the desk warms the lighted spot around me. I study, taking notes from Nietzsche's *Birth of Tragedy*. She talks to me from the cold darkness of the room behind me. I am annoyed by the interruption.

"I'll miss you," she says.

"Then why go?" I ask. There's a silence. As I look into the white wall in front of me, I feel the tension of her hesitation. I know she wants me to say more, and I want to talk. I want to hold her, to touch her and to feel her relax in my arms. I can hear myself asking her, "Will we be O.K.?" But I don't. All I can think is that I'm angry. She's cheating me. She'd rather be somewhere else with somebody else. I say nothing. I freeze her with the silence and then I realize that she isn't in the cold darkness.

I hear a radio, barely audible, playing the dirge of a country and western beat. We are driving on an asphalt road. On either side of the road are trees and almost total darkness. The warm glow of the radio and the dash lights are the only light in the car. She is telling me a story. Connie Smith, on the radio, is asking a generic man to help her make it through the night.

"I'm glad we left the interstate," she says. "This darkness and this road remind me of Sunday nights, coming home from the day at my grandmother's when I was a small child. After the "Hee Haw" gang sang their finale, the folks would make us put on our boots and coats and we'd drive home in the cold darkness from Sweetwater. Fun and good times were over. I'd be late to bed, and out to catch the bus to school early the next morning."

"I'm glad you're here with me," she says.

As we approach the town, fluorescent and neon lights appear. A black orchid blossoms on the front of a bar, outlined in purple neon tubes. The street lights cast a cold glow over the road as we drive through the middle of a ghost town, past a dead movie theatre, a crumbling garage and a post office . . .

"Rattle the bastard's cage." Two men are outside my cell door. I know there are two because one of them is talking. No one talks to me. Unless someone makes a noise, I don't even know when I'm being watched through the peep hole. The eye, the hole in the door, is like a bullet hole in the human body. It starts out tiny and by the time it gets to the other side they can see the whole room. The eye is watching me now. It sees me sitting at this desk, the fluorescent light on the picture and my hands and thick forearms in front of me. The back of my head is to the darkness behind me; but only the eye occupies the darkness.

A voice in the darkness laughs. "Stupid son-of-a-bitch never moves. I like to see 'em suffer more. Damn him. If I'd done what he did."

"I reckon they don't feel nothin'," another voice says.

"Philosophers." I laugh.

"Salt of the Earth," she says; and we both laugh.

"You know, morons," I say. But she isn't there now.

I've heard that in Russian prisons like this there's a hole in the door, like this peep hole, only big enough for the barrel of a gun. They come any time. No one knows when and the room is no longer occupied.

I see blood splattering on the picture, and I wonder if I have time for one last scene, or if the projector will stop lighting the screen. We are in the Nelson Atkins Museum in Kansas City.

"It's a sarcophagus," I say.

"Dead at last." She laughs. "We used to hide in the graveyard next to the parsonage when Dad got drunk and talked to the devil," she said. "When he got that gleam in his eye and went to the knife rack in the kitchen, we ran like hell, and the cemetery was the safest place. One night he lined us all up against the wall, saying if we flinched when he came at us with the knife, he'd cut the devil out of us. He 'taught us a lesson' all night long. By daylight Liz, my older sister, vomited blood. He made her clean it up with my new Levi's, saying to leave them hanging over the front door as our sacrifice to the Lord." She runs her finger along the imprint of a body carved in the soft limestone of the sarcophagus. She lies down on it and reaches for me.

"What about the guards?" I say.

"There are no guards here," she says. I sit on the edge of the sarcophagus. Her face comes alive with a worried look.

"Are we O.K.?" I ask.

"Oh no," she says, sitting up and looking into the darkness behind me. She laughs and the sound reverberates in the empty grave. I realize she isn't here.

They are laughing again. I can hear them in the hall when they clean up at night. One of them is looking through the hole.

"Poor son-of-a-bitch," he says. "Bet he'd like to have a drag on this joint."

"Shit. He don't even know where he's at," the other one says.

"Oh, well," I hear the first one say as they walk down the hall, "Got to go home to my trouble."

The other one answers, "That's the thing about trouble. It's good to have a place to keep it."

I take the picture off the casket. Fronds of leaves and garlands of flowers reach to the floor on both sides of the casket. A black orchid blooms in the fluorescent light.

"I'm here," she says.

The Black Orchid

THE SUN IS HOT. The hearse is white. I see it now in its darkened garage. The chain link gate revealing the Cadillac elegance. There is no chariot like a hearse. I suppose it's when you realize that only velvet death and silken elegance accompany you that you think of Emily Dickinson and the Grangerford house in Mark Twain's *Huckleberry Finn*, surrounded by death, romance and the parody of Emily Dickinson's work in the paintings of the dead sister. And the sister in *Harlan County U.S.A.* singing, "Oh Death!" like Death was a spirit to talk to in a land that reeked with the smell of blood.

The police are drawing the chalk outlines. A white-haired, leathery-faced man is pointing to the splatters on the cement driveway. They are dry in the sun. One of the policemen is taking notes. It is so hot you can fry an egg on the hot concrete. The protein and the blood almost instantly absorb the moisture in the air as they dry. There must be a difference in drying time between the two substances.

We are standing in this very driveway. I am oblivious to the heat as I push the shiny black hair away from her face and kiss the salty tear flowing onto her full lip. Again, I hear Emily Dickinson saying that she knows it's poetry when the chill runs up her spine and through her scalp. The face, the feeling (the senses *are* windows to the soul) is poetry.

The voice grates from the window of the unmistakable, metallic blue

The Black Orchid

low rider pickup. He still stalks in my mind. I know now he's locked up where I can't kill him, and his voice rings from the street toward that spot where the police are taking their samples and their notes. I see them both yelling. "Hey Baby Doll. I'm luffin' you." And his glare makes the irrational connection between love and hate, sadism and compassion, accepting separation only in death.

Her soft brown eyes register sadness. She understands separation. There is a scar.

"Love without fear?"

I see the soft, deep dark eyes. We sit in the floor of the empty concrete house.

"My first thought when I heard the car start was, *He's gone*," she said. She looks out the window. I watch the profile of her Aztec nose, the dark Chamorro face.

On this white marble floor, in all this whiteness, her dark face and shining black hair absorb the damp encroaching jungle outside the window and I know, except for the spirits in those twisted trees and the dark recesses of her soul, she is alone in this brilliant tomb.

I see the picture sitting on the Egyptian sarcophagus. The same dark face, the same shining black hair, the same profile—in the museum—the vain attempt of an Egyptian Orpheus to dream her back. I lost her for a minute. The memory of the portrait in the museum. "Do not touch." the sign said. Did I look back? I don't want to look back. I can't know. I *will* see, feel, taste, touch and smell her.

"You have to touch," I say. The sun shines on the mountains to the south as they rise like a brilliant green and blue three dimensional mirage. A curl of smoke floats from the hidden valley between us and the mountain.

She laughs. "His touch sure did hurt," she says. She turns toward me, her fingers locked just below her knees. She rests her voluptuous body on firm thighs and her eyes sparkle, laughing into mine.

Past the jungle, past the hot concrete, into room 107 on the second day of class. She is writing her name, year and contact number on the front of a file card, on the back she writes: *I am the girl with the long black hair. You will always remember the scar on my nose.*

I see the face now as I saw it then. I see the artifice preserved in constant perfect temperature by the Nelson Atkins family, having acquired it from the grave robbers, they left another's body to preserve their monument. It's turning cold. In this heat can something turn cold? The wind is stirring and I will not look back to the concrete.

The proud, dark aquiline face, made human (less perfect is more perfect) and sensual by the scarred flesh, leaving the mark that aches, chills and binds. The eyes—dark, lovely and deep, reveal a soul of pure misery. She laughs. Her eyes sparkle in the coal oil lamplight. Darkness fills the room; and the lamp, meant for power failure, spotlights the beauty in our dream of life. The light is soft and yellow in the globe. The darkness flows into, surrounds and protects the body. In this lamplight, she takes my breath away.

"My second thought was to leave as well," she says. "Then, I realized there was no car." The flame wavers and the light touches her face. She laughs.

"That happened to me once," I say. "My first realization was the grief. My second was the entrapment." I meant that she drove off in the car. I see her face turn solemn at the word 'entrapment.' Tears come and one flows down her cheek. In the lamp lit eyes are both the promise of life and the certainty of death. I taste the salt as I hold her. I do not see the warning in the tomb. *Do not touch.*

Velvet is her skin, softer than velvet is her voice. She murmurs the words and, engulfed in the soft yellow and brown world, I see, feel, taste, touch and smell every varying shade, texture and form until the pain of the joy is more than I can bear. Lying back in the darkness, feeling her diaphragm move while my fingers tickle the moist flesh of her soft skin and firm stomach, I wish there had never been electricity, lighting the cold hard concrete and the darkness could hide us forever.

The coal oil lamp lights the patch of marble floor in front of me, blending softly with the darkness. It flickers, drawing my attention to the face, raised on the pillow, asleep and surrounded by the quilted silk lining of the casket. With the soft light I conjure her out of the darkness.

I am lying next to her. She is asleep. I worry. Is she breathing? I reach to feel her diaphragm and touch the soft warm lips. She comes alive, in the fecund darkness, her warm, dark body closing around me as the soft light flickers.

The jungle is alive in the darkness. The flowers open and the warm, heavy air is scented with the perfume that breathes romance and life. A gecko screeches a warning. I awaken from my dream to realize the white coffin and the white silk.

I look to the face again. The lamplight is a kind of scrim, that with its movement, causes the illusion of warmth and life. I know now why Grandma Buckner talked, late at night, to my dead grandfather.

"I took the tickets back today," I say to her face, shrouded in darkness. It is her face but I can't touch it. I can't bring it out of the shroud of darkness. "We'll be staying here." I look around. The room is empty. Only this small marble stage is lighted by the lamp. "I'm sorry. We are trapped."

Stainless Steel

ENRICO ALVARADO SAT on the bare dirt bank of the river in handcuffs and chains. The dirty water sloshed against the bank about five feet beneath him. An empty cigarette package floated on top. Enrico wanted a Pall Mall.

"Got a cigarette?" he asked the man in a gray suit standing to his right. The stocky character with bulging red veined eyes looked at him, amused. Enrico noticed that his blue tie didn't reach the belt of his trousers.

"Bad for your health," the man said. He reached into his shirt pocket and took out a package of Marlboros. He gazed across the river toward a barge that appeared to be crawling down the river on the other side as he lit the cigarette. Then he returned the package to his pocket.

A tall, thin man, with short oily hair, looked over Enrico's head at a point halfway across the river. "Motherfuckers shore took a beatin' last night," he said. He stuffed his blue work shirt further down under his carved leather belt. The buckle was cast iron with two crossed rifles on a gray background, advertising Remmington. He tugged at the corner of his jeans jacket, trying to make the bottom line up with the top of his Levi's.

"Bastard's had it comin'," the stocky man said. He flipped the Marlboro out into the water. Enrico watched it bob on top as the water began, gradually, to soak into it. The wind, blowing across the river, was cold. Enrico wore only the T-shirt he was sleeping in and a pair of old bell bottomed Levi's that had been the first clothes they could find when they picked him up. He dug his bare toes into the dirt and leaned his forehead forward, resting his chin on his wrist in the space between the handcuffs. His long, wavy black hair fell onto his shoulders.

"Huh, Alvarado?" the stocky man said, looking at Enrico with his bulging blood-laced eyes. "Ain't a spic in the world that the best part of him didn't run down his daddy's leg. Ain't that right, Enrico?" he mocked, grinning for the tall man's appreciation.

"This one shore is a piece of work," the tall one said, glancing at the back of Enrico's head. "Jesus!" he said, and spat a glob of phlegm about two inches from Enrico's right foot. Enrico watched the bottom film pick up the light brown dirt as the glob rolled slightly. Then he looked down toward the rusty, abandoned bridge that spanned the river about a quarter of a mile away.

"Enrico," she drawled, "that's a name to remember." Her hair was short and blonde, and her light blue eyes were that color that made Enrico think of stainless steel. Tanya Tucker wailed on the jukebox. A dark complected girl wearing black shorts, a white long-sleeved blouse with a small, black tie and a very friendly smile on full lips, approached the table with a tray of beer mugs. She could see over the heads of the men slouched at the bar into their cowboy doubles behind it. The line of whiskey bottles behind the bar made a double partition between the bar and its reflection. Enrico was certain it was the best watered whiskey in Rosedale. The name of the town was pretty, like the dark Spanish Rose that brought the beer.

Her dark eyes glistened and her face turned serious as she set his beer down on the walnut table. Her thigh muscles flexed slightly as she put the drinks down. Enrico thought about the butterfly tattoo on the soft skin peeking out from under the shorts. Her firm hips and flat stomach shifted rhythmically as she moved away from him. It was as if she read his mind and winked.

She became hostile, serving the blonde women with the fascinating blue eyes. They didn't remind her of steel and she wanted to put out their fire. The fat man winked and grinned at her when she gave him his beer. He looked knowingly at Enrico, still grinning, "Damn!" he said. "If I weren't a married man, she'd have all my money before the night was through." The blonde broke her mask with a perceptible grimace of contempt and disgust. Enrico's mask didn't crack. He smiled at the man with the conspirator's smile that he was supposed to wear. His mind flashed to the knife in his pocket. He imagined the fat man's tie replaced by a Columbian necktie. Still smiling, he said, "For sure! Someday maybe I'll see that you get your fill." The fat man's face become serious for a moment. As soon as he turned to study the waitress, Enrico gave the blonde lady a different kind of conspiratorial look. She smiled.

"God, in all his glory, could never give me my fill," the fat man said, cupping his hands around his beer mug. He grinned at Enrico. Enrico doubted that. "The fat man's blonde did not appear to be filled to the brim," he thought imagining to himself. The fat man laughed with him, thinking it was his humour stirring Enrico to laughter. Now the blonde woman's foot was touching Enrico's leg under the table.

Outside, in the darkness of the Spanish style courtyard, Enrico pulled the blonde woman to himself. The soft flesh of her back transmitted erectile energy through his fingers. In the darkness he could not remember a body more exciting. His lips moved from her mouth down to the hollow of her neck and her body relaxed into his.

Inside, the fat man was distracted by what he called "chiquita bananas." He bought them drinks, growing drunker himself. The band played loud Spanish music and Rose, carrying her tray, moved with the skill of a dancer through the crowd of excited customers, their oily skin shining in the light from the dance floor.

Sitting on the grass outside the courtyard, Enrico leaned back against the wall, lit a Pall Mall and handed it to the blonde woman. She took it, murmured "Thank you," inhaled and, hugging her knees, said, "That was nice."

The strains of the girl singer crooning "Heaven's just a sin away," floated out into the darkness. Enrico watched the clouds drift across the white moon with its rugged face and thought about Rose. He saw her serving the fat man and his "chiquita bananas." He was certain she noticed the missing pair. He would have to explain.

He saw her face, framed by turbulent black hair, amazed and angry as if she couldn't believe her own mind. Her brown eyes flashed. "That pig?" she would say in amazement. Then in sad disbelief, "That pig."

He looked at the woman. She looked older now. The dim light had lied. Close up, without the music and the lies, her features were harsh. Her chin was sharp, and what she said rang with an emptiness easily recognizable.

She put her hand on his leg, just above the knee. "I could do that forever," she said and shivered.

"Yeah," Enrico said, and flipped his Pall Mall into the darkness. He wanted to go back inside. He thought of the dark girl singing on the lighted bandstand, watching the audience. Entering seemed much more difficult than slipping out. He thought about Rose, watching the door occasionally, as she hurried from the bar to the tables, angrily and anxiously awaiting his appearance.

From the top, he pulled the blonde lady up and over the wall. Hurrying through the trees, he felt as if he were shaking an unpleasant dream from his mind. The night air seemed cool and clean. He felt sorry about Rose, stuck in the hot roadhouse, working into the night.

Enrico felt the blood trickle down the side of his face. His head ached and he couldn't hear out of the ear on that side. He belched air into his mouth and tasted the gas, damp with blood. He thought he swallowed the blood. He could taste fresh blood in his mouth. He thought about Rose and his folks in El Paso. He saw the large fading photograph of his grandparents and his missing uncle, that he'd never seen in the ornate gold colored frame. The glass front was shiny and bubbled out. As a child, he spent hours studying the little boy's face. When he asked his father about the missing child, his uncle, his father simply said, "I don't believe he's dead. He's somewhere. He'll be back." Enrico studied the little fellow's dark, sad face under the bubble. He knew the melancholy that the face felt. He knew the face was dead.

"He went to dance," his grandmother said. Her face was like leather. She wiped her hands on her apron that hung over her protruding belly. Enrico thought the belly was somehow related to having seven children. "He went to a dance and he never come back. He won't be back," she said and looked at the picture over Enrico's head. Tears still came in her eyes. When Enrico saw tears he saw the boy as a teenager, somewhere lying in that unnatural position that he knew lifeless bodies fell into, his black hair matted with blood on one side and blood trickling from his mouth. "They don't never come back," she said. "We told the police. The policeman just looked at us the way they always look at us. Looked about for a pad. Yelled at somebody to bring him one. Said they never had nothin' handy. I said, 'You'll find him, won't you?'" He just looked at me. I could tell I wasn't even there. I wanted to say, 'I love my son! Please, please, Mister.' But another officer was already saying, "We'll let you know if we pick him up.'" Enrico didn't know for sure when he heard her tell him that.

He thought of Rose. "Shit." he thought and he felt something well up in his throat. He suddenly became aware of the two men.

The tall, thin, greasy one was laughing. His teeth were stained with tobacco and some of them were missing. "Yeah," he said, "that Myrtle's something else."

The stocky one was grinning, his eyes crinkled at the edges and his pudgy cheeks formed little pink cushions at the cheekbones. "Remember when he found her with Rafe? I was drivin'. I thought I'd die when we come up on them two cars right here on this very dirt road." He shook his short, stubby finger at the dirt road that went by the river bank. "There was her red '78 Impala, as plain as day, in our headlights. I didn't have to do no license check. And there was Rafe's old green Ford truck right in front of it." He laughed. "They was in her car. Even if there was a place on earth to run, old Rafe's truck was in the way."

The tall, thin one shook his head, grinning. He squatted, studying the dirt road to his left. "I shore would like to get some of that myself," he said. He slowly turned a twig between decayed teeth.

"I thought the Chief was gonna' kill old Rafe," the stocky one said. "There was them two heads, right up against each other, lookin' like two scared chickens into the Chief's headlights. I could have died. I knowed they couldn't see it was the Chief. The Chief, he just left them lights on and got out his door. I went as quick as I could thinkin', 'Oh shit, Rafe's finished.' The Chief moves quick for a fat man. When I got there he had that gun right up side Rafe's cheek. I thought I smelled shit. I didn't know if it was Rafe or both of 'em."

The tall thin one laughed as he stood up and threw his twig in the direction of Enrico. "Looks like she got into some shit this time," he said.

Enrico wondered who they were talking about. The sun, from behind a cloud, brightened half the river and the yellowed leaves of some dying brush on the opposite bank. Rose would be sleeping now after working late. He saw the white sheet pulled part way past her slim waist up her naked back. She liked to sleep nude. Even now, the thought of her cute butt, shifting slightly from under the edge of the sheet and her flat tummy beneath the curve of her slightly raised thigh, made him stiffen. His eyes moved, almost with a sense of touch, up the small, well defined body to the dark, sleeping doll's face and his fingers touched its pouting lips.

He saw her at the police station with both anger and anxiety reflected in her large dark eyes. The white police officer grinned at her with flirtatious contempt. "We ain't got him," the cop would say, "but I'd like to have you."

"Shit," said the tall, thin one, rubbing out a cigarette and looking down the dirt road. 'I wish that fuckin' Chief would hurry."

"Take it easy, Cowboy," the stocky one said, turning to look down the road as well. "It ain't every day he gets to do something like this."

"Piss on it," said the tall thin one. "I want breakfast before noon. Damn if I don't." He began to pace back and forth behind Enrico.

"What about the poor Spic?" the stocky one laughed.

The tall, thin one looked at Enrico and grinned. "Miss yore Tequila Sheila, boy?"

The stocky one laughed, reaching into his pocket for another Marlboro and looking casually down the road. "Looks like he's had one Tequila Sheila too many."

"He's probably got the clap," the tall one said. "What's the Chief gonna' do if he gets this boy's clap?"

"It won't be the first time the Chief's had Tex Mex clap," the stocky one said, looking absently at Enrico. "He likes Mexican women." They both laughed. He thought a minute, still looking at Enrico. "Don't mind 'em myself," he said. "I like the way some of that dark meat moves when you stab it."

He droned on into a story about this Mexican girl he saw sometimes when his old lady wasn't looking and Enrico stopped listening. It was hard not to listen for clues. They hadn't exactly come with a warrant and read him his rights. He thought about Rose again, and heard her voice saying sadly, "That pig."

He saw his dad's face and felt the homesickness in his stomach. The leathery face was tired and wrinkled. He was still handsome with his iron gray hair. "He don't like for folks to die," Enrico thought. Enrico saw his own high school graduation picture sitting on the mantel. He was dressed up in the only suit he'd ever owned. His mother's eyes had filled with tears at the graduation. They'd all come. He'd been embarrassed all the way to and from the parking lot. Three fucking generations of spics for a silly high school graduation. Grandpa in his baggy wool pants and brogans, Mama crying. "Shit," he thought.

"If it ain't about time," the thin man said. They grabbed Enrico, turned him around and stood him up.

"Time to meet your maker, boy," the stocky one said. A large white Chrysler came down the dirt road from the left. Dust welled up in funnels behind the rear wheels. It pulled up in front of them.

Enrico saw the blonde woman on the passenger side. Her pale blue eyes looked at him without expression through the window.

Cat and Garbage

The sign said, "City Limits, Birmingham" through the red-tinted light of the disappearing sun. The population figures made no impression on my mind. I have no real concept of what figures mean anyway. Then I saw her. Pushing her brown hair back from her tan face, she waved, first as if she were frantically saying "Hi," then palm down, asking me to stop. Tired, barely able to see in the fading light that was neither darkness nor fog but some other mystery having something to do with the way eyes work, I pulled the already slowed '69 Chevrolet onto the gravel shoulder. I looked back past the car's prominent, white, right rear and felt it's old age tiredness. I'd been in it so long I felt like it could actually feel, and in my head it felt tired like me.

She hurried toward the car, her thin body barely visible through the baggy, army fatigue pants. The large, snapped pockets bulged. She carried no other baggage.

She opened the door with a weak, fake smile. She looked too drained and tired for it to be real. Then she slid onto the seat beside me, looking directly down the empty highway as if it was interesting.

I was tired. I didn't hurry to move and she said nothing. Then, realizing that I hadn't moved, I said, "I guess this isn't it," motioning toward Birmingham with its dirty gray factories and a rotting wooden house or two. The factories with their dust covered windows, some of them broken, and their soot covered walls, hit me with depression. They were bad enough to look at from the outside. I thought about the hundred degree temperature, the roar of the machinery and the grime that collects on the human body that works inside them. I'd been there.

"You'd better believe it, Mister; and start movin'," she said, still looking at the highway. No part of her tan face resembled a Barbie doll. It was a bit too long, her nose was off center to the left. She pursed her full lips and her forehead wrinkled with anxiety, the marks of which people who are always worried carry.

"Look. I'm tired," she said.

She started unbuttoning her khaki shirt and said, with the same boredom, "Sure Mister, anything you want, but can't you wait to get out of this dump?"

"That's not what I meant," I said. "I didn't mean that at all. It would bore me as much as the thought of it bores you. Will you drive this damn thing?" I asked, motioning toward the large hood that I identified with to the point of feeling its heat after thirteen hours of driving.

"Why not?" she said. She opened the door quickly to change positions.

"I'll sleep in the back seat awhile," I said. I opened the back door as she took the driver's seat.

"Which way?" she asked. I was already curling my legs to fit the seat space so my head could rest enough to sleep.

"Anywhere," I said. "I was going north and it looks like you wanted to go that way. If you have any idea where the promised land is, head in that general direction, otherwise just drive." She didn't answer. She pulled the tired car off the gravel shoulder. I felt its movement as I relaxed to sleep.

When I woke up, rain flowed down on the windshield, making the slow efforts of the worn windshield wipers more nuisance than aid. Her motionless body simply held the car on the wide slab of concrete that I recognized as an interstate. I sat up in the seat and ran my fingers through my mass of black hair. Felt the flecks of gray that I knew were there without seeing them.

"You hungry, Mister?" she asked, still not turning her head.

"For two days," I said. The rain pounded the dulled white roof of the top of the car. "Gas comes before food," I said. "I don't think about food much any more. Without gas, you can't move. The last thing a man should be willing to give up is the ability to move."

She unsnapped one of her large baggy trousers pockets, pulled out a sandwich, wrapped in a wrinkled paper bag and handed it over the seat behind her.

"Just take half of it, Mister," she said. "I'm as short of food as you are gas."

I felt my mouth water as I took the sandwich. I broke it as a tractor trailer roared past, splashing a wave of water that cut off, for a moment, all view outside the car.

"You a school teacher or sumpt'n'?" She'd actually started a conversation.

"Why? I asked. What difference does it make what I once was?" I handed the larger half of the sandwich back over the seat to her. She took it and, feeling the size through the brown paper, turned her face around to look at mine for the first time.

"None," she said, "But," patting the pocket she'd stuffed the cheese sandwich into, "this does." Then she turned her face back into the darkness and the flow of water that was our view of the world.

It seemed like we rode an hour like that. Me watching the water, an occasional lonely green, fluorescent lighted sign that would predict anything from Knoxville, Tennessee to Chicago, Illinois. I could hear people from the past in both frivolous and serious conversations. I had meant nothing to them in a long time, yet I still rehearsed our conversations in the darkness. The windshield wipers clanked. Their main function seemed to be to make that noise of an autonome, an autonome where there were no musicians to play.

"You know where we are?" she asked.

"No."

"You care?"

"No," I said. "Just tell me what the gas gauge reads. It's tricky. You can't trust it and we'll probably have to fill it soon."

"I already did that,' she said. "It registers empty a long time before you find a truck stop."

She'd found a truck stop. Where did she get the money? I didn't ask. I knew it must not have been much money. She shared my philosophy about food.

"You eat yet?" I asked. I caught myself watching the back of her head. I was surprised that I really meant the question and waited for the answer.

"Tomorrow," she said. "We'll split the other half." She must have had something to eat before I found her in Birmingham. Another fluorescent green sign told us we were in Bucksnort, Tennessee. From the interstate, Bucksnort appeared to be the only Phillips 66 truck stop anywhere in the country.

"We're in the Smokey Mountains," I said. "They'll get steeper. Rain tires folks out. You better sleep awhile. I'll drive."

When we changed seats, I helped, with the instinctive manners I hadn't lost, her out of the seat by lifting her up by the hand. She was tired. I thought I felt her try to hold my hand a little longer than necessary, but I couldn't be sure. I dismissed it. I'd learned a long time ago not to try to interpret people's behavior. She was probably just steadying herself from hunger and fatigue.

I started to jerk awake, not knowing I had been asleep, so I pulled inside a roadside park where some people like me and a truck or two were taking the same rest.

When I woke up, the sun was up and a truck driver was racing his engine. At first, I couldn't remember where I was. I sat there, waking up, watching a thin gray cat, its body as flexible as a spring. It furiously ate a bit of something repulsive that somebody had thrown out and missed the garbage. I wondered if the girl was still there or if she had found a more dependable ride with a truck driver. For some reason, I hoped she had. I hadn't cared about anyone for a long time, so it struck me strange that I cared. Truck drivers were less likely to hurt girls. At the same time, I felt this other feeling like disappointment that she wouldn't still be there. I couldn't explain that either. It seemed obvious to me that I was on a one way trip to nowhere. I guess even people that aren't going anywhere would still like not to go alone. I thought about picking up the gray cat and then realized that I didn't have any more food than it did. Her saying we'd share the other half of the cheese sandwich crossed my mind. I just sat there thinking how nice a gesture like that would have been. The girl was alright. She did put gas in the car. She didn't have to do that.

Just to be sure, I checked the back seat and there was nobody in it. I sat there for awhile, seeing her face, the anxious forehead and the way it all came together to make her a person. It seemed silly even to me, but I hadn't had any human contact for a long time. I just rehearsed those conversations from a long time ago with people that didn't even know I was alive. I supposed they all lived normal lives. I could see them playing with their wives and children or standing around a barbecue in what I imagined their backyard had expanded to now, drinking a can of beer and making some joke about "the present administration" with their best friend while they turned a steak on the grill.

I could see the girls I had known, inside the kitchen. This time, two strangers would be at the grill that one could see through the patio doors. The women would be talking about what little Jimmy said last week that made that child so precocious and getting the silverware ready for the meal. Little Jimmy, at ten years old, would burst into the room wearing a ball glove and anxiously wanting to know if he and Arthur could go play with Jack and Cooter next door. I could even see his short cropped hair and smell that smell that kids have when they play hard.

The people around me were beginning to wake up. A new car with two parents, a red haired ten year old girl, an eight year old blond boy and a baby pulled in next to my junker to go to the toilets. The children stared at me and I knew that their parents had noticed. They were the same people I'd left years ago. There was a strange division in my mind between the man who sat there embarrassed, feeling his unshaven face and the professor that he used to be. I saw myself as this piece of human refuse that this man had parked next to. I noticed the man very quickly lock all of his car doors while the rest of the family headed toward the John.

I tapped my pocket for the bar of soap and razor that I carried and looked around for a spigot or some such thing. If nothing else, I'd wet my face from the water fountain. A truck stop would have a cheap shower. For right now there wasn't much I could do about the wrinkled cheap shirt and trousers. Funny how a man cares what he looks like right up to the end and how, if he has a family, they care what he looks like in the coffin.

I was walking into the john when I heard her say, "Glad you got some sleep. I knew you hadn't had none except that little bit for a long time." There she was. She was coming out of the woman's john and I couldn't even tell myself how I felt about it.

"I thought you'd gone," I said. I turned, forcing myself not to smile.

"Where?" she asked and then "Why?"

Yeah, I thought, I guess that's it. She's not going anywhere and a kid like that can catch a ride any time. I felt a bit more empty and embarrassed as I pissed into the stinking urinal, remembering the days when I used to take these trips as vacations and I'd be smelling that same stinking urinal while little Billy, who'd already peed, as he called it, was outside overjoyed by all these strange people in this strange place. He'd be trying to catch that damn cat. And then I saw him as I imagined he looked now. He'd be about the same age as that girl outside waiting to take her one way ticket ride.

Then I thought, "at least nobody'll hurt her until I run out of gas."

I drove and the signs began to predict Memphis more often now. Then somehow, by magic, she handed me a whole sandwich and pulled a can of Budweiser from under her shirt for me. I could feel my face blushing somewhere between confusion, gratitude and some emotion that almost made me cry.

"Where'd you get this?" I asked. She had already opened the can so I sipped the beer first, leaving the sandwich lying in my lap.

"Don't worry. I had mine. Even folks in Cadillacs, that take along stuff like this to eat between meals, have to pee." She laughed. It was the first time I'd heard her laugh.

"You little thief," I laughed, "You're O.K."

"So're you," she said. "Don't let nobody tell you no different. A person's what he thinks he is. Them folks in the Cadillac thought I was some kind of rich punk rocker because I was day dreamin' about bein' one. They even said 'Hi' real friendly like when they went to pee." She laughed again.

When the laugh died there was a long silence and the green signs said "Memphis" more often all the time. I began to feel this fear in my gut at the loss of something.

Something was on her mind. Her forehead was wrinkled with anxiety again and those rich mellow lips were sealed tight together again. Finally she said, "Where you goin' professor?"

She'd guessed it. She was the smartest person at reading human beings I'd ever seen.

"Nowhere," I said. Now it felt like doom. Before it just felt like fate. The traffic was getting thicker. A huge truck blew his horn, as if we'd threatened to think about moving into the space in front of him.

"That's what I thought," she said.

Then it occurred to me that nobody but some girl that had stolen a sandwich and a beer for me even gave a damn.

"Where you come from?" she said. And I felt the tightness in my stomach that always came with that damn question, my compulsive revelation and the boredom of the listener who wasn't looking for any answer except a birthplace anyway and wouldn't really have heard that.

"Them folks don't even think about you. And they ain't nobody in this world who thinks about folks like us, anyway." She used the word "us." I hadn't heard that word for so long that my stomach began to tighten. I pulled in front of a truck and the cussing bastard almost took the front off the old Chevy. He deliberately shifted back into the same lane after he'd passed me.

She didn't even notice.

"I talked to some folks in the park," she said. "They's waitress and factory work in Memphis."

I looked straight ahead. I didn't turn to see her looking out the window like somebody does after they've done their good deed, passing on some two bit philosophy that's supposed to get you through life as an excuse for why they won't be in yours.

When I did turn, she was looking at me. "We could both get them jobs and if we shared rent 'en food and stuff like that, we could even afford some fun," she said.

Thread of Light

"In the room the women come and go, speaking of Michelangelo," Harry said.

The sound of the saxophone seemed to curl like a disembodied genie as the colored lights caught the smoke that rose from the golden bell.

"Pardon?" the girl said. She leaned toward Harry with an earnest look on her face. "I want to know the English," she said. Her dark hair fell in waves to the shoulders of her black leather jacket. Harry watched her full lips move as the gentle light of the candle between them lit her cream colored neck, gradually softening as it reached her dark eyes. He was lost in the flame, dancing in her large, dark pupils. He floated into the dark cavern lit by the torch, and in the warmth of her body beside the fire, the darkness and cold went away. Outside the wind whipped. Harry thought aloud. "It must be ten below out there." He could see the kapici, waiting in the cold, watching intently for any available opportunity to extort money from an arriving gentleman. He, in his thin uniform coat, would park your car, begging for a few more lira and waiting for prayer time, the first thread of light, to be off duty. He could neither hear the music nor afford the dreams that came with the wine. At home, a large woman, fat from eating only bread, waited in a cold, sparsely furnished room for him. One of the kids was crying. One of the kids was always crying. Maybe the girl across from Harry was one of his daughters. Harry swished the bourbon in his mouth, swallowing slowly and concentrating on the flowing forms of dark figures that moved with the charm of the music.

"You are American?" the girl asked. She smiled. Her teeth were white and even. She was not the kapici's daughter. Her hair was alive. She was not poor, at least not real poor.

"Not really," Harry said. He smiled. "I'm odd."

"What does that mean, odd?" she asked. "Is it a country or a place?" She pulled her hair back from her face, unveiling it to make her confusion more apparent.

"No," Harry said. "Odd is everywhere. It's cold and it's dark, and I can't seem to find a match." Harry had a cigarette in his mouth and was fumbling in his pockets. The girl took the packet of matches from the ashtray and, lighting one of the matches, held it to his cigarette. As she leaned toward him, her coat opened slightly revealing a trim shape in a white 'v' necked sweater on dark skin.

The saxophone filled the air with a crescendo. The girl moved closer, touching his knee with hers. He moved his hand to touch her back under the leather coat. He felt warm flesh through the thin sweater, and her firm body relaxed against his. The touch closed the distance with its warmth.

The next day the sky was still overcast. Harry caught a cab on Cinnah Street and told the driver to take him to Ulus. The driver, his brown eyes flashing with understanding, said "Evet" in an excited voice and began rapidly driving the wrong way. Three blocks later he stopped in front of a casino with a neon sign that wasn't working and faded pictures of buxom, blonde-haired, brown-eyed Eastern European women. He turned his unshaven face and demanded to know where Harry wanted to go. Harry laughed.

"Not here," Harry said, and again repeated, "kale (castle)," with directions. Once into Ulus, the driver again appeared confused as he continued to beep his horn in competition with the hoards of people that looked like extras from an American movie set in the 1930s, and warned other drivers that he had no intention of slowing down at the traffic signals. Harry continued to direct him up the hill to the Citadel. Harry stopped him when they arrived at the market section where the vendors were set up in front of a retaining wall that had been there since the Romans. It had been rebuilt with the old Roman stones, occasionally patched with pieces of ruins from different periods. Three-wheeled motorcycles, left over from World War II, were parked next to a green Mercedes across from the makeshift stores made of tents. Harry approached the tent that was filled with sacks of nuts and feigned interest in the pistachios. The leather-faced old man with a cast eye grinned and offered him a handful of pecans. Harry took them and ordered a kilo of pistachios.

"Merhaba, Hoca." Harry turned quickly to see Okey standing, almost touching him, and wearing a Western style, pin striped blue suit on his lean body. Okey gave and expected the usual Turkish greeting, a kiss on each cheek. Harry felt awkward. He seldom touched anyone, and before coming to this region never touched other men except to shake hands.

"You are here," Okey said as if it was an unexpected pleasant surprise. "Would you like some refreshment? Perhaps some Coca-cola? Some tea? Coffee? Something to eat? Some wine?" Okey's unblinking black eyes focused intently on Harry's face. Okey guided him, holding his elbow, into the Ottoman House, a dwelling within the castle that housed a working museum of bakers, weaving village women and craftsmen. They climbed up a narrow, winding staircase and proceeded down a narrow hallway. Entering an antique study on the right of the hallway, they were shown to a table overlooking Güven Park. From this vantage point, you could see most of the eastern part of the old city. The bright sunlight belied the cold winter season. Inside the room, antique swords and firearms hung beneath the portraits of General Ataturk.

Okey's dark, ageless face wrinkled in a fixed leather smile. "It is history," he said with a sweeping gesture that indicated everything from the wooden minaret just beneath them to the crumbling red-roofed houses further down the mountainside. Just across from them, the aluminum teapot and white cotton curtain on the window of one of the deteriorating dwellings indicated that Gypsies lived there. If he walked down the alley on the other side of the building, Harry knew he would be accosted by any number of girls, small for their age, who spoke English, as well as maybe three or four other languages, and begged and stole for a living. "Sir?" they would say, demanding that he exchange money for some item of needlework created by the women inside. Their arms and legs were tiny and brown, their hair dark and their eyes black. "Sir!" they would demand again as if annoyed by his lack of the proper Western interest in their poverty. Harry had learned not to acknowledge them. If he saw them he knew that the next step would be to embarrass him, making the sensitive Westerner pay for their poverty and his guilt. His manners and pretense of respect were the first step into the trap. His realization of his hypocrisy was the last. Soon, like everyone else, when a scarfed peasant approached Harry with a "Sir!" expressing anxiety and shoving a baby, red faced from scabs, Harry knew better than to acknowledge such a creature as a human being. His only thought, as Okey held forth on the wonders that were the Ottomans and those that were the Romans before the Ottomans, was "They must be wicked to deserve such pain."

"You mean the terrorists," Okey said. Okey always made statements. He never asked questions. You were guilty either way he meant the statement. If you agreed with him, you were guilty of complicity. If you disagreed with him, you were guilty of the opposite crime. If you said nothing, you were guilty of conspiracy. You could guess which conspiracy. Okey walked on the bed of hot coals that was Turkish politics. You understood that you were always under the light that made his sardonic eye never blink.

"We have a problem, Hoca," Okey said. The tone of his voice made it Harry's problem. "You go out much?" Okey said and cocked his head so that his black eyes studied Harry's face as if to say that he knew what he was talking about. The question was rhetorical.

"I don't understand," he said. "I think I told my teacher friend he should stay in his own community." Okey shook his head. His full head of black hair flecked with white testified that, except for inescapable exceptions, Okey had always taken care of himself. Even during those periods, Harry knew Okey had survived because of his habit of taking care of himself.

A waiter approached the table. He held a silver tray. His thick black hair flowed back in waves from his pale face. Harry thought of Johnny Rivers singing "A Whiter Shade of Pale." Gül played American music for him the night before. Gül was a common name. It meant Rose. There were BinGüls, AsliGüls and BirGüls, anything from one to a thousand roses. Harry watched a tall dark girl leaving the restaurant. Her long dark hair flowed down her erect back. She danced energetically forward, her long legs clicking the heels of her leather boots. At first, Harry thought it was Gül, not seeing her face. Then he realized it couldn't be.

Okey was ordering. He snapped the order quickly for both of them and the waiter responded, moving quickly toward the kitchen. "Just a minute," he said in Turkish, realizing that Harry was back from his dream of life. "Would you like wine, Professor?" Okey's eyes gleamed with a knowing smile. "Pretty isn't she?" he said. He was looking out the window and Harry knew he wasn't talking about the Gypsy hag fetching her water pail.

"No thank you," Harry said. He grinned with no intention of elaborating. He lived inside his head. Okey could intrude. The conflict interested him and it interested Okey, but he had no intention of inviting Okey into his thoughts.

"You don't like them?" Okey said. It wasn't a question. Maybe it was an insinuation. Harry didn't know and it was automatic with Okey, so the tone didn't trouble Harry. He didn't answer. The waiter waited politely.

Okey waved his hand and said, "Never mind." The waiter left and Okey began studying his glass of water, turning it between his thumb and fingers. Then he looked up at Harry, grinning, as he began a thoughtful monologue. Harry knew by the gestures and tone that this was as serious "as a Turk could be serious" to quote Okey. Harry wondered if this Turk was even serious when he killed. Life was not particularly important either, at least not most people's lives. Harry had difficulty predicting what people wanted, or at least their reason for wanting it. They'd let you know what they wanted if they thought you had it.

"They came across the border from Syria again last night," Okey said. "We're chasing them back to the mountains right now. We'll catch them and kill them." "*Mutilate them,*" Harry thought. "Then we'll broadcast pictures of them to their fellows across the border. They will be frightened but they won't stop coming. Their leaders will threaten them."

Harry thought about the basement of the police station and Kayahan standing in the doorway. He would be loafing there today when Okey and Harry came from Ulus. He liked to watch the girls in the street after lunch. It was just one of the many things Kayahan seemed to enjoy. He wasn't avoiding his work. He liked his work, especially his work in the basement. Harry saw Kayahan as a sort of bedouin Iago. His hooked beak, dark eyes and dark skin on the lookout for Desdemonas to interrogate. The feeling that Harry got was foreboding.

Okey was watching him. "Back from the dead, Professor?" Okey said. "I go there sometimes," he said. He grinned. "It's a refreshing pause in the cycle of life. It keeps one aware." He raised his eyebrows as if in warning at this last statement. Then he smoothed the tablecloth, looking down at it as if it meant something and said, "I suppose it doesn't matter, 'Eh Professor? The best things in life are dead." He grinned and paused. "How about Shakespeare?" He raised his eyebrows and pursed his lips. "How about Desdemona?" His eyes cocked. "The girl you met last night is from the Southeast. She has brothers that Kayahan believes to be terrorists. I don't know if it is true."

"How would you know?" I asked, surprised at his network of spies.

"I know you, Professor," he said. "I know as you know what we are talking about. I don't think our Iago will be in this play if you continue to see the girl. Honey will work better with her anyway. I'm certain she isn't a terrorist." He wasn't looking at Harry now. Harry could tell from his face that he was really serious this time. "She is too pretty, Harry." Now he was watching Harry. "A Turkish girl that pretty should not be exposed to Kayahan, Harry."

Back at the police station on Ataturk Boulevard, Harry hung his coat on the coat tree in the hall just outside the office that overlooked the street through barred windows. Kayahan was inside behind a large ancient desk, his back to the drab green wall, playing backgammon with himself. "Fuck it!" he said, shoving the backgammon set out of his way. He grinned. He was entertaining Harry with his knowledge of English cursing. Then he immediately jumped up, exchanging Turkish greetings with Okey. Turning his attention back to Harry, he said, "Salaam a-lakum." It was the Arabic contact greeting shared by workers, and sometimes by members of the Turkish mafia. The use of Arabic, being frowned on since Ataturk's Westernization of Turkey, was occasionally employed by the subcultures and as a medium through which to infiltrate terrorists.

"A-lakum au salaam," Harry returned, smiling. Kayahan liked to impress Harry with his criminal mentality. Once, when Harry had said, "It takes one to know one," Kayahan had tried out the idiom in every situation that he thought the phrase suited, looking to Harry for approval or correction. "I want to learn the English like the people talk it, Harry," Kayahan said. "Not how it was taught me in the Turkey." Harry laughed. Later he realized that, in every way, Kayahan was more like a pit bull than a comedian. He did know how criminals thought; and he reasoned from himself to everyone. He was fond of Harry and Harry didn't know why. Kayahan recognized Harry's weakness right away, often teasing Harry with his reckless driving, and, noting what worried Harry about driving, would say as he narrowly missed a pedestrian, "We can kill that one, Harry." He would laugh, his black eyes blazing with delight.

Harry's reaction to the near miss amused Kayahan; and, although Kayahan lacked a certain respect for human life, he seemed to admire Harry's respect for life. More than that, he seemed to want Harry's respect.

Okey watched with the usual sardonic look on his face. He was drawing water from the lower portion of the samovar for all of them, and then filling the top half of the glass with the strong constantly brewing tea from the pot over the fire.

"Speak English," Okey said to Kayahan. He laughed. "I will send you back home to the southeast if you continue to speak Arabic. You would like that, wouldn't you?" A map behind the desk displayed that part of Turkey. Kurdistan, the original homeland of the Kurdish people, was the pink area overlapping all the bordering countries. "The mountains are your home, aren't they?" Okey winked at Harry, handing Harry his cup of tea with a small silver spoon to stir the sugar cubes. Harry sat down on the sofa and began to stir his tea. Through the window he could see the busy street, vehicles honking as if to identify themselves, people hurrying across in front of them until the light turned green and the traffic moved at murderous speed for awhile. A vendor swung a large bread doughnut in his hand. He was hawking the doughnuts that he carried, stacked on a mortarboard, on top of his head. Harry noticed that his head was dirtier than the rest of his body. *"Not much water in his part of town,"* Harry thought. *"If you can't see the germs they don't exist."*

"We see them," Okey said, appearing to read part of Harry's thought. "And when we catch them we will exterminate them."

"Mehmetci will watch us fuck his mother," Kayahan said. He was furious. A civil war was the worst. You hated enough to kill your enemy, mutilating his mind and his body. "*Or her body,*" Harry thought. In a moment of realized horror, his eyes watching Kayahan, and seeing Gül, he said aloud, "Why?"

"Not because we love the old bitch," Kayahan said laughing. "How would you feel if your worst enemy was fucking your mother and you were watching with this wire around your balls?" Kayahan held up a piano wire with a loop at one end. "Those bastards should have been born with this around their balls. Then they couldn't reproduce themselves."

"Shut up," Okey said. "I'm tired of this conversation." Outside it had started to snow. White flakes were falling on the long thick black hair of a young lady hurrying down the street, her boot heels clicking. She was oblivious to Mehmetci, to death, to the street vendors and to the trio inside the police station. Harry was, as usual, outside looking in, peeking through the barred windows at people living and thinking about how they felt, how they lived, what they thought and what the next line in that story would be. Then, the two inside the barred window crossed his mind. He felt uncomfortable and slightly anxious. Getting up from the couch, he hurried out the door hearing Kayahan calling after him.

"Wait for me! I haven't been out of this stinking hole all day." Harry held his breath, not answering from the hallway as he put his topcoat on. Then he heard Kayahan say, thinking Harry was gone, "Fuck it. Fuck him. Fuck them all."

Outside the snow began to fall faster. Harry hurried along the crowded streets toward the bus stop. A green Fargo truck turned the corner from the side street next to the police station in front of Harry as he waited for the stoplight to change. Harry noticed the silver wreath on its side. It pulled into the street behind a line of traffic, its two coffins, side by side like toolboxes, under the canvas top. These were recyclable coffins. They took the body to the cemetery, put it in a winding sheet and into the grave. Muslims believed in returning the humus to the Earth. "Ashes to ashes, dust to dust," Harry said to himself out loud.

"You think about death too much Harry," Gül stood beside him and he hadn't seen her. She hunched her shoulders, collar up on the long black coat she wore against the cold. She laughed at Harry's surprise.

"Thank God or the Devil for your life," Harry said, happy to see her. The light changed and he grabbed her arm, hurrying across the street. He was relieved now that Kayahan was out of sight. "Lunch? Breakfast? Dinner?" he asked as they cleared the last honking car, making the safety of the sidewalk that by now was slightly muddy from the combination of falling snow and heavy pedestrian traffic.

"All of those," she said, smiling and looping her arm through his. Harry felt the curve of her hip against his leg as she walked effortlessly in rhythm with him. A rush of excitement touched off a much more lively chain of associations. He imaged Gül's body talking to the rhythms of her walk. "But not now," Gül said. "How do you say in English? I have to take care of business." Harry almost bumped into a large peasant lady bundled up in bright clothes that covered her to her ankles. The snow would build up soon, and Harry imagined the soft glow of the street lights, the bright pastels of the neon signs in the city covered with fresh snow that evening as a background to Gül's dark warm beauty. "Tonight?" he asked.

"Tonight," she said, standing on the tips of her boots to kiss his cheek good-bye. She hurried off down the street, her hair streaming, waving her small hand at Harry.

Harry shook his head. He must be asleep. He was in a small gray room, a kind of oversize cement pillbox. Kayahan stood by a small window, looking out at the slim spire of a single minaret. There was no mosque. The village guard that Harry had seen hanging from a telephone pole with American money stuffed in his mouth swung lazily from the minaret. He needed a shave. "*They always need a shave,*" Harry thought. The guard's eyes bulged from their sockets as his face came alive. Looking at Harry, he began to laugh, "Allah mu akbar," he chanted, "*God is great.*"

Harry said gravely, "God is great. God is good, and we thank him for this food." The village guard swung dangerously. His hands were tied. Harry could see stigmata. "But he is a muslim," Harry said. "I don't think Muslims are allowed to eat American money."

"What time is it?" Harry asked. Kayahan turned from watching the village guard. He looked at Harry with the mixture of mockery and gravity that seemed to be genetic in Kayahan. "It is the first thread of light," he said. Then, turning back to the village guard, he yelled, "Cut him down! Give him my tomb! I won't be needing it today. We can exhume him later and transfer him to a mass grave somewhere in Germany. The Germans are experts at this sort of thing."

Okey, in his full dress policeman's uniform, turned toward the window smiling at Harry, and with a gesture denoting the uniform said, "It is American." He began violently shaking the minaret.

"Stop that!" Kayahan shouted. "Have you no respect for American dollars? What if they were to fall from his mouth and touch the ground?"

The guard's face loomed huge. It appeared as an elephantine balloon in Macys' Thanksgiving Day Parade. Harry was cold. He stood beside Ataturk Boulevard and wondered why the parade was in Ankara this year and why he had forgotten his trumpet. He wasn't prepared. He had forgotten all about his trumpet for years. Anxiety overcame him. He was forgetting to pay attention. "What time is it?" he yelled at Kayahan.

Kayahan turned from the window annoyed with Harry. "The first thread of light," he said. Harry was unable to comprehend. "It is time," Kayahan said, "to bury our differences." He turned to march gravely beside the coffin. The guard's bloated face was covered with a ski mask.

"It is American," Okey said, denoting the ski mask. It is the latest thing in Palestine. "Will you be bringing your pretty young lady to see our fashion show?"

Then Harry was with Gül. He felt her body against his own. He touched her warm soft legs, holding her thin waist. When he awakened he was on top of her. She clung to him, her long legs wrapped around his buttocks. It was the first thread of light. Harry realized the time as he heard the call to prayer from the neighborhood mosque.

When Harry awakened again, the room was much brighter. For a moment, because of the white lace curtains, the steamer trunk at the foot of the bed, the quilted comforter and the bright red, white and black designs on the tapestry that hung behind the mahogany dresser, Harry thought he had awakened in his grandmother's bedroom. Then he realized the similarities between these people, himself and his dead grandmother. They shared tastes and colors. They even looked alike.

Gül's face lay on his chest. Harry noticed that she wore no make-up. Her dark eyelashes were long and the eyes were Mongolian. Her black hair, against his shoulder, was thick and full bodied. It fell in waves and Gül said it was difficult to manage. Harry doubted that. Even now she looked as if she was on a movie set playing a Hopi Indian. She dreamed. Her oriental mask pressed against his chest, and her fingers gripped his pectoral muscle. Harry touched her hip as it curved into her small waist, his arm and hand beneath her, and looked about the room.

A tall, thin middle aged man stood beside a dark complected middle aged lady. They looked at Harry from an eight by ten photograph on the dresser. The lady's face was kind and open. She wore a scarf and a long black coat. She seemed to be smiling at Harry. The man, his black hair flecked with gray and cropped short, stood in his three piece suit in front of a pine tree studying Harry. His face was only slightly wrinkled at the corners of his eyes. He was on the verge of breaking into a smile.

"If they were really looking at us, they wouldn't like what they saw," Gül said. She was awake. She reached across Harry with her entire body, straddled him and turned the picture toward the tapestry. Harry appreciated her firm muscular thighs as her knees clinched his hips. "Don't move," he said, looking up into her smiling face. "I want a photograph in my mind's eye." Her black hair, cascading down her shoulders, complemented her body. Outside, the world stood still, frozen underneath the deep snow on a Sunday morning. He touched her perfect body with his mind.

China Doll

HER FACE was the most open face he had ever seen. The snow, before melting, sprinkled her short, black hair. Her bright brown eyes were prominent. He could imagine his reflection in them. She smiled.

"Hello," she said.

He stood beside her, looking into the plate glass window, only occasionally glancing at the eyes that were fully focused on him, taking him in. For a minute he protected himself, thinking, "*like a large black spider takes in a defenseless insect.*" Then he lost the thought. He couldn't see her that way. Sometimes, when he wasn't around her, he saw her as the abstraction that was her profession, wearing the glasses she didn't like to wear. He knew that because she only wore them when it was unavoidable, or when she thought she was alone.

She was beautiful. And she was conscious of it. She stood beside him in the snow dust that barely covered the sidewalk. The shine on her black, designer boots would be slightly besmirched by the wet snow that sprinkled the toes. The boots were small. Her feet were small. Her petite body must have been a size six. He tried to think of her as a manikin in a fashionable store window. It was about as successful as his other attempts to reduce her to reality, or not to love her.

"She's small," he once thought. "Why did she seem larger?" Then he found himself lost, imaging the immaculate body that seemed to him sensually perfect, as if Michelangelo had sculpted it. "Too perfect," he thought. "I have cheap tastes. Whores turn me on. I'll tell her about this whore I spent a week with in Memphis. How much I loved that whore." And, in his mind, he obsessively told her about the whore, imaging in every detail the whore's sensuality and sensitivity. And he related to her a very different ending from reality. At the end of his story the whore . . . and then her voice interrupted, "with a heart of gold," she said. Her face smiled, understanding. Her brown eyes were delighted. Angrily he thought, "*She was right. She was always right.*"

She reached down, scooping up a handful of snow, and, laughing, threw it, loose, hitting the side of his face.

He laughed in spite of himself, turned from the plate glass window and grabbed for her. She dodged, and as quickly as a wild deer, sprang backward and away, just out of reach. She had a habit of doing that, both physically and spiritually.

She kept going, turning back to look at him when she reached the street lamp. The light from atop the post caught her hair and her smiling oval face. "*God! She is beautiful*," he thought and he felt a visceral surge of excitement.

"You're wrong," he said.

Her face sobered. "Do it anyway," she said.

"How can I do something I don't want to do?"

"Do you want it or not?" she asked.

"I want you!" he blurted.

He felt a rush of embarrassment. He felt foolish, like the time he told her he loved her. The next time he saw her, he had carefully intellectualized that sentiment. He had explained how there was nothing emotional in what he felt, that in his isolation he just used her as some kind of symbol to talk to.

Her face, those eyes, the movements of her lithe, responsive body accompanied him everywhere. He saw her dance, pick up a fork, reach for a withering daisy on the ground. He watched the rhythmic movement of her body as she walked effortlessly beside him. Most of all, he saw her face, open, vulnerable and free of protective emotions, listening intently while he built his intellectual and artistic snowmen. Then, laughing, she would cause them to melt. He grew angry.

"You're always telling me to do things," he said. "What difference does it make to you?"

She just stood there looking at him. She wouldn't answer. He knew she wouldn't answer.

"Are you coming or not?" she asked. She turned, and began, threateningly, to walk toward the edge of the lamplight.

"Why?" he asked. He was already following her. He often thought about telling her, "*crook your little finger, and I'll follow you anywhere.*" But it never occurred to him to say that when he saw her. She had something he didn't.

She stopped in the snow just beyond the point at which the light from the lamp imperceptibly blended with the darkness on the soft, white layer of snow that by now completely covered the flagstone street.

"Are you okay?" she asked. "If you don't want to do it—I can go back."

He thought of ways to tell her. He ran all the images of all the petite, dark girls he'd ever known through his mind. Li Ching, brown Mongolian eyes and dark hair among the brightly lit yellow and white signs of Taipei, saying, "I get through the days alright, but at night in my bed" —And she didn't spend the nights alone in her bed. At least not for awhile. In the end he always saw, not the blank, hostile look of contempt that he wanted to see on Li Ching's face, but her bloodshot eyes. She'd come to see him again after all he'd done, asking the same question, "Are you leaving?" He could hear the phone call after the despicable thing he did. "Are you okay?" Jesus! She should have wanted him dead. He saw the hostile stare in other Chinese faces. Why not hers? She told him once, "You show your passion on your face." She knew him. She could not understand why he would do this if she had done nothing wrong. Searching desperately for the cause, she had cried out, "You don't understand!" She believed that he thought she had betrayed him while, whimsically, he hurried away from her, giving her no chance to explain. Explaining was not her custom. She would never even attempt to explain. Until the end, only asking, "Are you leaving?"

That was not the story he told. He talked about a hard, calculating girl who would do anything to get to America. If you knew her, you would have known different. The Chinese knew different. Unlike Americans, she would say nothing rather than lie about important things. The Chinese thought the word "love" in the American language did not translate into Chinese. When he was taught the word in Chinese, he was told never to use it. "It means something very special to the Chinese." Of course, he used it. What red-blooded American boy wouldn't use such power? Don't we hear stories about Spanish Fly? He had never told anyone that he loved them since.

He didn't talk about the letter and the baby. He lied as loud as he could, attempting to drive the truth from his own mind, hoping to convince himself by making other people believe a lie. He tried to realize the geographic and cultural distance from his dishonor, but Li Ching was inside him. Against his own will, he imaged her face constantly. "*If she had only hated him,*" he thought.

"Tell me," she said, "Either do it, or tell me why." She was looking at the snow growing deeper and pushing her small boot into it. He thought of Li Ching's small feet.

"I'd rather lie," he said.

She looked at him. "But not to me?"

"I want to," he said.

He stopped and looked at her. Her open face was smiling knowingly. His mouth became dry. The cold that he felt a moment before, he didn't feel now.

"American soldiers did worse," he thought angrily. "They get away from home, and they're mean, malignant and cruel."

"She had dark hair and brown eyes like you," he said. "She wanted to come to America."

"Oh." She smiled. She looked at him with that teasing look on her face. It was as if she believed she knew everything. Just that one detail and Li Ching became a selfish, conniving little bitch. "*Things don't translate,*" he thought.

"I see," she said, turning and looking at a bare tree, its black skeleton being frosted with snow as the flakes sifted down, carried by the slight North wind. He didn't see the tears on her face, but he knew they were there, because he saw her wipe them away with her small black glove.

"You think you do!" he said, looking at her.

She turned, looking at him with surprise and hope on her face. There was silence. He started to talk, then shifted his gaze to the ground.

"This is all a bit like the ending of Hemmingway's 'Farewell to Arms,'" he said. "You know, when Frederick Henry is walking home in the rain after leaving Catherine and the dead baby."

He looked up in time to see her face relax into disappointment. She turned and began to walk hurriedly forward.

"Wait a minute," he said. "I—"

She turned back, looking at him, waiting with resigned patience. "Yes?" she said.

He caught up with her and without finishing his sentence, began to walk beside her. He felt really awkward and silly. "Jesus! It is cold," he said. She looked at him with a quizzical expression on her face.

He had never seen the little Amerasian boy that he created in the imagination of Li Ching. But he knew the child existed. He could see the slight difference in facial structure that made the child stand out among the odd collection of merchandise in front of one of those little stores on a busy street in Taipei. It was dusk there. Dusk was a split second in Taipei. The bright yellow and white lights were on. Chinese calligraphy filled the darkness with the excitement of exotic messages. The child's large, brown eyes were sad. There was no excitement in these lights for him. Both his own face and the face of Li Ching were apparent in the child. The part that was him wanted to cry. The part that was Li Ching was stoic. He watched other children, either with their parents or together. He was alone. From a fruit stand on the corner, an old Chinese man looked at him, then went casually about the business of survival, holding up a few sprigs of owl eyes, smiling behind a mask and saying something in excited Chinese to a passing American.

"What's wrong?" she asked. "Was there something you wanted to say back there?" Then, hurriedly, as if it had been a rhetorical question, "No. I guess not." She turned her body to face him.

"I—" he said. Then he reached for her waist and kissed her.

"You!" she said. She pulled loose and hurriedly began walking down the flagstone street covered by billions of tiny geometrical snowflakes. Li Ching would have said "thousands and thousands!" He could see her delighted face watching the snow. She, of course, had never seen snow. It would be something new. "It would be something foreign," he thought, hating himself.

The snow continued to sift down, covering the top of the stone fence beside the road. He watched her small body in its conservative wool coat, tucked in at the middle to reveal her shape.

"You've never loved anyone," she said.

He looked at her. He didn't hear her. He'd tried to tell her once. He compulsively grabbed the phone, realizing that her husband might answer. But nothing would stop him. He would let the phone ring until someone answered, overcoming the difficulty when it happened. He had lived his life that way before. As the phone rang, he saw her lying asleep in the bed next to her husband. Shame rushed to his head, but he would not hang up the phone. It continued to ring. Then it occurred to him that they couldn't be sleeping through this. Were they trying to ignore it? He saw them making love, but not really. He saw her making love.

He had never seen her husband. Her husband was only a shadow, an engineer. Someone she often quoted with admiration and respect. He believed him to be athletic, calm, always in control. He saw him acting, always certain, accustomed to and speaking with authority. Not pretentious authority. He was the kind of man who gave one sentence commands, often expressing ten pages of opinion in the innuendoes of one sentence. His world was not complex. He didn't analyze people or agonize over whether or not he had made a good impression on them. He liked himself and assumed that they wouldn't be around him if they didn't like him. He was rational, except for once in his life. She never told him the particulars of that time, but he believed that one of them had had an affair.

Analyzing people was her way of life. She liked art. Subtleties effected her. You could tell more of what she thought from her emotional expletives than her rational thought.

Her husband answered the phone. His voice was deep and asleep. "Yes," he said, after a moment's silence, waking up.

He said her name. Then, as if the call had to be explained, he lied. "A patient."

Then, calmly, from the other end, "She's not here." Her husband waited.

He hung up.

"What's wrong with you!" she demanded. She stood there with her hands on her hips, looking angrily at him.

"I was thinking about something else," he said.

"What?" she demanded to know.

He reached down, picked up a handful of snow and let it sift through his fingers. He looked up at her and grinned, "Well, first there was this lovely lady with dark hair and dark eyes. Her soft, nude body undulating under a dogwood tree on a warm day in the early spring. Then a coyote howled somewhere in the darkness as I sat in a dark theater in Taichung watching a beautiful Chinese girl urgently delivering a monologue on a black and white screen."

"You son-of-a-bitch!" She grabbed a hand full of snow and angrily threw it at him.

He laughed. Then his face sobered. "The Chinese girl lay in a rosewood coffin made in Ireland. Her face was porcelain. It was a mask, like one of those stylized china dolls. It was then that I noticed the baby, lying nestled in her arm, by her side. Its little Amerasian face stared at me with dead, open brown eyes."

She stood, shocked, perfectly still, listening for a moment. Then he laughed. Her whole body plunged into violent action and she began to beat his chest, crying.

"You crazy son-of-a-bitch! Why do you do that?"

He sobered, grabbed her wrists and glared into her face. "In lies, my dear, is the truth," he said quietly. "Nestled away somewhere in the hollow of a dead Chinese arm is a little, dead Amerasian baby." He let her go and then began laughing again.

She collapsed into the snow, her hands over her face, crying. "Why do you do that? It's a perfectly lovely day and you ruin it with your craziness. You lie, and you laugh, and you ruin everything with your craziness."

Suddenly he broke into song, "My baby is American made, born and bred in the U.S.A." then, grinning, "Isn't it true? Perhaps you should discuss the frightening effect that this whole thing has on your psyche with one of your colleagues." He grew suddenly angry, then surprised that this whole thing could have happened.

He reached down, took hold of her arms and tried to lift her from the flagstone street. She continued to cry, her face in her black-gloved hands.

She went limp when he tried to lift her, becoming dead weight, like a child. She didn't want to get up. He sat down beside her in the snow.

"I'm sorry," he said. Then, in frustration, "I was joking."

"It wasn't funny," she said.

That night, in the soft light coming from the half-open bathroom door, he watched her sleep, imprinting on his mind that it was her. She was asleep, here, in his bed. Her short, dark hair and her dark complected face were on the pillow by his side. He normally slept with the bright overhead light on. He couldn't do that now. The images in the darkness were living and generating new combinations of images, like an infinite number of snowflakes, all geometrically perfect and original. The apparitions came blooming like flowers, most of them malignant ones. He could feel them. He heard himself telling her the next morning, "People who harbored Josef Mengele in Sao Paulo say he had nightmares, screaming out all night long. Perhaps he should have confessed to a priest and sought redemption." He followed this statement with a bitter angry laugh.

He thought of the blue and white winter scenes of Monet and looked out his bedroom window as the snow continued to drift. He looked at the small body beside him and felt the bitter sweet sense of nostalgia for American girls bundled in sweaters and wool coats, their smiling blonde faces and warm bodies in opulent rooms. He reached over and touched her.

"You don't feel," she murmured in her sleep.

Then Van Gogh's restless, swirling, bright, angry images vibrated before him. Van Gogh, mutilating himself for his lover, desperately attempting to show the intensity of his feelings, imagining his lover opening the envelope and seeing his ear. His lover would see the pain, the frustration, the hate and the isolation. They would be whole again.

He thought about telling her about this in the morning, but he wouldn't. He would tell her a lie. No matter how he said it, he would tell her a lie. Picasso said, "Art is a lie that makes us realize the truth." If you mutilate yourself and send it in the mail with her husband looking on as she opens the envelope and he sees her fall to her knees in horror and grief, is that a lie? Socrates said, "The truth, not being art, is a lie," he thought bitterly. Even now, he was thinking of sending her the ear with a note that said, '*now*, you know how I feel.'" For a second, he could hardly control his angry laughter.

She asked, "Do you have other lovers?" She knew the answer. She knew the answer because he told her about the aborted twins. How he said to the doctor who reported the miscarriage to him, "It's my fault." The doctor said, "It's nobody's fault." Nothing is ever anybody's fault. Then when his relatives, enjoying their saccharine discussion of this premature loss of twin heirs, expressed their condolences around the breakfast table, he heard himself say, "Had I known you would be so fond of them, I would have pickled them and brought them to you in a Mason jar." They all looked at him with horror, disgust and anger.

"I sleep around because I come from trash," he retorted. Did he tell her the truth or did he lie? Any respectable psychologist knows that you sleep around for acceptance. He didn't believe that she was looking for an answer. It was an accusation. If he hurt her enough, would she send him an ear?

He heard Jeannie Sealey plaintively begging for the illusion, with the sincerity that "struck a cord." He laughed at himself. She sang, "Tell me a lie."

He heard her say, "You divide everything by its lowest common denominator. What do you have left?"

"Bitch!" he said.

He imagined Sybil Shepherd. She became the blonde singer he knew in Atlanta. He saw her singing Rock-a-Billy songs, a laugh always in her voice and on her face. She spoke with a Georgia accent. She sang the up-tempo songs, laughing, teasing the audience with her body in tight leather pants or dark green slacks that revealed her firm, pneumatic body. She often laughed at her sensuality, saying things like, "Blow me up and I'll follow you anywhere." But she never let anyone close enough to blow. She just had one after another of aspiring lovers who would follow <u>her</u> anywhere until she whimsically and sadistically "reduced them to shit," as she put it. He imaged her laughing eyes and flirting hands, her body dancing slightly back, away and sideways as she sang, "Just out of reach of these two empty arms." It was her show from the beginning. He followed her in spite of her cruelty and the continual presence of a new victim that he had to watch mutilated before his eyes, because she was an artist. She made music, her body, and even her despicable life style, an art. She never sang the same songs in the same way and she never told a joke or introduced a song with the same humorous line. He knew she ad-libbed them.

In his mind, he heard and saw her introducing a song. She couldn't remember her own lines, but he never forgot any of them. "This song should give John the Baptist head. Crazy man. Crazy as hell. Used to sing this shit to Mary Magdalene 'til Jesus would tell him, 'Go, take a bath John.'" Then she would introduce the band with a drum roll and a crash of cymbals and launch full tilt into the saddest song you ever heard.

Toward the end, she would call him when she got home from work, high on smoke, amphetamines and booze, wanting to know, "Did I wake you up?" and laughing. It did no good to be angry with her. If he hung up, she'd just call back. And he didn't want to leave the phone off the hook. He wanted her to call. She'd talk until the sun came up, ridiculing herself and everyone else. Then one night, as she talked, the whole thing got crazier than ever. She began crying, wanting to know why he couldn't be there when she got home from her dates, like he used to be, fixing breakfast for her as the sun came up. She called him Daddy. Said she missed him awful. He knew she had never been talking to him when she called. Now he knew who she'd been talking to.

She dropped the phone. When he got there, she was very dead, her pale blue eyes staring directly into the sun.

Then he saw the fan that Li Ching had brought him. An overweight blonde he had picked up in a country and western bar, had found it lying on the bedroom floor among unpacked boxes. She had been attracted to it, calling it "unusual." And in some sort of domestic fit, helping him organize his house, had hung it on the living room wall.

It was of green silk, the color of jade, and rosewood. Jade meant something so special to a Chinese lover that you seldom saw anyone wearing it. On it was a tree limb with impressionistic, soft, pink blossoms, like a dogwood. The limb was various shades of olive, white, black and green. The painting became palpable in its expression of a spiritual union. The Chinese calligraphy expressed the same quiet, everlasting sentiment. Something very different happened with the fat blonde in the heat of passion and drunkenness that night in the bedroom.

He saw himself standing in front of the sparsely furnished room in which Li Ching's mother lived. She sewed buttons on clothes that American women rummaged through, looking for bargains at Sears. He heard himself, at this late date, frantically begging, pleading, threatening to kill himself, collapsing into tears. And she stood before him, looking at him with the blank, contemptuous look that the Chinese reserve for the dishonorable, pretending that she didn't know him. She motioned for him to go away as if he were a diseased animal. The shame of the situation overcame him and he ran from her like an idiot, through the teaming streets of Taipei where no one seemed to notice him. He stopped for a breath and beat his head against a brick wall that partitioned a pig sty from the street.

He heard himself, drunk, in a bar bragging about his exploits in China. A mechanic next to him at the bar, laughing, took a drink of beer. He grasped the glass with his stubby, grease blackened fingers. "Do Chinese women really have it on their side?" he asked, snickering.

Sometime toward morning he knew he was asleep. The malignant spirits in the darkness of his mind engulfed him. Li Ching lay next to him on her back. Her normally dark face was tinted with gray. It was the Chinese mask of death, but she was alive. A tube, extending from a bottle, released measured doses of morphine into one arm. Other tubes released other liquids into her veins and there was a tube in her nose. He watched her throughout the night. He was taking care of her. She was alive.

Once he roused enough to go to the bathroom. In the foggy, surreal light, as if coming out of an anesthetic, he realized for a moment that it wasn't Li Ching in the bed, but her. He lapsed back into the blurred half-light of the reality of his mind.

He awakened to the smell of bacon. Don McLean's "Starry, Starry Night" was playing on the stereo. Van Gogh's self portrait vibrated in his mind and he heard Browning's Childe Roland say, "They must have been wicked to deserve such pain!"

He went to the kitchen sink to take his dexadrine. He could never drink the water from a bathroom sink. It seemed dirty to him. She was in front of the sink washing dishes.

"Excuse me," he said.

"What are you taking?" she asked.

"Aspirin," he said. He drank the water and reached for the cup of coffee she handed him.

He controlled the urge to begin a long discussion of McLean's perception of Van Gogh. Instead, he delivered the monologue to her mentally while he drank his coffee.

"I miss you," he said. He looked at his coffee cup.

"Of course you do," she laughed.

"In a way, you are here," he said. "I talk to you constantly as if you were."

"Write it down and send it to me," she said.

There was a bit of disappointment in that. He knew she had taken out a post office box, especially for him. His would be the only mail going there. He imaged her going to the mailbox, opening the letter, and finding his mutilated ear. In the bright light, reflecting off the snow, he laughed.

Outside, the snow had become quite deep. The sun was shining and the bare oak tree just beyond the porch cast a skeletal shadow on the sparkling room. She was vibrant in her tight jeans and heavy sweater.

Later, in the bedroom, as he watched her undress with all the simplicity of movement and creativity that made sex symbols goddesses, he thought, "*The man that said sex was purely animalistic, had to be either a hopeless degenerate or a hopeless puritan.*" They were the same thing. They didn't even look different, like the North Pole and the South Pole. He thought of Jerry Falwell and Larry Flint. Yukio Mishima would have called them brothers separated by Hitler's lamp shades.

Through the bedroom window, the slightly melting snow sparkled as if sprayed with diamonds in the bright sunlight. In the warm bedroom, he knelt before the pristine body that embodied all of his fantasies. Her dark hair, soft brown eyes and open face bent in acceptance of adoration. Her open arms reached to pull his head and face into the flesh of her soft womb.

Outside, the wind died. The bright sunlight gave motionless life to the glistening snow. And the bare, black trees stood quiet guard.

That afternoon, he passed the people picketing the clinic, annoyed by their blank, hostile eyes, signs and irrational pamphlets. The nurse was surprised to see a man attempting to make an appointment for a woman. After all, it was a female problem. It was her body. There might be legal complications. God knows. He would have to wait and talk to the doctor. Would he like a cup of coffee while he waited.

It happened like that. He felt as if he were having a realistic, chronological dream in which appearance made everything safe and logical. You just handed all your problems to authority figures. Give up control and they, being more objective, would decide. They would protect him from his demons.

"The sun was blood red and going down," he thought as he climbed the steps onto the porch that evening. He stamped the now damp snow off his feet in front of the door. He had seen her watching and waiting anxiously from the living room window as he drove up. When he entered the living room, she was in the kitchen pretending to have just finished the dishes. She looked up and smiled. He said nothing, went into the bedroom and took two dexadrine capsules from the bottle underneath his underwear in the bureau drawer.

As he entered the kitchen, unable to hide the nervousness, she asked, "Did you do it?"

"It's arranged," he said.

He saw her begin to tremble, but continued to pour a glass of bourbon.

"It's not too late," he said, taking his pills with the alcohol.

"What's the choice?" she asked.

"You know the choice," he said angrily. "My choice is obviously not yours."

"How do you know?" she asked.

"I asked!" he yelled. "I begged!"

"Yes, but you didn't mean it," she said.

He looked at her furiously. Then controlling his fury, poured another glass of bourbon and extended it.

She hesitated. "I don't think I better," she said.

"What the hell difference does it make NOW!" he yelled.

She flinched as if he'd hit her. "None, I guess," she said. She took the glass and, bracing herself with one hand on the sink, began to drink it.

He went into the living room, sat down and glared out the window.

She came into the living room, standing to one side of him, clasping her hands and looking down. In his peripheral vision, he saw tears running down her face. She raised her head and, with rapid motions, rubbed the tears away. "I won't see you again after tonight," she said.

"Sure," he said. This sounded terribly familiar. And the feeling that he felt in his gut was familiar, too. But it was like sex. You can never remember how it felt before. Like when they tell you somebody you love is dead. You feel terribly lost and homesick, but you know it can't be fixed.

He heard her crying from the bedroom far into the night. He wanted to go to her, but he couldn't. He couldn't stand to go and talk to her. When the crying stopped and he thought she was asleep, he went to his typewriter and began to type. He wrote one absurdly comical scene after another. He laughed as he wrote.

He thought of the masks back to back, of tragedy and comedy. They were the same. Analyze how they worked and they came out the same, tragedy was funny. "Leave 'em laughin'."

Toward dawn, he stopped. He went to the window and stared into the darkest night he could remember seeing. He saw his Amerasian child on the streets of Taipei. The Chinese people in hoards around him. Cars of all descriptions and nationalities raced through the streets. He realized that the child's face was his face. He was seeing what the child saw. And with it's face of himself and Li Ching, he felt the most horrible homesickness and isolation that he had ever felt. Groans welled uncontrollably up from his chest.

The Bedraggled Dead

"There were two of them and one of them used to kill himself," I said. "You'd know it if you saw him do it. His laugh felt like somebody vomiting blood."

The man's eyes were jaundiced. They didn't move, just waited. They hadn't heard a word yet. Cuts under his chin made half-mooned patches of skin among his gray whiskers. His grizzled eyebrows stood out like dusty quills. I could hear my parents twenty years earlier, in a dream, saying, "He must be on dope," as the three of us looked with suspicion and disgust at myself twenty years later. I was four then. Somewhere I could hear a toilet running, or was it one of their instruments.

"Yes?" he said.

"Excuse me," I said nervously. It must be those pills I take for migraines. Then I caught myself. He couldn't know what I was thinking. It was like they say about a dream. What seems like an hour is only a minute. But I could never get over believing that I had just been standing there looking like "somebody on dope" for five minutes. And I'd come wearing jeans! What a place to come wearing jeans. I'd forgotten to shave. He wore a black pinstriped suit.

The blood was splattered like when you pull a chicken's head off, in the dust on the road. I held the broken bottle, feeling calm and really good – not pious like when I testified for God in church.

"Well?" the man said. This time it had been a long time. I had only one explanation.

"He's my father," I said. The man recognized the pretended disorientation from grief. His left hand took my arm. Short gray hairs sprouted like pin feathers around a ruby Masonic ring.

"I understand," he said. "Please sit down." He guided me to a gray, heavily cushioned divan. He motioned to another man who stood waiting for attention. The attendant left, his feet floating on the thick gray carpet between himself and the floor. The man sat next to me, folded his hands and waited. I expected more.

I smelled perspiration odor. I looked at him quickly, too quickly, hoping he didn't smell it. I could feel it trickle so I clamped my arm to my side. I thought about formaldehyde, decided that he used it for deodorant and then I could talk.

"Where is he?" I asked.

"If you'll give me the name, I'll go with you," he said.

I looked up. A plump couple with moist eyes stood in the hall. The woman lifted a black net veil and dabbed her eyes. The attendant reappeared and removed them quickly.

The man appeared not to notice.

"Go ahead and help them," I said. "I can help myself."

They appeared to be part of his world. His attention seemed too expensive for me to use.

He glanced in the direction of their disappearance. His face talked for the first time. His lips firmed, and the mescaline allowed me to see an otherwise imperceptible grin. The jaundiced eyes looked at me again.

"Why are you waiting?" I asked. I was too down. I didn't like it. Now I wished that the grass I smoked after I took the mescaline had been hash. It would have lasted longer. I wanted the combination back now that I was about to be left alone. Even the gray velvet divan felt thick with the heaviness of blood splattered wool. The air was sweet and pungent.

"I'm waiting for the name," he said. His eyes were yellow from fatigue. Yet he said the words as if he didn't need either rest or excitement. "You said that there were two of them and that one of them used to kill himself," he said. "That I'd know it if I'd seen him do it. He laughed like somebody vomiting blood."

"I was talking to myself," I said. "How could you have heard?"

"I ain't deaf," he said. The voice was still a monotone.

I looked at him. I must have missed it. Then I couldn't tell myself what. His face was blank and his body was tailored as if he had walked out of a bank.

"If you'll just give me the name," he said. Organ music started. He raised his hand and an invisible attendant must have seen it. The music stopped.

"I dislike organ music," the monotone said. "I play it for them. Not because I love them."

"Why?" I asked.

"Have I asked you why you came looking for what you call your father?"

"Call?"

"Very well then," he said. This time the monotone showed signs of severing whatever relationship it had started. His hand started to rise. I didn't want the attendant. Now, in the heavy, fog-yellow light, I wanted his time.

"No." I said. He lowered his long, thin hand. "I didn't ask you if you did it for money either," I said.

His eyes expanded and contracted viciously. "Are you about to?"

"No," I said.

"My time is valuable," he said. "I have my work. I am never hesitant to admit a mistake. Even if ending a thing is a mistake. That kind of indecision can destroy a man. *Benefit of doubt* is cowardice not consideration. So watch what you say."

"My time is not that valuable," I said.

"That doesn't mean you may waste mine with such statements about your past. Please restrain yourself. Self-indulgence will also destroy a man. Ask your father."

"How did you know?"

"What a stupid question!" The monotone intensified. "This is the last time that I will waste time answering such a question. The statement or question implies generality, especially if the son indulges himself."

"You mean if people waste time?"

"Did Benjamin Franklin teach you such an inane question? Do not underestimate me again. I hope I'm not lying to myself about you. That would be self-indulgence."

"Not indulgence of me?"

"There is *only* self-indulgence. Elevated, it is called pity. That doesn't mean it isn't work. All kinds of torture are work - even idleness. Complete rigor mortis sets in only with death."

"There's something better than work," he said. "It must be what you came here to see. You admitted that it wasn't your father."

I had been asked for a name. I had come to give one. I knew better now, but I still didn't know what I wanted to see.

"A chicken?" I asked. What a foolish question. Someone must have mixed speed with that mescaline. Jesus! And I thought it was the answer. It had to be covered. He'd throw me out. I had to stay now, for the trip. Nothing ever climaxed.

"What?" The lips almost parted. It was the mask's version of a smile. A real one would be self-indulgence.

"Sooner or later everyone comes here to see a chicken?"

He allowed himself the joke. No. The point was something else.

"Without a head," I said, tasting the air that was the breath of things dead.

"Birds are the oldest beings alive," he said. "They can't die. The buzzard is the oldest of them. He and his kind have been alive longer and will remain alive longer than any other species."

The monotone had changed. The man now spoke in the rhythms of the priest of a superior religion.

The chicken's head, severed from its flapping, bedraggled body, lay with membrane eyelids covering what? Its affinities with its brother the buzzard?

The organ music started to play again. There was no transition necessary in his face. The mask had never broken. The monotone came back.

"This time it is for a funeral," he said. "All things have their own validity. It is not the infinite. It is religion. But, after all, even a sculptor must pay money for his materials. Anyway, my attendants take care of these things. I no longer have to dirty my hands acquiring materials."

Then he took me to see *it*. It lay far back in the basement. "I waited years for the proper materials," he said. "Don't worry about the bier. At the proper time I embalmed and disinfected it."

Lying on a mass of amorphous, decadent, gray tissue lay the tiniest human body I had ever seen. The buzzard's head was grafted on perfectly.

"Beautiful!" he exclaimed and looked at me. For the first time, the mask, on the verge of tears, begged for recognition.

Fairy Tales

Darkness covered the face of the earth. The people talked all night long in the dimly lit room, speaking quietly, and the old, silver gray haired woman that Preacher had called the Lord's gift to him, lay with her head on his arm, her tiny body moving no more than that of the old whiteheaded exhorter who, in dream, raised his thin gray hand mapped with the purple veins of blood rivers and said: "Bring unto me the maiden, Philomela, whose Christian name I shall call Sarah Elizabeth. It is she who shall bear my Abram."

Philomela (Sarah Elizabeth) began to wail in her Choctaw tongue. There was no breeze. There was no lightening, and her darkling child, Abram Rexford, was in the federal penitentiary at Leavenworth, Kansas.

The old woman dreamed of a tall, hard young man who held and loved her body with the soft touch of his lips and the hardness of his loins as the soft coal oil lamplight caressed her tawny skin and flickered over his rippling muscular body. In the dream, he gave the young Philomela, trapped in the skin of the old Sarah, the ecstatic freedom from body that had given her Abram. As the old Preacher, young in the dream, caressed her with his lips in the peace and joy that followed the turbulent crescendo of love, she died.

Standing a necessary distance from the cage, Abram watched the guard at the penitentiary check his few personal items as they were handed to him. Abram, eyes dark brown enough to appear to be almost black, watched with the energy of silent hate and electric anger.

"The tobacco pouch," Abram said. He wanted the carved leather gift from his mother with her father's red stone pipe that they took from him on his entry. It was the one gift, valuable to both himself and his mother, that Abram could give back to her for her journey. The Preacher, as Abram called his father, disciplined her harshly when he caught her smoking, but she saved the pipe and passed it on to Abram in the buffalo skin pouch.

"What tobacco pouch?" the guard said. His eyes bulged with a contemptuous stare, baiting and sadistic.

Abram took one step across the painted line, his body poised like that of a wolf, hungering for the throat of his prey.

"Watch it, boy!" the guard standing at Abram's right blurted with the explosive force of a genuine warning. "You're almost out. Don't fuck it up over a tobacco pouch."

"You mean this here one," the guard pulled it from his pocket. "Happy hunting, Chief," he said, and threw it through the hole in the cage.

It was afternoon when Abram got on the bus in Jefferson City. He was wearing the Levi's and blue cotton shirt that he wore into the prison. Real clothes felt strange, the way a suit used to feel on special occasions. The Preacher's image crossed his mind; Preacher standing behind the pulpit in his one blue suit, gesturing with his hands as he exhorted his audience to call upon the Lord for forgiveness. The child, Abram, watched the Preacher's weathered, leather face and dark eyes for signs of the malice he was familiar with at home. The old man inspired fear. As a very small child, Abram believed that the wages of sin were real fire and brimstone, hotter than the volcanic eruption vomited by the devil from the bowels of the earth.

Abram's mother told him different. She told him there were spirits, some of them whimsical, and that they had to use their wits, and each other, to live in a world of spirits. She told him Preacher was not evil, and that everyone was a human being with feelings. Abram doubted that. He called his mother Phil for Philomela. He knew that was her name, not Sarah like his father said. He was a freshman in college before he knew what the name meant in Greek mythology. Philomela, wandering without a tongue in foreign lands, creating the music with which she told the story of her rape and mutilation to strangers. The story was a tragedy.

He saw her now, the way she must look. High cheek bones, brown face and closed eyes, her long hair nested around her shoulders. She wore the death mask that belied the escaped life. Preacher, from the pulpit above the casket, raised his hands to heaven, asking his Lord to please accept the soul of his faithful servant as Abram slipped the tobacco pouch and pipe into the casket for his mother's final journey to the sand hills.

As the bus moved like a heavy whale, its air brakes sounding like the plosive force that precedes a breathing mammal's surfacing bid for air, he watched fence posts, fields and an occasional gray deteriorating wooden barn.

He paid no attention to the girl sitting next to him until she spoke.

"Where you going?" she asked. "Not that it's any of my business, but you look familiar."

At first he ignored her. He had decided not to talk to people, at least not in idle conversation, when he was arrested and court martialed in North Carolina for international distribution of cocaine. He didn't say anything then, and he wasn't going to say anything now. He was surprised by the arrest. He took off his green beret uniform, and wore it only for his trial. Now he was no longer a Major and had lost all rights and privileges of most citizens. Why talk to them. He felt like he was a stranger in foreign lands "who had lost his tongue outside language" as Holderlyn said. He thought about saying that to the girl. She would think he was crazy and leave him alone. Instead he said, "You're right. It's none of your business. It's no one's business." He stared straight ahead at the back of the seat.

"Just making conversation Mister," she said. "It's a long way to where I'm goin' and I won't be anywhere when I get there."

That made him turn toward her. He was surprised. She looked like Phil must have looked in her twenties. She wore her dark hair in a single braid down her back, and sincere brown eyes encompassed his face. She wore no make-up and a plain print dress.

"Sounds like where I've been," he said, surprised at his own decision to talk. "I've been staying in a place where talk is cheap and there aren't any human beings to talk to."

"Leavenworth," she said, looking out the window. "I thought you looked familiar. I saw you in the bus station. I once had a brother," she said. "Remember Austin?" She took a picture out of the small leather bag in her lap. Abram as a captain, wearing fatigues and combat boots, laughed in the picture. A pretty Vietnamese girl stood between him and a lieutenant holding both their hands. He looked enough like Abram to be his brother.

"He sent this saying you married the girl. That was a long time before you were arrested." She looked out the window. "What happened to her?" she said. She said it as if she knew. Abram tried to think. He looked at the picture again. It was a haze, colored by the work he did and the pills he took not to feel.

"I was an assassin," he said, staring at the picture. They gave us the pills. The pills made me more efficient. There were no feelings, no hesitation, nothing. I could do things I'd never do normally and depend on the pills to separate me from the act." He heard himself saying this to the picture. He was afraid to look at the girl.

"Was my brother an assassin?" she asked.

"No." He lied. Abram remembered the first man he killed. He, Rex, as he called himself, put the pistol to another man's head. The South Vietnamese officer in Khakis wearing Captain's bars knelt, his hands tied behind his back, beside the standing green beret officer that was the historical Abram, younger and dedicated. The man wept, begging, his eyes open. Abram squeezed the trigger. The man's face turned to a mask, the eyes snapping shut. A glob of red colored matter came out the other side of the man's head in slow motion, spraying the sand with blood flecks in intricate patterns like dark snowflakes. Abram watched as the body followed the force of the explosion. He still saw the image of his handiwork. Horrified, he backed away from the man.

"Austin?" He said.

"Dead," she said.

"I'm sorry," Abram said. The bus exited the interstate. The driver down shifted and followed Missouri Highway 7 south. Abram looked across an open field into the orange sunset. He thought about himself as a child, at sunset, reading Zane Grey's *The Rider's of the Purple Sage*. The characters were either good or bad and the romances were sad and forever.

"Why?" she asked. Abram sensed that she was looking at him. She waited for him to turn and look at her.

"I remember when you first came home with him," she said. "It was an evening like this one and you said how mom reminded you of your mother. You said you might have been Asian a long time ago. I didn't know what you meant." The bus slowed as it passed a city limits sign. "Now, maybe I do."

The bus rolled easily into a small town with green lawns, landscaped in patterns of bushes and manicured trees. At the edge of the business section, a sign in front of a large colonial-style white house advertised *Clinkingbeard's Funeral Home*. Abram thought about the concept of a mortuary as home, the pale men who labored in basements embalming bodies and the made-up finished product lying on a bed of silk creating the illusion of an opulent and peaceful rest. He saw Phil's face surrounded by silk and lace, wrinkles and hollow cheeks all ironed out by the skills of the embalmer.

"I didn't know, then, that anything was wrong," she said. I thought you and my brother were perfect. Maybe you stepped right out of one of those old movies where American soldiers are romantic gentlemen, righteous and handsome. I laughed the first time I saw a training film teaching soldiers manners and proper etiquette. "Still, I suspected that your *'yes ma'am'* and *'this house looks so much like home'* were you. What happened?" The bus rolled south out of town in darkness. The interior lights replaced the sunset, and people settled back to rest.

Flight 801 in the Heart of Guam, USA

THE CANDLES FLICKERED on the makeshift altar in the dimly lit hotel room. The linen-covered board extended the length of the wall, and the flickering candles conjured, in dream like imagery, the young Korean faces hanging on the wall. Carl watched quietly from the back of the room as some of the people cut kneeled before the altar quietly weeping, while others spoke in hushed tones of the faces that looked into the room from the aura of the soft candle light.

Carl understood that, to these families of those faces, the young Korean women and men were not yet gone. Their spirits hovered on the verge of darkness in the faces illuminated by the soft light. The faces faded with too much light or too much darkness into the empty room decorated by glossy pictures, *in memoriam*.

An older man with a hard, weather-beaten face recognized the Governor and turned on the harsh overhead lights. He bowed. Carl returned the bow and reached for the man's callused hand.

The young faces on the wall froze into one-dimensional pictures and the grief-wrung faces of gray-haired grandmothers, angry fathers and shocked brothers and sisters turned to the Governor, demanding an answer. At first, Carl felt as if he were outside this scene, watching the Governor as the people held him accountable for this tragedy that, to a parent, meant an empty house, an empty life and an empty future. He merged with the

Governor's image in his mind, and looked directly into the eyes of the leathery face that had introduced him to the people and the faces on the wall. Carl began to tell them what he knew, all that he knew.

At 1:42 A.M. on August 6th, Carl lay sleeping no more than a quarter of a mile from the spot where Korean Airlines, Flight 801, while aborting a mistaken landing, slammed into the side of a steep embankment. Minutes later, the huge aircraft burst into flames.

Being human, Carl awakened only to the eerie sound he heard when the plane made its unusual approach to the airport. At first, sensing that something was wrong, he reacted to the sound, then dozed off again to be awakened by the rude ringing of his telephone some time around 2:05 A.M. He reacted instinctively as the message coming over the telephone blazed with the reality of the burning plane just over the ridge from his bedroom.

When Carl arrived on the crest of Nimitz hill (named for Admiral Nimitz of World War II fame in the Pacific theatre) with Officer Carlos Ramon, no one was there. The beacon loomed white under the dark skies that obscured the normally apparent stars that guided the ancient Chamorro sailors. Almost instantaneously, Officers Chargaulauf, Cecil Sula, James Santos, John Aguon and Jesse J. Mendiola arrived with Sargeant Fisher. Knowing of a road into the jungle that paralleled a gas pipeline, Carl commanded, "Let's Go!" and jumped into Cecil Sula's four wheel drive.

Twenty-five minutes had passed after the flight disappeared from the screens of the airport monitors. Its failure to appear on the tarmac began to concern the controllers. Carl, being the closest concerned person, was the first to cut through the dense jungle. With the flashlight, he illuminated the thick foliage and led the way through the tangle of brush, sword grass, and vines into the jungle. Directly in front of Officer Ramon, Carl led the way down into the arroyo, planting one foot and then the other in the clumps of grass, seeing for the first time the flames of the huge airship and smelling the burning rubber of the gasoline fire.

"You sure you want to walk into that?" Ramon said. Neither Carl nor Carlos slowed their pace. The flashlight was no longer necessary.

Carl began to register the hoarse calls for "help" from the area outside the plane. He focused on the horror and his image of trapped people. The fumes and fire, as in a dream, were not related to himself except as he saw himself as an inextricable part of this surrealistic funeral pyre. Trying desperately to reach the people inside the fire, Carl felt everything happen in slow motion as if all his efforts would never bring him to the huge tail looming behind the giant rib cage of the burning 747. The tail assembly proclaimed KAL in the circle with the unreality of the most vivid dream he would ever have.

As Carl strained forward toward the wreck, an explosion lifted him off his feet. The shock of the screams overwhelmed him as the officers began calling out of fear for their friends around the crash site.

As if it were the next frame of a nightmare that he dreamed, Carl reached for the child holding the flight attendant's shoulders, crying and begging the semi-conscious woman to please wake up and come with her. The woman laid still, her legs collapsed underneath her; her head lolling behind her shoulders in a puddle of something dark and wet. The first officer replaced the child above the woman as Carl lifted the girl.

She turned her head and eyes as he started to carry her and grabbed hold with all her strength. Looking in the direction of the burning section of the plane, she said, "My mother." Carl walked toward the hair-singeing heat. The smell of burned hair and burning chemicals stung his nostrils.

"She's dead," the child said. Carl groaned, realizing for the first time the impossibility of anyone being alive, and that human beings were the source of the unmistakable, heavy odor of burnt flesh. How, on his island, practically in his neighborhood, could people be dead and dying? He had felt nothing like this since the weeks of deliverance from captivity in World War II.

Climbing up the steep hillside, he heard the child saying in perfect English, "My daddy is at home in Tokyo. We must tell him. My mother is dead."

The crash destroyed all of Carl's illusions of security from the violent, coincidental death that had lurked in the dark jungle and in the darkness of his mind since his childhood. Now, as he returned to the site, he was drawn by feelings of kinship to these people, fighting death in the darkness. Their fight was his fight. He was one of these people, and some of them lay in agony as he barked orders to clear a road and activate rescue efforts. He pushed his driver to get him back there to the remaining bodies and pull them from the jungle, the wreckage and the fire that was devouring them.

At daybreak, the giant tail section loomed like a KAL monument to the carnage that, everyone knew by now, lay buried beneath it. Carl turned from the still body, entangled in the wreckage at his feet, to look, from his vantage point beneath the giant rudder, over a field of remains. Tatters of gold cloth, royal purple uniforms, garbage, luggage and people were strewn over the hillside. The gigantic bird smoldered and burned in the chemical fire of its own fluids, the fumes drifting above it in a haze of smoke. Rescue workers scrambled through the brush and the trees throughout the surrounding area, calling out when they found something and Carl responded instinctively, leaving the dead, to find and save the survivors. He was numb to his own pain and the heat. Carlos handed him his hat as the sun exposed the carnage and burned from above. Carl took it, wiping his forehead and plunging into the underbrush in response to cries of "Here! Over here!"

Carl was threading his way up the steep embankment at the front end of a stretcher, a child writhed and groaned on its canvas, when he saw his first television news cameraman. His first thought, the salty sweat running down into his eyes and stinging, was anger. Here came a man, seven hours late, to take pictures. *People need help,* Carl thought; *and he comes dragging in here, after the engineers have cut a path for him, to take pictures.* Then, the questions that Carl hadn't yet considered, started.

"Why? What happened?" the large, casually dressed reporter who accompanied the cameraman asked. "Can you tell us anything about this crash, Governor?"

"No. Not now," Carl said. "I came as soon as I knew and too many are dead. Everyone must help."

The day passed and the living reported as investigators followed the rescue workers. Carl learned, from an Australian helicopter repairman, that the plane appeared to be coming in for a landing. Survivors were taken to the Naval Hospital and Guam Memorial. The more serious were transferred to burn centers in Texas. Carl tried to be everywhere, at the hospital, in the field and in his office. Questions were to be answered and Carl learned, answering those questions, what Harry Truman meant when he said, "The buck stops here."

Carl remembers the days and nights of the following week with the poignancy of a horrible dream. The families demanded to see the remains of their dead children, husbands, brothers, sisters and wives. Carl took them to the ship in which their relatives were entombed, and answered the living with telephone calls, reporting the progress of the survivors and the fate of those remaining (through the nights) at the crash site and in the morgue.

At daybreak, Carl lead those condemned to searching through the wreckage to collect the remnants of the once living bodies for identification. There is a film clip of him, sweat running down his face, answering a question for another reporter for the evening news. From a miasma of ashes, scattered wreckage and strewn remnants, Carl reports (as if interrupted in this hell by the camera) that counting is difficult. The scene and the people are like pieces of a puzzle scattered beyond recognition. Carl turns away from the camera and back to the puzzle with the urgency of his realization of the scavengers surrounding the people in the hot sun.

The families continue to arrive. Angry at Guam, angry at America, and angry at God. Grandfathers demand the bodies of their children and attack the executives of Korean Airlines. The dead are identified while body bags and caskets replace the carnage in Carl's days and nights. Carl refuses to appear on talk shows to answer charges of publicity-seeking by people who spend their time, and earn their living, reporting on those condemned to the responsibility for collecting the pieces and answering to the families. He appears before the wall of still photographs in the Pacific Star Hotel room and answers to the grief-stricken parents, sisters and brothers for Guam and America.

Carl looks out at wrinkled, grief-stricken and shocked faces and says: "I'm sorry." Again reporters catch this on film and we see it on the evening news. What we don't see is Carl Gutierrez, *in the stillness of the midnight,* awakening to the horror of death and separation. We don't see his "hands on" assumption of responsibility for and to the people in rescue, identification and confirmation. We don't see these things because they are filtered. The television cameras don't show us Carl in action, because we don't want to see it. Only those condemned to responsibility for closing the chasm that opens to claim the dead, leaving only the still photographs hanging on the wall, have to see it. They, necessarily, by sharing the horror, transform it into a tragedy that we can live with. The rest of us go on with our lives, and the candles that illuminate the photographs above the makeshift altar remind us of the fact that Guam is, as always, at the heart of the human community.

The Plays

The Recommendation

a play in one act

CHARACTERS:

Smith
Marian
Winters
Colonel
Minister
Audience

[*When the lights come up, they reveal a thirty year-old man, sitting at a rectangular walnut table. A single electric bulb hangs from the ceiling by a worn cord. The man's white shirt and black trousers are wrinkled. He has obviously been sleeping in them. His black hair looks as if he has been combing it with his fingers, and he needs a shave. His elbows are propped on the table. He stares out into the audience. His name is SMITH.*]

SMITH: [*Staring at the audience*] I would like to call your attention to myself.

[*There is a long uncomfortable pause during which SMITH and the audience exchange stares.*]

SMITH: Before I went to the war, I was often considered a normal human being. I wore clothes on the street. I didn't sit in restaurants and stare at people. I didn't even join in their conversations the way I do now. I don't often go out, but at least once every three days I have to eat. Just yesterday a man hit me. I sat next to two men who were talking about their wives. All I said was, "I married a bitch. I'm sorry it happened to you, too. You'll have to learn that even your mother and sister often screw." Then the one with a big stomach and butter on his chin hit me in the mouth. There was a big mess, and the restaurant owner told me never to come back; said he'd been keeping an eye on me. Wanted to know if I was a dope addict or what? Said he didn't like the way I looked at his women customers. I told him it was okay, that I didn't screw any more, and that if I did, I wouldn't do it right there in his restaurant. He kicked me out anyway.

Before the war, I was a quiet boy. People used to say to my mother, "Boy, that Smitty sure is a good kid. Quietest kids are always bright. And I just know the Lord is working with him. He'll be a great man someday." My mother wanted me to be a Baptist minister, so she had me saved and baptized. Twice, before I was fifteen, the Lord came to me in a dream and I loved him, but I was afraid to tell anybody. They might have thought I was a homosexual. Later, I decided that I loved him because he looked like a woman in all the pictures.

Anyway, I grew up and quietly married a reformed prostitute like all the heroes in the best movies. Then the war came along, and I knew what would happen. I couldn't work the way it was. One day at the machine shop, I made two giant-sized candlesticks that were supposed to be gear shift levers. I kept thinking about her in bed with the smiling fellow next door who chewed juicy fruit gum, and was all the time coming to visit in the daytime when I wasn't supposed to be home.

At that point I wasn't a particularly valuable employee, so when the draft notice came, my boss said how sorry he was to lose me, but he was sure I could get a job somewhere else when I got back from protecting my country. One of the other fellows looked at the candlesticks, they hadn't been thrown out yet, and said he was even sorrier thinking about what it would do to the country to have me protecting it. But the generals have a place for all of God's children and they put me in mine.

[*The lights go down. When the lights come up again, only stage right is lighted. SMITH is wearing a private's uniform. He is standing next to a COLONEL. The COLONEL is a slim, clean-cut, middle-aged man. He is studying the darkness off-stage right.*]

SMITH: [*Salutes. The COLONEL notices him and returns the salute.*] Private Smith reporting as ordered, sir.
COLONEL: Smith, we've got to cross that river. Who's the most expendable man here?
SMITH: I am sir. My squad leader relieved me of all duties.
COLONEL: Why, Smith?
SMITH: Well sir, I'm the ammunition bearer for our squad.
COLONEL: What does that have to do with your being relieved Smith?
SMITH: Remember that last engagement, sir?
COLONEL: Yes, Smith?
SMITH: Well, sir, I forgot to bring the ammunition. I explained to him that anybody could make a mistake, sir, but he wouldn't listen. I told him I'd never forget it again, but he relieved me anyway. He was really mad about having to tell the Captain his whole squad didn't have any ammunition. Said if his weapon was loaded he'd shoot me right there. The Captain said I was a crazy son-of-a-bitch and ought to go back in irons.
COLONEL: [*Grins*] You want to redeem yourself, Smith?
SMITH: Not particularly sir. I'd just as soon go home. One of the medics said I might be able to get a medical discharge for being crazy.
COLONEL: What about your country, Smith? [*The COLONEL looks off into the darkness.*] You want your country to lose this valuable swamp to the communists? Think about your wife and family.
SMITH: (*Looks out into the darkness*) I guess you're right, sir. You never can tell when we might need this swamp.
COLONEL: That's right Smith. Daniel Boone didn't blaze trails in virgin timber land for nothing, even if it did kill a few trees. (*Looks at Smith*) Think of yourself as a tree, Smith.
SMITH: I often have, sir. That's why the medic said I might get a medical discharge.
COLONEL: You want that on your record, Smith? How many businessmen do you think would hire a man who thought he was a tree?
SMITH: I hadn't thought of it what way, sir. I guess I'd like to carry the ammunition after all.
COLONEL: [*Points into the darkness*] See that brush on the other bank, Smith?
SMITH: Yes, sir.
COLONEL: I want you to walk straight toward that bank. While you're doing that, the rest of the company will charge across on your right. You'll get a medal.
SMITH: Sir, those bushes are moving! There are guns in those bushes. I'd rather not go.
COLONEL: It's the logical thing. Redeem yourself!

SMITH: No, sir. That doesn't make sense at all. I'll be killed.

COLONEL: We all take that chance Smith. Act like a man!

SMITH: Send the Captain, sir. That's what King David did. My wife doesn't look at all like Bathsheba. When I married her, she was a whore, but after I reformed her, she got fat. She just sits around all day and eats chocolate covered cherries, and without the exercise, well— Everybody likes the Captain's wife, sir. You'd like her. She's very generous, and she doesn't discriminate. She'd like you too.

COLONEL: Do you know what you're saying Smith? Get across that river now, before I shoot you here!

SMITH: No logical reason, sir. If you sent the Captain, things would be easier for everybody. You might even get something yourself. Send the Captain, sir. I won't forget the ammunition again. I promise.

COLONEL: [*Throwing his arm violently in the direction of the river.*] Move, Smith!

SMITH: No, sir. I won't go, sir. Please sir, try not to think of me as a tree, sir. Let me go home, sir. I'll be alright there, sir. I can live a normal life.

COLONEL: [*Grabs Smith's coat and slaps him violently*] Coward! Move, Coward!

SMITH: [*Falls to his knees*] Please, God. Save me. Let me go back and carry the ammunition. I'll never forget it again God. I'll always go to chapel God. Oh, please, God, don't let them kill me!

COLONEL: [*Slaps SMITH who falls on his back. Then yells.*] Put this despicable coward in irons. (*The lights go down. When they come up again, SMITH is still sitting at the table.*)

SMITH: [*Talking to the audience*] When I came, unexpected, back from the war, I couldn't find my wife for two weeks. She finally wandered home drunk, with a bruised face, and cussing some man she'd been shacked up with. She'd lost a lot of weight and when she sobered up, she cried and was very attractive, so I forgave her. She reformed and started eating chocolate covered cherries again.

Everybody at the machine shop was surprised to see me. They all looked at each other and grinned and the boss said, in front of the whole group, that he couldn't afford to have a war hero like me working for him. You should have seen them laugh. It would have brought tears to your eyes to see those poor people so happy about a dishonorable discharge.

It got so I was begging for jobs in my dreams. Huge, puffy men would ask me if I was a veteran, just when I was about to get the job. Then they would go into rages, screaming, "Move, coward!" Typewriters would pick up speed, IBM machines would roar and I'd wake up.

My wife was beginning to be very angry. I couldn't afford chocolate covered cherries anymore, and I suspected that she had taken up her other luxury. I didn't blame her much. The job paid well and it kept her in clothes and food. She'd gotten fat, so it didn't pay as well as before we were married. You see, I didn't know this for sure. I didn't dare ask or try to find out. But she had an awful lot of new clothes. With all this in mind, I called on the Lord again.

[*The lights go down. When they come up, only stage left is lighted. A minister stands behind an ornately-carved pulpit that sets on a stage-like platform. He is middle-aged and fat. He wears a loose fitting black suit. He arranges a large Bible on the pulpit as if he were a funeral director preparing a body to be viewed. A fluorescent lamp, attached to the pulpit, illuminates the Bible. The large print is divided into three different colors of ink. A wine colored carpet leads up to the pulpit. SMITH, wearing a black suit, approaches the MINISTER.*]

MINISTER: [*Looks up from the Bible and down at SMITH.*]
SMITH: Brother Fulbright, I need a job.
MINISTER: Well, as you see Mr. Smith, this isn't an employment agency. [*He smiles at his own joke.*]
SMITH: I know, sir, I've been there. I've been everywhere since I came back from the war. I've tried to help myself and—
MINISTER: Now you want the Lord to help you. I'm glad you came to me. [*Smiles affectionately at SMITH*] What did you do in the war?
SMITH: I carried ammunition, sir.
MINISTER: And the business world doesn't need very many ammunition carriers. Is that it, Mr. Smith?
SMITH: No, sir. You see, I left the war early. In the middle of a battle.
MINISTER: Didn't you trust the Lord to save you then, Mr. Smith?
SMITH: He did sir, but He didn't take care of the loose ends. You see, sir, there was a case of mistaken identity. Somebody mistook me for a tree. There was no other passable way. I called on the Lord and He got me a dishonorable discharge. Now I need a job. My wife's not happy, and I don't eat well.
MINISTER: Place yourself in God's hands Mr. Smith. You have strayed somewhere. Sometimes we mistake what we want for what God wants. Maybe you made that mistake in the war.
SMITH: No, sir. They wanted me to die and save a swamp. They thought I was a tree and that it wouldn't make any difference. They never did realize their mistake. If the Lord had just made them give me back my job as ammunition carrier everything would have been alright. Then I could have led a normal life.

MINISTER: We must not question the Lord's way, son. The Lord works in mysterious ways. That swamp might have become the sight of a great temple. Millions of heathen peoples might have come to know the Lord. You have deserted the Lord through your own selfishness. You have been cast out into darkness.

SMITH: I didn't know, sir. I thought they were killing them. At least that was the way it looked.

MINISTER: It is not ours to know why, my son. The Lord works in mysterious ways. We must not question them. To question them is to be cast out into darkness where there is weeping and gnashing of teeth.

SMITH: My wife weeps a lot, and my teeth are gnashed, sir. I know now sir, I should not have questioned him. Please, sir, if I could just get a job. Do you know someone, sir, who could help me?

MINISTER: [*Gravely*] I know someone.

SMITH: Maybe you could give me a recommendation? I'd never doubt or question again, sir. I'd always do as I was told and try not to forget important things.

MINISTER: I can give you a recommendation, but you must accept the Lord's will of your own accord.

[*The MINISTER reaches into the open back of the pulpit, takes out a sheet of paper and hands it to SMITH.*]

SMITH: [*Takes the paper and reads*] For The Unemployed. No man can serve two masters; for either he will hate the one, and love the other; or else he will hold to the one, and despise the other. Ye cannot serve God and mammon. Therefore, I say unto you, take no thought for your life, what ye shall eat, or what ye shall drink; nor yet for your body, what ye shall put on. Is not the life more than meat, and the body more than raiment? Behold the fowls of the air; for they sow not, neither do they reap, nor gather into barns; yet your heavenly Father feedeth them. Are ye not much better than they?

MINISTER: Remember those words from "The Sermon on the Mount" my son. I can tell you nothing more.

SMITH: I'm not questioning, sir. I will never question the meaning of the Lord's ways. But to whom am I to give this recommendation, sir?

MINISTER: The Lord's commands are clear and not to be questioned. Go home and wait upon the Lord. He will not fail to serve you if you accept him with an open heart.

SMITH: [*Exiting stage left*] Thank you, sir. You don't know how much I appreciate this. I thought it was hopeless and now I have a recommendation. I understand that I am to never question again, sir. The Lord will forgive me.

[*The lights go down. When they come up again SMITH is still seated at the table as in the first scene.*]

SMITH: I took the recommendation to a lot of employers. They asked me if I was selling Bibles or if I was a Jehovah's Witness or something like that. I told them that it was a recommendation for a job. Most of them laughed and said they weren't buying any today. One of them, a Mr. Winters, almost understood.

[*The lights go down. When they come up again, stage right is lighted. A well dressed, middle-aged man with graying temples sits behind a gray metal office desk, leaning back in a swivel chair. SMITH sits to stage right of the desk in a straight backed metal chair. He wears the black suit.*]

WINTERS: [*Reads SMITH'S recommendation. Then studies SMITH for a minute.*] Where did you get this recommendation, Mr. Smith?
SMITH: My minister gave it to me, sir.
WINTERS: [*As if he is talking to a child*] And where does your minister live, Mr. Smith?
SMITH: I don't know, sir. He never told me. He doesn't like to be disturbed at home. We just talk to him at the church. He's there every day if you'd like to call him. He only gave me the recommendation, though, sir. It's from someone else. Don't you recognize it?
WINTERS: [*Leaning over the desk, closer to SMITH*] Who is your recommendation from, Mr. Smith? I think I know, but I'm not certain.
SMITH: God, sir. Haven't you seen one like it before? Maybe it's the paper it's printed on. Our minister saves money on paper. I'm sure God would prefer watermarked paper. (*He pauses, worried*) But I'm not to question his ways —I must remember that. No. The paper is fine. If God uses that paper, we should all use it. I will not think about water marked paper.
WINTERS: [*Leans back, away from SMITH. He talks in a calming voice.*]Okay, Mr. Smith. Your paper is fine. I didn't mean to question it. But you must understand that we have to take precautions. We have to be sure that the recommendations are valid. Almost anyone could copy that down. We can't always tell that God himself wrote it. [*Pauses, looking at SMITH, than off stage right, then he says, more quietly, attempting to sound official.*] The paper certainly looks like the kind

God uses. [*Reaches in his desk.*] Here, let me check it with a letter I got from God last week. [*Looks in the desk.*] It's the same alright.

SMITH: [*Looks puzzled. He begins to suspect that WINTERS is off balance.*] You get letters from God?

WINTERS: Only on important occasions, like at Easter and Christmas. [*He gets up from the desk and starts to pace behind it.*] Now, let's see what we can do for you, Mr. Smith. Where did you say you worked last?

SMITH: In the war.

WINTERS: Were you a general, or did you have a more important job?

SMITH: No, sir. I carried ammunition. But I questioned God's ways and was relieved of my position. I won't do it again, sir. Honest! I'll never disobey orders again.

WINTERS: Okay, Smith. It's okay. I know you won't. All I want to know is why God sent you here, and where he sent you from.

SMITH: I'm a machinist, sir.

WINTERS: And I bet you are a good one, too. Did they tell you that where you came from? Were they nice to you? And did they say you were making progress? I bet they liked you so much, they wouldn't let you go and you had to escape. Is that right, Mr. Smith? Well, we aren't about to let them have you back. Such a valuable employee. Just tell me who they are and where the place is. I'll make sure they don't sneak in here.

SMITH: I don't think they want me, sir. I often made the wrong things.

WINTERS: We all make mistakes, Smith.

SMITH: Thank you, sir. Most people, especially my squad leader, couldn't understand that. He should have known it was a perfectly normal mistake.

WINTERS: That's when they put you in?

SMITH: Yes, sir. And now that I'm out, with the discharge they gave me, I can't find a job.

WINTERS: [*Picks up the recommendation and looks at it.*] I guess not. And you want to go back? Is that it?

SMITH: No, sir! I want to live a normal life! Just help me live a normal life! You can do that?

WINTERS: Easy, Smith. Of course we can. I just want to know their names so I can warn the boys to watch for them. We wouldn't want to lose you.

SMITH: Well sir, there was a Colonel Holgrave, Captain Robinson and Sergeant Fuller. Is that enough, sir?

WINTERS: [*Pauses a minute, watching SMITH*] Fine! Just let me put in a call here to the boys. [*He picks up the telephone receiver and dials a number.*] Is this the uh — I can't talk frankly, but I would appreciate it if you would send a car to 26 Franklin Street. I'll send someone out to you. [*Puts down the receiver and looks at SMITH.*] Everything's taken care of

The Recommendation

now. I can put you through to the man who's really in charge. He can give you a much more important job than I can. [*He looks off stage right anxiously. A police siren can be heard in the background.*]

SMITH: Thank you, sir. I knew I could depend on the recommendation. Everything's fine. God has forgiven me. You have no idea how happy I am. [*The lights go down.*]

[*When the lights come up again, they reveal SMITH sitting in his original position.*]

SMITH: You have no idea how upset I was when I discovered that Mr. Winters was a madman. He led me to the door and kept insisting that a police car across the street was an office and the policeman was God. He said God always interviewed his employees personally and that I should go explain my situation to him. I didn't argue with him. I suspected that something was wrong when he told me about the letters from God. I just thanked him and told him I would go right over there. Then he got emotional and shook my hand. Said I was a pitiful case and that he hoped I'd find fulfillment. I left. When I got home, my wife had prepared all the fulfillment I'd ever need.

[*The lights go down. When they come up again, stage left is lighted with a rose tinted light. The light reveals a small blond, maple table. On it is a portable stereo. Throughout the scene, this stereo plays country and western music. There are two gaudy easy chairs on each side of the stereo. One is covered by a bright green slip-cover and the other is upholstered with red plastic. SMITH sits in the green chair. He isn't wearing his coat and tie. His shirt is wrinkled. SMITH holds his recommendation. His wife, Marian, sits in the red chair manicuring her fingernails. Her hair is long and bleached white. She wears a thick crust of makeup. Her dress is both too short and too tight on her fat figure.*]

MARIAN: [*Sarcastically*] Well, did you get a job?
SMITH: I almost got one, Marian, but the employer turned out to be a madman.
MARIAN: [*Laughs harshly*] I suppose he couldn't understand your recommendation?

[*While SMITH speaks, MARIAN files her fingernails and shakes her body in time to the music.*]

SMITH: He might have been able to, before he went crazy. I thought I had the job. We've got to eat Marian. What are we going to do? You know how much I love you and depend on you, Marian. I couldn't stand to lose you. You must love me an awful lot to understand this. You're a fine woman, Marian. We've gone through a lot together. I stood by you when men brutally took advantage of your kind heart. Now you're standing by me. As long as we've got each other we've got something to hang on to, even if callous men take advantage of you and employers don't understand my recommendation—What're we going to do?

[*MARIAN stops wiggling to the music and looks up as SMITH speaks the last line.*]

MARIAN: [*Speaking in a harsh, low voice*] Where do you get this we stuff? You got a turd in your pocket? [*She laughs.*]

SMITH: [*Startled, leans forward*] What's wrong with you Marian? Why are you talking like this to me? [*Pleading*] Be nice to me, Marian, please.

MARIAN: [*Rising and yelling*] I've had it mister! [*Draws her finger across her neck*] Up to here! Job! Job! Job! How could a coward like you get a job? You're not a man. You deserted your country. You turned into a hunk of shit when you were asked to do one little job. And you come back here and think you can satisfy me! [*Swells up*] I'm a woman! I need a man who can fight my battles for me. I can't stand to go to bed with a hunk of shit any more. Find yourself some trash to screw. I'm a woman!

SMITH: [*Rising*] Marian, please, Marian. Don't talk like that. It's the pressure. I'll get a job. You won't have to have those awful men touching you. I know, Marian. I've known all along. You've been prostituting yourself for me. I couldn't admit it. I couldn't face it. But now, Marian, you've got to stop! Even if we starve, you've got to stop!

MARIAN: [*Yelling*] Are you calling me a whore? You filthy coward! Are you calling me a whore?

SMITH: No. Marian. No. I never have in my life accused you of that. You know that, Marian. I accepted you, Marian. I love you for what you are, not what you've done.

MARIAN: That is the last straw. That is all. You low, filthy, useless son-of-a-bitch.

SMITH: [*Desperately*] We've got the recommendation, Marian. Please listen, Marian. Please believe me. Believe in the recommendation with me, Marian.

MARIAN: Not only are you a weakling and a coward, but you're a crazy man. Do you know what that recommendation is, you fool! That's one of thousands of scripture helps. That foolish Baptist church passes them out every Sunday to "people in need." Thank God we never did anything like that in the Church of Christ. Coming from a low family and a low religion, you were never my equal! You should have made your bed with your own kind.

SMITH: [*Falls on his knees in front of Marian*] Please, Marian. Please believe in the recommendation with me. I love you, Marian. Take off your clothes, Marian. Please take off those awful clothes and we'll start over. You'll see, Marian. I can satisfy you. We'll believe in the recommendation and the men will go away. Please! Please! Please!

MARIAN: Do you know what you're saying! Me, Marian, be satisfied with a cowardly piece of insane trash like you! (*She stammers in mock hysteria*) Get out!

SMITH: Please, Marian!

MARIAN: [*Simultaneously yelling and slapping him violently*] Coward! Move, Coward! Get your filthy body out of here!

[*The lights go down. When they come up, SMITH sits at the table.*]

SMITH: You might say I was looking for something to worship. I spent a hell of a lot of time on my knees. [*Laughs, then looks around the room.*] I moved myself and the recommendation in here. I don't go down on my knees much any more. I only have to go out once every three or four days. People bump into me on cross walks, automobile drivers honk their horns and curse me, elevator doors slam in my face. Occasionally, I get beaten up just trying to tell people what I've learned. It happens most often in restaurants where I see people talking about the weather conditions, and whether or not they'll get a Christmas bonus. I sometimes talk to them about the war, sometimes about God and sometimes about sex. I'm beaten most often for talking about sex, so I've decided, although I no longer feel anything, that it's the most important problem. You see, they don't know who I am. It's not often I get a chance like this to call attention to myself. But, as I was saying, it doesn't matter. I've found a new source of power so I can't feel or be hurt any more. [*He raises his leg and reveals an electric cord wrapped around it. It plugs into a socket that has been tacked on to the table leg.*] A skeptical encyclopedia salesman asked me how I could get electric power if I wasn't wired for it. I told him I had become mechanical. Then he told me that the plug wasn't attached to anything. That I should learn about electricity before I started depending on it. That worried me. You see, I'd depended on so many undependable things before. Finally, I just put it out of my mind. There's some things a fellow's just got to not think about, if he expects to live a normal life.

In the Stillness of the Midnight

a play in one act

CHARACTERS:

Man
Crowd
Policeman
Demonstrator
Riot Policeman

[*The stage is almost bare. In the center of the stage, a middle-aged policeman sits behind a gray metal office desk. There are papers spread over the desk. Behind and stage left of the desk, is a voting booth. It looks like a telephone booth with a solid door. A sign on top of the booth says "Voting Booth." The heckling sounds of a riot are heard from off stage right. A Black man enters, and the policeman looks up.*]

POLICEMAN: Now what're you doin' here? You know you niggers can't vote. And what's all that crowd doin' out there? Them white beatniks bring you up here and put you up to this?

MAN: I'm looking for my wife's body. I told her I wasn't going to take it any more. That she'd have to stop getting drunk while I stayed home and kept the baby. But she just smiled and went out anyway. I'm sure she's dead or she would have come back home. I didn't beat her, or hurt her or anything.

POLICEMAN: [*Grins*] And you think she might be layin' around here somewhere, huh? You niggers are all alike. Have you checked any other black beds lately?

MAN: [*Motions toward the voting booth*] She might be in there. You can't tell where they'll put bodies nowadays. One of the professors where I went to college killed his wife. He put her in a trunk and kept her in his office for three weeks. The janitors thought the smell was coming from the chemistry laboratory.

POLICEMAN: Yeah, sure. Peter Peter Punkin' eater had a wife and couldn't keep her. Put her in a punkin' shell and there he kept her very well. You Peter Punkin' eater? Maybe you put your wife in a shell? If you don't want to go to jail, maybe you'd better get out of here.

MAN: No. I want to look in the booth, to see if they put her there. That's all. Just let me look in the booth. Nobody can vote if she's in the booth, anyway. After a while she'll stink up all the ballots.

POLICEMAN: Yeah, sure. You want to sneak in that booth and vote, don't you? You think I'm crazy? That crowd out there brought you down here to sneak in that booth and vote. You ain't even registered.

[*Outside a bottle breaks and the crowd cheers. The MAN moves toward the booth and reaches for the door. The POLICEMAN rises and jerks his billy club out of his hip pocket.*]

POLICEMAN: Get away from that door! Keep your fingers off that door!

MAN: [*Backing away*] She's in there, isn't she? You know she's in there and you won't let me look.

POLICEMAN: Why don't you just be a good nigger and go home?

MAN: I bet you've had her in there for a week. I think I can smell it now. Your voting booth stinks.

POLICEMAN: Maybe it used to be an outhouse. That's it. Why don't you go look in an outhouse. Maybe she had a heart attack while she was on the pot.

MAN: There are no outhouses in the city. You can't fool me. Everything's mechanical here. She's in that booth. She couldn't be anywhere else. The professor put his wife in a trunk and kept her in his office for three weeks. In class, we thought what we smelled was his breath. He read to us from these yellowed notes that he must have taken in graduate school, all about the eighteenth century and reason. His hair and mustache had turned a dirty yellow color. I thought it was him. I thought he was rotting.

Logically, she couldn't be anywhere else. He used the trunk. You can't use the same gimmick twice. The police aren't stupid.

CROWD: [*Outside, chanting*] Dumb cop, dumb cop, dumb cop.

POLICEMAN: That's right, buddy. So why don't you give up tryin' to sneak into that voting booth. We haven't had any bodies in voting booths for years, nor maniacs trying to get them out. There ain't no precedent for it.

MAN: That's just it. The unexpected. That's why she's in there. How many bodies have you found in a professor's office?

POLICEMAN: And we ain't gonna find no nigger bodies in voting booths, because we don't even let them vote.

MAN: That's why! [*He moves quickly toward the booth. The POLICEMAN jumps up and pushes him back just as he touches the doorknob*] I thought if I could just get the door open she'd fall out and you'd see. [*Looks at the POLICEMAN suspiciously for a minute*] But you already know, don't you?

POLICEMAN: Yeah, I know. I know you're the nigger them white liberals brought down here from a lunatic asylum to sneak into my voting booth. Then the newspapers could take pictures that said, "See the cop, see the nigger. The cop's letting the nigger vote. The cop loves the nigger."

MAN: Did you see them put her in there? Is that why you won't let me open the door? You're afraid they'll take pictures of her in your voting booth?

POLICEMAN: Hell, no. I'm afraid they'll take a picture of you in my voting booth.

CROWD: [*Outside, the CROWD becomes noisier, another bottle breaks and they scream*] Cops eat shit!

[*There is a struggle off stage. Then a policeman, wearing a riot helmet and face mask, shoves a young man, wearing a navy pea jacket and a fatigue cap, on to the stage. The DEMONSTRATOR carries a sign that says, "SAVE US FROM SLAUGHTER" in large red letters.*]

DEMONSTRATOR: [*Speaks mechanically*] I'm being beaten. The police are brutally beating me with cattle prods and nightsticks.

RIOT POLICEMAN: He hit me with that sign. [*The RIOT POLICEMAN leaves.*]

DEMONSTRATOR: It's not true. I don't believe in violence. I'm being brutally attacked and charged falsely. Go ahead. Arrest me. Throw me in jail. You people crucified Jesus and poisoned Socrates. A sensitive human being cannot live in a police state governed by manikins in police uniforms screaming about democracy.

POLICEMAN: What were you doing out there? [*Motions toward the CROWD*]

DEMONSTRATOR: You call this democracy? We're supposed to vote? What good would it do? We're all being sent to war. We're all being herded into battlefields and slaughtered.

POLICEMAN: [*Motions toward the Black MAN*] You bring him here?

DEMONSTRATOR: (*Noticing the Black MAN*) What are you doing to my brother? You've already deprived him of his right to vote. Have you brought him here to slaughter him?

POLICEMAN: We don't kill very many crazy people. There ain't no precedent for it. Did you people really think you could sneak a crazy nigger into my voting booth? Huh? You think I'm dumb?

DEMONSTRATOR: Dumb? I'm demonstrating against your ballot box. Against a democracy that puts people in boxes and slaughters them.

MAN: [*Talking to the DEMONSTRATOR*] How'd you know?

DEMONSTRATOR: Know what?

MAN: My wife's in that voting booth. It hasn't been done before. The professor used a trunk and kept his wife in his office. That's why she's in the voting booth. She's been there for a week. How did you figure it out? Did you smell it?

DEMONSTRATOR: Yes, my friend. This whole world stinks. It stinks of people being slaughtered in the name of abstractions. That voting booth stinks in the name of democracy.

MAN: No. Her name was Isabel.

DEMONSTRATOR: Was? You said was. You mean she had a name but that ballot box deprived her of an identity.

MAN: I don't know. You might not be able to recognize her. She's been in there for a week. I didn't look at the professor's wife. After we found out what the smell was, we were horrified. Everybody smelled it for six months. The janitors were even afraid at night. It wasn't the idea of her having been there dead for three weeks. It was the smell that hung in the air. I almost suffocated once with a cold. I couldn't stand to breathe through my mouth. It seemed like I could taste it and that the gases from her decaying body were getting into my system.

DEMONSTRATOR: That's it. That's bureaucracy, my friend. You're a poet. Together we'll face the world. Somebody said Christ was either a savior or a crazy man. I'll become your disciple. I'll wear sandals, and you can let your hair grow. It doesn't matter that you're the wrong color. That's better! That's much better! You'll become known as the black Jesus. And disciples from all over the world will follow you. [*Thinks a minute*] No. We must keep it small. Christ chose twelve for a reason. Avoid the bureaucracy. Pretty soon, parents would be sending their children to you so they could get good jobs in banks and insurance companies. Then we'd have an alumni and people would send us money for gymnasiums. I don't believe in physical fitness and we can't allow ourselves to compromise our ethic. We can't take money and send out specially printed Bibles and scripture helps like Billy Graham. No. We'll have to keep our number down to twelve and go around the country teaching multitudes and eating loaves and fishes. I'll be right beside you all the way.

MAN: Then you'll help me?

DEMONSTRATOR: I'll follow you anywhere.

MAN: All I want to do is to open that door. [*Points at the voting booth*] Then she'll fall out and he'll know, and I can take her home before she stinks up all the ballots. He surely doesn't want to breathe her and taste her for six months.

DEMONSTRATOR: I see. He asked Peter to walk on water. I'm not a doubting Thomas. [*He walks toward the booth.*]

POLICEMAN: [*He has been leafing through papers on the desk, either laughing sarcastically at the talk or ignoring it. As the DEMONSTRATOR starts for the door of the booth, the POLICEMAN rises and takes the billy club out of his hip pocket.*] Stay away from that door!

DEMONSTRATOR: I have faith.

[*The DEMONSTRATOR keeps walking, then puts his hand on the door knob. The POLICEMAN shoves him back, but the DEMONSTRATOR simply stumbles backward, uses this to gain momentum and lunges forward. The POLICEMAN slams the billy club into his head. The DEMONSTRATOR sits on the floor.*]

POLICEMAN: I said stay away from that door, and I meant it. The state didn't put this property here for lunatics to play with.

DEMONSTRATOR: [*Stunned, still sitting on the floor*] It worked better for Peter. But this isn't the age of miracles. This is the age of non-violent demonstrations.

MAN: See. He won't let you in. I bet he won't let anybody in, because if he did, she'd fall out and he'd have to let me take her home.

POLICEMAN: Look buddy, I'll let anybody in that's registered. Neither you nor that kid is registered.

DEMONSTRATOR: Registered what? Sheep, cows, goats? I'm registered with the draft board. You can send me to the slaughter and all I can do is protest non-violently.

MAN: That's what I did. I didn't beat her, or hit her, or kick her, or anything.

I kept the kids, I washed the dishes, I emptied the trash and I begged her not to go.

DEMONSTRATOR: That one's too obscure for me. [*Looks at the POLICEMAN*] You can't understand everything these poets say, you know. I never did understand what Bob Dylan meant by 'come and lean upon the river.'

POLICEMAN: [*Laughs*] Maybe you two oughta go lean on a river somewhere. Then I'd know what to do with you. We'd put a tag on you at the city morgue.

MAN: They refrigerate them there, don't they? They should have put her there. It's too bad they had to put her in the voting booth. But, logically, there was no other way. After what the professor did.

POLICEMAN: (*Smiles at the DEMONSTRATOR*) And you people really thought I'd let that crazy nigger sneak into my voting booth.

DEMONSTRATOR: You cops are all alike. We don't operate like you. We don't plant spies. Wolves in sheep's clothing, that's what policemen are.

POLICEMAN: At least we don't dress like women.

DEMONSTRATOR: The one that came to our party wore long hair and a beard. He was a Judas.

MAN: That's it. Maybe you didn't recognize her. Maybe they painted her white. They're always painting things white. That's the official color. You could tell it was paint real easy if you'd look. Paint cracks in places, especially if she's started to bloat.

DEMONSTRATOR: Aw! He won't listen to you. You're a voice crying in the wilderness, a man with no place to lay his head.

MAN: No. I own a home in the suburbs. It's a very good neighborhood. I only found one cross burned on my lawn and nobody broke out any windows or anything. [*Proudly*] It's almost all white.

DEMONSTRATOR: [*Dismayed*] Suburbia!

MAN: I thought it was heaven, too. But my wife, she's not like us. She kept hanging around cheap bars, had no respect for our image. I told her it was dirty to do what she was doing, that she was a wife and a mother, that her place was in the home.

DEMONSTRATOR: Are you crazy? That kind of talk's not good. Somebody might take you seriously. We have a commitment to our followers out there. [*Motions toward the riot*] We leave all bureaucratic goods behind us.

CROWD: [*Chants*] Police brutality, police brutality. [*There is the sound of an explosion. The crowd cheers, then starts to sing a protest song.*]

DEMONSTRATOR: We will start by going into the street and leading them to the voting booth. Passively, we shall endure nightsticks, cattle prods and tear gas for the sake of freedom.

MAN: No. You've got it all wrong. We'd never get her that way. Maybe if the crowd went away he'd let me look. Maybe he's afraid they'll see, too. Then they wouldn't vote if they knew. The newspapers would take pictures and people would be afraid to go in voting booths. It's almost impossible to get the smell out. Once they knew what it was, they couldn't stand the smell and the taste. You said you'd help me. Maybe you could get them to go away. They wouldn't want to know. It's a terrible thing to know. I wish I'd never known about the professor's wife. I still wonder if some of her gases aren't circulating around in me.

DEMONSTRATOR: You were serious about suburbia. You've been brainwashed by the bureaucracy. We've been betrayed! Something must be done. We cannot allow this kind of thing to happen. It sets the movement back years!

POLICEMAN: [*Listening intently to the conversation and noticing the split*] We can't have niggers in our voting booths. There's a precedent here somewhere. A way to keep them out.

MAN: I only want to look. She'll fall out if you open the door. She's very fat, so she must be packed in tight. They probably had to kick the door hard to make it shut.

POLICEMAN: Yeah, we know. But once you got in, you'd play havoc with the machine. I've had dealin's with niggers for years. There used to be a way of handlin' niggers like you, before this race business come along. It don't look much like you're gonna leave.

DEMONSTRATOR: He can't leave. I can't allow it. He would disillusion the multitude, and it would be years before the crowd would reach this emotional peak again. This is the time and he ruined it. He's a traitor. Suburbia, wife, mother, home, he sounds like an IBM machine. Can you imagine what it would do to the movement to hear him talking that way?

POLICEMAN: If he did leave, he might lead them right back in here, babblin' about the body again. The boys'd have to swing those sticks. Jesus! I'd be crucified.

DEMONSTRATOR: At a time like this I've got to think about the movement. If Jesus hadn't been crucified and resurrected in three days, where would Christianity be now? Up from the grave he arose, and the whole thing blossomed.

POLICEMAN: Never too many niggers came back from the dead after what we did to 'em. If they did, they weren't much danger to the women, that's for sure.

DEMONSTRATOR: If he goes out there, he's a traitor. If he stays in here, he can become an example.

POLICEMAN: An example. They haven't had an example in a long time.

In the Stillness of the Midnight

Those niggers'd take over the whole country if we gave 'em a chance. Can't have the boys beatin' that crowd with sticks. The newspaper men'd have a field day.

DEMONSTRATOR: This is the day of non-violent suffering. People burn themselves in front of the Pentagon. Do you have any gasoline?

POLICEMAN: That ain't the way it's done. We only burn the cross. We mutilate the body. Nobody'd know why it was done if we just poured gasoline on him and burned him. Besides, that's the way you people do it.

DEMONSTRATOR: You want rid of him, don't you?

POLICEMAN: [*Worried*] I didn't say that.

DEMONSTRATOR: Okay. We'll just let him do whatever he wants to with that crowd.

POLICEMAN: What do you think he'll do?

DEMONSTRATOR: [*Nonchalantly*] That's your problem. I just protest non-violently. Sometimes we're beaten with nightsticks and electrocuted with cattle prods. Policemen come and go, but we're always there.

MAN: Maybe if I went out there? Then would you let me look, if the crowd wouldn't look? I could explain to them about how it's my wife's body. I'm sure they wouldn't want to see. It's a horrible thing to see. I've been seeing it in my imagination for a long time. It causes insomnia.

POLICEMAN: You must'a been born in that asylum. That's all they'd need. They'd pay ten dollars a head just to watch us castrate a nigger. They stand under a building when some guy's jumpin' off, excited as hell. The whole damn block's depressed for a week if he don't hit the net. They don't seem to understand what bad publicity the police get if he misses that net. I knew three policemen that got fired just because some lunatic was a diving champion.

MAN: I'll ask them. [*He moves toward the riot. The DEMONSTRATOR steps between him and the exit.*]

DEMONSTRATOR: [*Looks at the POLICEMAN*] Well?

POLICEMAN: You think he really believes his wife's in that voting booth?

DEMONSTRATOR: We could show him.

POLICEMAN: Naw. He'd mess up the machinery. Besides, there ain't no precedent for givin' in to niggers.

DEMONSTRATOR: What about that other precedent? You said something about an example.

POLICEMAN: I guess maybe if we had a little kerosene we might clean the spots off a' that voting booth while he was in there.

DEMONSTRATOR: Ask him.

POLICEMAN: [*His tone toward the man changes*] Say old buddy, how'd you like to take a look in that voting booth?

MAN: You're going to let me look? [*He starts slowly toward the door of the voting booth.*] Could I have a sack to carry her in? We wouldn't want nobody else to see her. Even now I have to leave the lights on all night in the house. Sometimes I talk to interrupt the dull glare. Then my own voice makes me afraid. You see, I can't talk and listen for small noises at the same time, and my voice echoes in my head, especially if I have a cold—I'd stop real quick, thinking I'd catch the noise, but it always stopped at the same time. That's how I found out it was the cold. Do you have a sack?

POLICEMAN: Yeah, sure buddy. [*To the DEMONSTRATOR*] Under the desk, get him all the paper he needs.

[*The DEMONSTRATOR goes to the desk, reaches under it and starts taking out wanted posters, ballots, paperback mysteries and pictures of mutilated bodies. Then he takes out a long paper sack and a bottle of kerosene. He hands the paper sack to the POLICEMAN.*]

POLICEMAN: [*Hands the paper sack to the MAN*] Here you go buddy. Now just open up that door.

MAN: No. This won't do. She'll leak through the paper. You know how when it's hot and you have your lunch in a paper bag, the grease all leaks through and makes big spots? I wouldn't want her grease touching me.

POLICEMAN: It won't. Now just open up the door.

[*The DEMONSTRATOR moves up next to the POLICEMAN and they start to herd the MAN toward the door.*]

MAN: [*Beginning to see what is happening, looks around frightened*] Why don't you look and see if there's another paper bag? If they were double it wouldn't leak. Okay? Let's go look under the desk again. [*The MAN starts toward the desk. The POLICEMAN steps in his way. He backs up and tries to go out the DEMONSTRATOR'S side. The DEMONSTRATOR blocks his passage and he steps back, holding his hands, palm upward, at his sides helplessly.*]

MAN: Maybe she isn't in there at all. I guess I was wrong. She probably isn't in there. I've decided she's not in there. I'll go now.

POLICEMAN: [*Coaxingly*] Just open up the door and see. That's all. Try me. See if I won't let you in. Why, you can even go in and look at the machine if you want to. I bet you haven't even seen one. Nobody's gonna hurt you. You've convinced us. Let's be friends and you just go look at our machine. You can even play with it a while if you want to.

MAN: No. I want to go home. You can have your machine all to yourself. I might wear it out. I've got machines of my own. I'll just go home and use them. [*He starts to move between them. They grab him, he struggles.*]

POLICEMAN: [*To the DEMONSTRATOR*] I got him. Open that door.

DEMONSTRATOR: [*Picks up some of the papers and the kerosene off the desk*] Let's get it over with quick, before anybody comes in.

[*The POLICEMAN helps him, spreading papers and pouring kerosene around the voting booth.*]

MAN: [*Inside the booth, trying to sound innocent. His voice shakes*] Hey fellows, what're we going to do? There's no doorknob in here. I can't get out. Let me out now fellows. It's dark in here. I can't see the voting machine, anyway. Open the door a little bit fellows so I can see the machine. Don't you want me to see the machine? Isn't that why you put me in here? (*He laughs shakily*) Okay fellows, which would you like thrown under the door first? The nuts from the machine, or the bolts?

[*The POLICEMAN and the DEMONSTRATOR set fire to the papers and rush off stage, left. The voting booth continues to burn.*]

MAN: Hey fellows, we going to roast weanies? Huh? What's the fire for, fellows?

[*Then he becomes desperate and starts to yell and scream as the booth burns. But his cries are almost drowned out by the noises of the riot when they see the smoke and smell the fire.*]

CROWD: Fire! Something's burning in there! Let us in! He's burning himself! [*Bottles break. The audience can hear objects hit the police helmets, scuffling feet, screams, cheers and all kinds of yells. The noises occur simultaneously with MAN'S screams. Then, part of the crowd breaks through the line of riot policemen and comes onto the stage. Seeing the burning body inside, they become almost artificially quiet. A bass voice starts to sing, then the crowd joins in, exuberantly. They sing the funereal song with the joy of a mob.*]

Precious memories, how they linger,
How they ever flood my soul.
In the stillness of the midnight,
Precious, sacred scenes unfold.

CURTAIN

Hellas and Death

a morality play

CHARACTERS:

Lady
Prostitute
General Cain
JoAnnie, body of a dead prostitute

[*The scene is laid in the theater of the world down-under in the year of decadence.*

When the curtain comes up, a woman appears, timeless in age, wearing a white wedding dress of Victorian vintage and a white hard hat of the type construction workers wear, attached to which is a decal that says, "Bring our boys back." Her hair is almost white, but the texture reflects its present and past thickness and beauty. She occupies a straight-backed wicker chair. Her well proportioned and expressive hands, hands of authority; hands that when they gesture speak, hands that direct and order the lives of men and women, lie on the two large arms of the chair. Behind her, a dim light shines through a stained glass cathedral window. The panes are leaded and the style is gothic. Directly above the window is a sign that reads: "HE WHO LOOKS UPON THE FACE OF GOD

SHALL SURELY DIE. Author: God." Underneath, someone has scrawled, "As told to Moses when he questioned the view from the rear."

Spotlights alternately illuminate the posters and graffiti, written on the walls of the set large enough for the audience to read. To the right of the window is a full color poster of a young lady, lying on her back, wearing a bright red bikini. One leg is twisted in an unnatural position with the calf and foot up under her thighs as if she were unconscious before she fell. Her head lies in a pile of blonde hair stained with blood that apparently came from her heavily bruised and made up face. The caption reads: "MAKE WAR, NOT LOVE."

Another poster (this time an ex-congressman's wife) reveals that lady getting out of a Mercedes, smiling and saying, in cartoon style: "You have no idea how nice it is not to be wrapping Red Cross bandages and being a hypocrite." Someone has scrawled underneath it: "We would have included the centerfold, but unfortunately we could only afford the magazine where we found the Gideon Bible."

A picnic table sits just stage left of the room at a right angle to the audience. Benches behind the table face the lady. A single light bulb swings over the lady's head. She looks into the darkness of the audience and begins to speak in what appears to be some sort of sign language, occasionally clasping her hands in frustration, folding them in prayer, saluting a mysterious figure back stage, etc.

Finally, she points an accusing finger at the audience, indicates the literary and pictorial set, and proceeds to give the audience a standing ovation.

A young girl, apparently a prostitute, in a low cut acrylic blouse— sleeveless, enters from stage right. Her tight black skirt reveals sensually molded calves, thighs and long legs, much of which are exposed. Looking about, she brushes snow out of her wet, bleached hair.]

PROSTITUTE: Where am I?
LADY: America. Don't you recognize it? Perhaps you've been here before, but you just haven't looked around.
PROSTITUTE: Jesus! What a dump! I haven't missed much.
LADY: [*Looking worried*] I'm really sorry. I guess it would be better if we had some music. [*Thinks a minute*] I used to sing. Long ago when I knew some things, I could sing. I even had a bird that could sing. I called her Sister Angela. But you know how birds are. They're terribly moody and they're so selfish. They sing for themselves. Never for other people. Then, when the food ran out . . . they're so small. They starve more quickly than people. I came in one morning and there Sister Angela was, her feet sticking straight up in the air. Her eyes

were all glazed over. Even that was a kind of relief. She'd been looking at me for days, refusing even to chirp. Treated me as if I were refusing to feed her. I never kept her in a cage. I even left the door open. It was raining all that week and I even had to turn the heat off. That was before the landlord did. But she wouldn't leave. I cried and begged her to look out for herself. Explained to her that everyone else did.

She just kept looking at me as if I was eating and wouldn't give her any food. I even kept making myself vomit to show her I didn't eat.

She just looked at me in that sad, accusing way. Wouldn't even chirp. It's almost impossible to communicate with anyone. That's why I signaled to the audience my appreciation for the gallery of art they came to see. You see, I got these posters very inexpensively. Thanks to people like those in the audience. There's a great demand for this material. I was able to steal it easily, except for the picture of the congressman's wife. The maid at the motel was upset when I came in while she was cleaning and took the magazine. I showed her the spots on the centerfold and she said, "*Well*, he didn't leave me enough tip to cover the postage anyway."

I knew you'd like those pictures in the magazine wrapped with brown paper much better. But they're very expensive. Even the wealthy men don't leave them lying around. I've seen them buying them. They can't waste money, you know. The store owners won't even let you look at them without paying for them first. They must be terribly good art.

I'm really sorry [*looking at the audience*] that someone got spots on the best picture of the congressman's wife. She said herself that it was the best. Said it was so *elegant*. That it made her feel *so* beautiful. I do wish I could show it to you.

PROSTITUTE: God it's cold out there! My old man'd kill me if he knew I's in here. I keep tellin' him there ain't no johns on the street on nights like this. He just says, "You are, bitch." Tonight I said, "Ace, honey, they's ice on the street. Nobody cares about pussy when they's ice on the street." He just said, "The hell you say," kicked me between the legs, handed me some pills, and said, "If you care about yours, you better find *one* cock that does before it hurts worse."

He was real nice to me at first. Still is nicer to me than my folks. I forgot and went home once. Daddy said every time he thought about what I'd done, it made his skin crawl. He kept scratchin', makin' mine hurt!

Got a job a month ago. Workin' in a health studio. Heard someone outside sayin' he wanted chicken meat. Daddy had his pants halfway off before he saw it was me. He beat the hell out of me and drug me out. Ace beat the hell out of me for stable jumpin'. I won't try that any more.

It was then that Ace explained loyalty to me with a steam iron. I understand loyalty now.

[*The women glance toward stage right as someone approaches, singing loudly a version of a familiar lyric. The sound rings throughout the entire theater. The prostitute becomes frightened.*]

When Joannie comes marching home again, Hurrah, Hurrah!
When Joannie comes marching home again, Hurrah, Hurrah!

LADY: [*Turning toward the prostitute, who appears to be very frightened, looking about in desperation*] Don't be afraid, it's just General Cain.
PROSTITUTE: Not my Ace, I hope. [*She raises her short skirt, pointing to a large red tattoo on her thigh. Large black letters on a red heart spell, I AM LOVED*] He'll know me anywhere, forever. All he has to do is pull up my dress. Says it's his corporate seal. You know, like the revenue stamp on a pack of cigarettes. It makes me his property, you know. (*Proudly*) He owns a lot of whores! Claimed Brother Fulwell, the T.V. preacher, stole the mark from him and is selling those buttons on T.V. for *his* whores to wear. Talked about suing for a while, but then Hutton's started giving them away as logos to men that could afford to own a whore and not even share her. Ace just slapped the shit out of me and bitched about how rich men got everything and a poor man didn't have no legal rights at all any more. Not even the right to his own mark.

[*At this point, a tall, thin man, resembling a cadaver; wearing a military helmet with five red hearts saying, "I am loved" in gold letters, designating his rank, enters. He wears a black tuxedo T-shirt that says, "Morticians do it with fluid," and is pulling a cheap black coffin behind him on his version of a caisson. The wagon, is in fact, a version of the cart on which maids once wheeled tea and crumpets to the lady's auxiliary during the first big war. A banner hangs from the side of the cart. Bright red letters on a cheap, black velour background say, "STAND BY YOUR MAN." Underneath he has written, "IF YOU FIND THAT DIFFICULT, TRY FRANK SINATRA." A publicity poster of Sinatra advertising the movie "From Here to Eternity" is pasted to the coffin.*]

GENERAL CAIN: Omar Bradley was buried in Arlington today, you know. [*He muses*] Next to his first wife. Chivalry is not lost. His second wife kept quoting Gloria Steinem in senility, when she was eighty.

Said things like, "This chastity belt itches," and "Omar can never remember where he put the key. I never get none nowdays." Said them at tea parties.

Just before he died, a stone-mason carved "I am loved" on his first wife's tombstone. Mrs. Onassis and everybody must have been there to watch the engraving. [*He wipes his eyes with a dirty handkerchief. Then, in tears*] Some people still *do* feel. Brother Fulwell spoke at the funeral. He seemed a bit confused, though. Kept talking about how the great man had escaped the communist assassins all the way through the second world war, only to be cut down in his prime by old age. Went away mumbling something like, "We'll see what happens in three, in three days." When one of the four-star generals asked President Jennings, who was standing there with a campaign poster like the grave was one more homestead, sayin' THIS IS WAYLON COUNTRY, if an eternal flame was in order, President Jennings took a snort from his silver spoon and said with that gravity that only he possesses, "I don't know. We'll wait three days and see what turns up." Vice-President Nelson threw down his Jack Daniels and couldn't stop laughing until one of the secret service men distracted him with a secretary in the back seat of the presidential limousine. Politicians are all alike! I remember the blessed days when they at least practiced hypocrisy like the rest of us. Why, just last week, Dan Rather, on location in a massage parlor, posing as a naked Arab and claiming his microphone was a phallic symbol, interviewed Senator Haggard on nationwide T.V. Senator Haggard, laughing, told Rather about his new welfare legislation, part of which was to set money aside for delinquent girls. He proposes the erection [*at this point Haggard laughed himself helpless*] of ten story, all glass office buildings where problem adolescent girls could handle the paperwork involved in the government responsibility for importing oil by truck from Apache Indian reservations. "Congressmen," he said, "would check their works," again he started laughing, "on a regular basis." *Now*, they want to put the small whoremaster out of business! I have always said, and I quote myself, "Ruin hypocrisy and you ruin business."

[*As General Cain talks, the prostitute continues to stare at the cheap coffin on its makeshift caisson, occasionally looking at the poster of the scantily clad and battered body of the blonde girl.*]

GENERAL CAIN: [*Noticing the lack of attention, glares at the prostitute.*] Aren't you interested in anything important?

LADY: [*Looking at the prostitute with an ironic smile*] You must understand, dear, General Cain is our local politician. To him, government matters are *very* important. We get all our religious and political opinions from him. We must respect his philosophy, and in return, he pays our burial expenses. He even teaches independent businesswomen like me positive mental attitude. He has explained how difficult it is to counteract the "negativism" of those girls who already wear property patches. He does, however, sometimes give them money for drugs if they promise to support whichever politician he wishes them to bear, and they return the gift twofold when they find a generous john. General Cain is really *very* generous. He's a liberal. You see, at this political level he represents both parties, and is only concerned with the happiness of what he calls *his* people.

GENERAL CAIN: [*Smiling with benevolent understanding*] He gave his blood for you.

PROSTITUTE: Who?

GENERAL CAIN: Ace! The man who loves and takes care of you. He sold blood at the blood bank last week and, you know, Ace doesn't need the money. He does it because he cares. [*Approaches the prostitute and holds out his hands in a caring motion. Coming closer, he puts his hands on her hips and begins to feel the sensuous curves of the girl's thighs. Turning to the lady.*] I realize that, according to custom, we should continue with the funeral, but do you suppose that my newly found constituent and I could take a short break in the back room. [*Smiles at the girl showing two uneven rows of stained teeth*] I really *do* care about *my* people.

LADY: Please, Cain, not now.

PROSTITUTE: [*Again looking at the coffin*] What did you mean? You said Ace gave his blood for me?

GENERAL CAIN: I meant, my dear, that, as we all do, he cares for you. We're a family. Does Ace not feed you as if you were his child? Does Ace not provide you with a home? Does Ace not pay your bills? Ace does much more than give his blood for you. Ace gives you freedom. All Ace asks is that you give him your love. Where do you think Ace gets the money? And believe me, my child, it is not enough. Much, much more is needed. But Ace is loving. Ace is generous. Ace cares what happens to *his* girls.

PROSTITUTE: But the blood?

GENERAL CAIN: But all our children are not grateful, my lovely child. [*General Cain kneels and begins to knead the hips and buttocks of the prostitute. Some say to themselves, "Why can I not be as the girls in the magazines?"*] Why can I not pose as does the congressman's wife? Why must I labor for my drugs by the sweat of my brow, and never have enough?"

As a philosopher and a Christian, darling child, [*He moves his hand gently and softly up the inside of the girl's thigh*] I can tell you that is an historical question. Women as well as men have always asked, "Why me Lord? Why must I work in the fields? Why must I bear children? Why are my children hungry while there are those around us who 'Live in the sunshine.'" Even Ace, with his Porsche, asks, "Why am I not President Jennings?"

God and Ace have given you life. Do you not feel joy? [*Handing her a capsule*] I give you this pill. Will you not feel joy?

Now, sweet baby, [*touching her hair with one hand and her breast with the other*] let me speak unto you of those who have questioned the will of God and the will of Ace. JoAnnie who lies in the coffin, the coffin that I, myself, paid for, from my own meager earnings. Does this not show you that I care? [*Pulling the dirty handkerchief out of his pocket, the General again wipes his eyes.*] Ace gave his blood. Blood from all generous men like Ace was transfused into her veins at the hospital in an attempt to restore to her the beautiful gift of life. And she will receive no statement of charges. Does not the world care?

Again and again, Ace forgave her. She went to the police. Did the police give her food to eat? Did the police give her spiritual sustenance? Did the police give her a home? No. They imprisoned her. Three weeks after being given her *freedom* to seek a job she returned to Ace.

She was hungry. Ace gave her food. Her clothes were torn and she had sold the beautiful coat that Ace gave her, to buy *one* meal. Ace gave her another one. She was ill from sleeping with the dogs in the streets. Torn asunder by vomiting and shaking with fever. Ace gave her warmth, soft linens, rest, peace and freedom from pain. She came home to Ace.

Her penance was small. Ace would not dismember *his* girl. Ace would not make *visible* scars as the world does. But, tempted by the sight of college girls in cars, girls holding hands with young men, pictures in the magazines . . . All those things that tempt a beautiful child to ask, "Why me Lord?" she ran again.

This time, Ace, in all his kindness, could not forgive. She signed the man's statement. She signed the bargain with that evil world that does not want Ace to love and take care of you.

I talked to Ace when it was all over. Ace could not stop crying. I tried to calm him. I said, "Ace, I know you loved her. I know you loved her more than life itself. You gave your blood for her, Ace. You would have been willing to give your own life. But could you give the lives of *your* girls? What would they be without you?" [*General Cain wheels the coffin down front, center stage.*]

[*In a quieter, 'I do this because I love you' tone*] I was told by the mortician no one was to see this. You see, we have very little money.

We *must* care for our girls who are living. Life ... above all, life, freedom and the spirit of giving must live. I open it because I love you. I open it out of love for you.

[*The frightened girl prostitute stands, shivering before the coffin. The General officiously moves to one side and opens the lid, revealing the full length of the viciously mutilated body. The prostitute screams, the upper portion of her body falling into the casket with the mutilated body. She alternately screams in horror and sobs in repentance as the curtain slowly comes down.*]

The Compound

CHARACTERS:

HEAD LUNEY: *a young man, about 35 years old, an evangelist Jim Baker type, dressed in a blue pin stripe suit, a cross between cult leader and sales manager.*
PORTER: *a middle aged African-American man, distinguished 55 year old gentleman with silver gray temples, wearing a black tuxedo.*
DOUG WINTHROP: *about 40, Luney disciple and sales representative, long hair. A Bob Goldthwaite type.*
WILLA KAY: *about 25, blonde and athletic.*
CINDY DUBROWSKI: *about 25, brown hair, sensuous, firm and well built.*
WOMAN: *about 60, has earned the bitter, angry face that she wears.*
GHOULS LOADING BODY: *young men about 35, white, pasty skin, ill fitting clothes over misshapen bodies, dirty hair.*
BIKERS: *fit the stereotype of biker, long stringy hair, beards, leather jackets with the usual decorations, wearing their colors and black arm bands.*
BIKER OLD LADIES: *jeans, jackets, various forms of dress and undress, hair flying, trussed in black mourning ribbons.*
BODY: *dressed in cheap casket, covered with gray flowered upholstery.*

A Frankenstein image decks the top. MAMAS: *(Biker's) jeans, jackets with property patches, tight halters, various forms of dress and undress, wearing black bands around their necks as dog collars.*
FARMER: *about 50, wearing overalls and flannel shirt, grizzly and gray.*
SHERIFFS: *in cars.*
TEACHER: *a young man about 30, nervously attracted to Willa Kay.*
CHILDREN: *the usual 5th graders. They look human.*
BIKER AND HIS BOMB: *wimp in wolves' clothing.*
RICHARD GUNN: *stereotypical newsman, approximately 40, conservative dress.*
PETER EDWARDS: middle aged respectable newsman.
JONATHAN WAINWRIGHT: *awkward, fumbling, stereotypical F.B.I. agent. Don Knotts-type character.*
DR. AMANDA SKAGGSWORTH: *about 35 years old, dishwater blonde, dishevelled appearance. Phyllis Diller type.*
DR. JEREMIAH LINGSTROM: *elderly full professor of medicine, scholar noted for genetic research, tousled long, white hair. He suffers from osteoporosis and, in his dotage, takes advantage of exposure to T.V.*
OSCO: *Lingstrom's elderly African-American assistant and life-long companion.*
DERRICK LIVINGSTON: *approximately 30 years old, well dressed, conservative, young African-American reporter.*
SENATOR GOLDBLADDER: *dry cleaned, about 55 years old, neat hair, silvering in political style of the decade.*
HIGH CLASS PROSTITUTE: *beautiful, young, about 22, dark complected.*
AIR FORCE MAJOR: *uniformed, about 30, tall.*
CONGRESSIONAL AIDES: *stereotypes, conservative look alikes, about 25, male and female, blue suits.*
WINSTON: *local postmaster, thinker and political authority, about 45.*
MATTHEW: *local store owner, about 45, casually dressed.*
JACK: *local farmer, about 40.*
CLAUDE: *about 40, factory worker.*
YOUNG MAN: *young man about 25, bleached hair, earring.*
YOUNG LADIES: *about 22, nondescript, wearing jeans, fatigues etc.*
NADINE: *local woman, about 35, wearing jeans.*
LINCOLN "LINC" COMSTOCK: *attorney for defense, about 35, wearing an out of style, expensive suit.*
MRS. JOHN "MAUDE" CLINE: *ancient grandmother of the three*

young strangers.
QUENTIN RIMBAUD: *about, 60, thinning gray hair.*
EMANUEL STONE: *prince of the aryan nations, about 45, wearing full dress decorative uniform with wreathed cap bill.*
GUARDS: *dressed in nazi uniforms, riding boots, etc.*
VOICE OF THE FBI: *voice on a loud speaker.*

FADE IN:

INT. LUNAR TOILET FACILITIES AND CONFERENCE ROOM—DAY

CAMERA OPENS on a MEDIUM LONG SHOT of several, very reputable looking men in three piece suits surrounding a conference table in a large men's toilet facility like that of thirties-era hotels. A slightly overweight young man sits at the head of the table eating and playing with grapes. This is the HEAD LUNEY. A BLACK PORTER, dressed in a white coat and black tie, stands behind the Head Luney with a towel draped over his arm. The Head Luney occasionally wipes his hands on the towel as he leads the meeting. A large cake sits in the middle of the table. CAMERA MOVES IN for a MEDIUM SHOT of Head Luney.

HEAD LUNEY

Brothers and sisters, I've called this meeting here today to call your attention to my needs. I had a dream. (*aside to Black Porter*) Bring the towel here, boy.

Black Porter steps forward. Head Luney wipes his hands and mouth on the towel.

HEAD LUNEY

Thank you. You know, I have a black friend. (*motions Black Porter back*) Last night I had a dream. I was standing on a hillside when I perceived that my pants were unzipped. And then I had another dream. I dreamed that I had flooded the Communist bloc.
(*laughs*)
Just a little joke to get the testosterone stirred up. People say that we men of God lack humor. Anyway, let me be serious for a moment. I feel that the Lord has called me in this liberal age to fight the Communist philosophy that threatens the very fabric of the Protestant sales presentation. The Communist Chinese, on our very doorstep, are under mining the best Congress money

CONTINUNED:
HEAD LUNEY (CONTINUED)
can buy. This plague has not only invaded our colleges, reducing Lunar condom sales, but is encroaching on our fast food restaurants. Our President, who uses Lunar Industries latest plastic sandwich bags for herbal storage purposes, refuses to eat unless his food is one hundred percent American.

SOUND of music and lyrics of "My Baby is American Made." Head Luney stands and puts his hand over his heart for this LUNAR INDUSTRIES ANTHEM.

HEAD LUNEY
Gentlemen! On this, the first anniversary of the birth of Lunar Industries,
  (gestures exultantly toward cake)
I present my dream!

CAMERA FEATURES CAKE. The cake explodes, smattering the Disciples, and revealing CINDY DUBROWSKI. She is a tall, dark complected, dark eyed, young lady. She poses, delighted, on one foot, her bright eyes looking from one Disciple to another. She is clad only in the Lunar Banner. Breasts and shapely thighs protrude from its narrow edges. MEDIUM CLOSE SHOT of Cindy's entire body. CAMERA PANS UP Cindy's sensuous spread legs. Cindy smiles, her hands on her hips, at the Disciples who, rising to their feet, extend a dual arm LUNEY SALUTE. SOUND OF FEMALE LUNEY DISCIPLES off stage breaking into chorus of "Climb the Highest Mountain." CLOSE UP of Cindy's well formed size C breasts heaving with Esprit De Corp.

VOICES OF WOMEN DISCIPLES
(singing)
Climb every mountain. Ford every stream. Follow every rainbow, 'til you find your dream.

DISSOLVE TO:

EXT. HIGHWAY - DAY

DOLLY SHOT TRACKING. DOUG WINTHROP, Luney Disciple and Sales Representative, is driving down the highway with CINDY DUBROWSKI. Doug is in his forties. His hair is gray at the temples. He is dressed in a gray hound's tooth coat. Cindy is wearing a white sundress that emphasizes her soft, dark shoulders. Her black, mid-length hair is tied in a bun. Her ideal, dark complexion appears not to be covered with makeup. Here, as throughout the script, Cindy carries a bottle. MEDIUM CLOSE SHOT of Cindy.

CINDY
(*studying map*)
There's a town with a hotel fifty miles from here.
(*touches Doug's leg*)

DOUG
The Lord is my shepherd. I shall not want. He maketh me to lie down in green pastures.

CINDY
If you lie in a pasture, you can lie with the Lord. I ain't sleeping in no pasture.

POV SHOT of young girl hitchhiking. WILLA KAY tosses her long blonde hair back, smiles and waves. She wears tight jeans and a tank top. She is accustomed to the sun. MEDIUM CLOSE SHOT of Willa Kay licking her upper lip. Doug pulls the car over quickly.

WILLA KAY
(*hurriedly squeezing into the back seat of the car*)
Lord! Am I glad to see you folks. You can't imagine what I been through with them truck drivers and such. But them oddball ones is the worst.

Cindy gives Willa Kay a knowing look.

WILLA KAY
It sure is nice to get a ride with a couple of good lookin' people. Where you goin'?

DOUG
Does it matter?
(*watches Willa Kay in rear view mirror*)

WILLA KAY
I'll tell you mister, it sure don't.
(*pops head up, delighted, over the front seat*)
You got anything to eat?

DIRECT CUT TO:

MEDIUM CLOSE SHOT. Doug, Willa Kay and Cindy stand at the door of a suburban home. Doug holds a large case. Willa Kay moves restlessly from one foot to the other. A thin, grey haired WOMAN, about sixty years old, opens the door. CLOSE UP of Woman. Her face is bitter and angry. SOUND of loud television in background. The voice of an evangelist harangues.

WOMAN
(*annoyed*)
Yes?

Doug, Willa Kay and Cindy hurriedly push past the horrified Woman into her living room. CAMERA FOLLOWS ACTION. CAMERA PANS QUICKLY AROUND the dark living room, PAST the television set, and HOLDS on a picture in an elaborate gold frame. The picture sits on a table covered by a dark green, velvet cloth. A bronze urn sits beside the picture. CLOSE UP of the picture reveals a gaunt, fifty year old man with a full head of white hair, wearing gold rimmed glasses. His face is lined and bitter. MEDIUM CLOSE SHOT of Doug unpacking a vacuum cleaner from his case.

WOMAN
(*shocked and frightened*)
What are you doing?

DOUG
Ma'am, we were guided here by a power greater than both of us.

WILLA KAY
(*giggles*)
I hate to ask, but do you have anything to eat?

Woman stares, open mouthed in disbelief, at Willa Kay.

> WOMAN
> (*realizing Doug's mission*)
> I have a vacuum cleaner.

> CINDY
> (*looking about, hoping to find liquor*)
> I'm awfully thirsty. It sure has been a long drive. I need to relax.

> WOMAN
> You can just relax someplace else!

> WILLA KAY
> (*bouncing across room*)
> Lord! Doug sure relaxed me. Do you have a bathroom?

> WOMAN
> (*exceedingly annoyed*)
> No!

> WILLA KAY
> Well, I'll be!
> (*squirms*)

> DOUG
> Ma'am, this vacuum cleaner was created with the most powerful suction of the advanced technology of Christian engineers.

> WILLA KAY
> I like suction.
> (*Doug smiles at Willa Kay*)

> WOMAN
> Will you all please leave!

CAMERA FEATURES Cindy. POV SHOT. Cindy sees dusty bottle of Schnapps, apparently a keepsake, beside the picture of the man. MEDIUM CLOSE SHOT of Cindy pouring herself a drink in the dusty shot glass that accompanies the bottle on the table.

The WOMAN makes an involuntary sound and reaches toward the small shrine (table with urn, picture and keepsakes) in anguish.

POV SHOT of Doug reaching for urn. Takes lid off. Sees ashes, and throws them on the carpet. WOMAN makes involuntary guttural sound as if choking.

                    DOUG
                (*unabashed*)
Notice the nasty spill of cigarette ashes. No other vacuum cleaner will remove this stain.

Doug begins to rub ashes into carpet.

                    WOMAN
My husband!

                    DOUG
                (*realizing*)
Oh my God!

Doug shakily regains composure, and begins attempting to pick the ashes up a pinch at a time.

                    WOMAN
                (screaming)
My husband! My husband!

                                        DISSOLVE:

EXT. WOMAN'S HOME—NIGHT

MEDIUM SHOT. Doug, Willa and Cindy stand in lighted area outside front door watching two ghoulish looking men load the body of the woman into a hearse. CAMERA MOVES IN for a BIG CLOSE SHOT of the body as it is being loaded into the back of the hearse.

MEDIUM CLOSE SHOT of Doug, Cindy and Willa. Cindy is drunk and crying.

                    CINDY
I couldn't believe she just fell over dead. She looked so much like my dead Mother.

                    DOUG
                  (*gravely*)
    We don't know what tomorrow brings.

                    CINDY
    Do we have any money?

                                        CUT DIRECTLY TO:

INT. LUNAR TOILET FACILITY—DAY

MEDIUM SHOT. Head Luney sits at the end of the conference table. The Lunar Disciples surround the table, their heads bowed in prayer. A huge chalice of wine occupies the center of the conference table. Tin cups are scattered in front of the Disciples. Willa Kay sits, head bowed, nude, in the wine.

                    DISCIPLES
                  (*in unison*)
    Lord, smile upon our new member, brought unto us by Organ
    Doug and Sister Cindy.

CLOSE SHOT OF CINDY. CAMERA ANGLE WIDENS to include Disciples pouring wine over Willa Kay. Willa Kay rubs her body as the wine cascades over her nude body. As they pour, they sing, "Are You Washed in the Blood?"

                    DISCIPLES
                  (*singing*)
    Are you washed in the blood? In the soul cleansing blood of the
    Lamb? Are your garments spotless? Are they white as snow? Are
    you washed in the blood of the Lamb?

CLOSE SHOT of Cindy drinking from her tin cup. MEDIUM CLOSE SHOT of entire scene. The Disciples all fall into drinking enthusiastically from the tin cups as they splash Willa Kay. CAMERA FEATURES Head Luney. He laughs, delighted, then begins to pound his tin cup on the table. MEDIUM CLOSE SHOT of Willa Kay as she rises from the wine. The Disciples grab her voluptuous body and begin to toss her about the table. CAMERA FEATURES Head Luney.

The Compound

> HEAD LUNEY
> (*pounding cup on table*)
> Enough! Enough!

Disciples drop Willa Kay and come to attention.

> HEAD LUNEY
> (*piously*)
> Children! Children! The Lord meant us to have a little fun, but now let us begin the work of the new order.
> (*bows his head*)

A long moment of silence follows.

> HEAD LUNEY
> As I lay in my humble bed last night, exhausted from tasting the flesh of Sister Bathsheba and Sister Mary Martha
> (*looks alternately at the two beautiful female Disciples. They smile beatifically.*)
> I began to reflect on our recent accomplishments.

He looks about the table. CAMERA PANS AROUND table. The Disciples have become quiet and, as if they were unprepared students in a classroom, look about uncomfortably, avoiding his gaze. CLOSE UP of Cindy as she gulps from her tin cup. CAMERA FEATURES Doug, who also appears quite uncomfortable. He is very much interested in a wet spot of spilled wine on Organ McCallister's shirt. CAMERA FEATURES Head Luney.

> HEAD LUNEY
> Other than a recent grant of $3,000,586.26, thank the Lord for the assistance of Senator Goldbladder, for the development of fashion merchandising skills among our imprisoned brothers involved in the recent covert activities in the Pentup Mansion, we have generated very little money for the Lord's work.

CAMERA PANS AROUND the table. The Lunar Disciples have become extremely uncomfortable. The men are scratching themselves and moaning. The women are rubbing their bodies and beginning to groan. They speak in unison.

> DISCIPLES
> Father, forgive us. We know not what we do.

HEAD LUNEY
(*raises his hand*)
Go ye forth unto all the world, distributing the Lunar merchandise in the name of Lune the Father!

CAMERA FEATURES urinals. The Disciples rise and speak in unison.

DISCIPLES
Let us piss!

DISSOLVE:

EXT. HIGHWAY OZARK COUNTY, MO.—DAY

DOLLY TRACKING: Doug and Cindy are in the front seat of the car. Willa Kay is in the back seat, leaning her blonde head between Cindy and Doug. Her hair often brushes Doug's cheek, and she frequently touches him with her hand. They are singing loudly.

DOUG, WILLA AND CINDY
Jesus is coming again! Coming again! Coming again! Jesus is coming again!
(*Continue. Use complete song*)

Cindy interrupts by crying out loudly. She takes a drink from her bottle and begins to cry again. Doug and Willa are concerned. Willa puts her arm around Cindy. Doug pats Cindy's knee.

DOUG
Sister Cindy. What troubles you? Are you not on a mission for the Lunar Being? Should you not rejoice with Willa and I in our work?

CINDY
(*blurts out*)
You and Willa rejoice too much!
(*begins to cry loudly*)
I haven't been rejoiced in a week!

DOUG
Sister Cindy! I did not know! Perhaps I should explain.

The Compound

                CINDY
Explain! Explain! Explain! I don't want talk. I want sexxx!

                DOUG
            (*quite shocked*)
Sister Cindy! This indeed surprises me. And coming from you. The pure person with whom I have been united by the Lunar Being.

                CINDY
Pure! Pure! But I'm not satisfied! Sister Willa is getting all of Organ Doug.

Doug brings the car to a rapid halt beside the road. CLOSE UP from the rear seat. Sister Willa is watching. Brother Doug is out of sight in lap of Cindy. Cindy's face, above the seat, is contorted in ecstasy. She is making loud noises and moving rhythmically. SOUND of "Family Affair" playing in background.

                CUT DIRECTLY TO:

EXT. HIGHWAY—DAY

LONG SHOT: A funeral procession made up of BIKERS, OLD LADIES and MAMAS is passing the car where Doug, Willa and Cindy are engaged in sexual activity. The Bikers are wearing their colors, black arm bands and various forms of dress and undress. MEDIUM CLOSE SHOTS FEATURE various small groups and individual motorcycle gang members as they pass. At this point Willa's bare hips are draped over the seat and all three passengers are nude and exposed to the gazes of the motorcycle gang. SOUND of riders shouting obscenities, ad libitum, at the three people in the car. The funeral procession is moving slowly.

                MAMA ONE
Blow him and leave him, honey.

                BIKER
You can ride me anytime, Blondie.

LONG SHOT of Bikers going joyously over the hill, following the hearse.

                DIRECT CUT TO:

EXT. HILLSIDE LOCATION OF BIKER'S GRAVE—DAY

MEDIUM SHOT: A cheap, gray casket sits on the pall of a freshly dug grave. A wrecked motorcycle lies near the grave to be buried with the body in the customary manner. A large group of Bikers have rendezvoused at the grave. They and their women are busy drinking, snorting, smoking, shooting and weeping. Doug, Cindy and Willa climb up the hill and enter the group. Willa, breathing heavily, carries a box of small, red books. HOW TO FIND LUNAR PEACE is printed on the outside of the box. Cindy is carrying a bottle. Her clothes are askew and she is weeping sympathetically. Doug, with his usual decisiveness, moves to the casket and stands beside the tangled motorcycle. Doug turns to the crowd, takes one of the red books from Willa and holds it up. MEDIUM CLOSE SHOT FEATURING Doug.

> DOUG
> Our brother obviously cannot rise to the occasion.
> *(crowd laughs inappropriately)*
> His engine has turned over for the last time. But he is not dead!

MEDIUM CLOSE SHOT of vocal portion of crowd.

> MAMA ONE
> The hell you say!

> MAMA TWO
> He was stiff as a poker when we found him.

> MAMA THREE
> *(crying)*
> He could stay as stiff as a poker all night.

CAMERA FEATURES Doug.

> DOUG
> He has found peace. As a witness from the Lunar Being, I can offer you the same peace. You will not suffer when you're cold and dead, but you will rise again to join your loved ones on the other shore.

CAMERA FEATURES Crowd.

> BIKERS
> (*in unison*)
>
> It's the Lunar Being Witnesses! Those motherfuckers will go anywhere!

CAMERA FEATURES Doug.

> DOUG
>
> Consider how much of your hard earned money you spend on cocaine per day. What would you give in exchange for your soul? What would you give to join your dead brother on that morning when the dead shall rise again? That morning, when once again, you will frolic in the Lord's beautiful sunlight.
> (*pause*)
> If you pay the price.
> (holds up the red book)

MEDIUM SHOT OF CROWD. Crowd becomes frenzied. Action goes into slow motion as the crowed begins to shout obscenities and to throw bottles and the bits of lunch that they have brought.

> BIKERS
>
> M-o-t-her-fuck-er! No respect! Crucify the Son-of-a-Bitch! Roast his balls! Our warrior lies slain! The man pisses on our grave!
> (*they attack Doug*)
> Bury his whores with him! For it is written, "The Nomad Biker's grave is the only monument to his way of life!"

MEDIUM CLOSE SHOT of Willa and Cindy as the Biker's move toward them. Frightened, they begin to back toward the casket. They trip and fall into it, their skirts coming up. The biker's get a new idea and pounce upon them. CLOSE SHOT of casket. The casket reels, the bottom rips open and the body rolls down the hill. CAMERA FOLLOWS body. The crowd first opens up a path for it, then begins to grab at it as it rolls, yelling accusations at each other.

> BIKER
>
> I told you not to buy such a cheap casket!

> OLD LADY
>
> You begrudged our brother!

BIKER
You sure know how to ruin a good time.

MEDIUM CLOSE SHOT of Willa and Cindy helping Doug to his feet. As the chaos proceeds, the three of them stumble (falling and sliding) hurriedly down the hill to their car.

MEDIUM CLOSE SHOT of the crowd as it arrives at the body. CLOSE SHOT of them trying to lift it. An arm comes off. MEDIUM CLOSE SHOT.

BIKER
Jesus, it stinks! I told you to get that sucker embalmed!

LONG SHOT of road. Several Sheriff's cars arrive. A FARMER riding shotgun in the front seat of the first car jumps out, yelling.

FARMER
Trespassers! Drug addicts! Terrorists!

MEDIUM SHOT of the Bikers quickly deserting the body and scrambling to their bikes.

DIRECT CUT TO:

INT. LUNAR TOILET FACILITIES—DAY

MEDIUM SHOT: The Lunar Disciples surround the table drinking and splashing large chalice of wine as before. The HEAD LUNEY enters. The BLACK PORTER stands, as before, holding a towel. He comes to attention. CLOSE SHOT of Black Porter.

BLACK PORTER
All rise!

MEDIUM SHOT. The Disciples continue to drink, splash and make dirty jokes. Sound of hymn playing on a phonograph.

HYMN
Are you washed? In the blood. In the soul cleansing blood of the Lamb. Are your garments spotless? Are they white as snow? Are you washed in the blood of the Lamb?

CLOSE SHOT of Head Luney.

> HEAD LUNEY
> Are you ready to meet your God?

SOUNDS of sex in the background, coming from the direction of the urinals.

> MALE VOICE
> Just a minute.
> (*sound of long grunt accompanying ejaculation*)
> Now!

> HEAD LUNEY
> Think not of your body, but ask yourself, "Will my corpse be properly cared for?" And how will you answer in those last days when our Lord God asks the inevitable question, "What is your net worth?"

He looks about at the Disciples. POV SHOT of the Disciples who have fallen quiet and are trying not to be noticed. CLOSE SHOT of Head Luney.

> HEAD LUNEY
> Look about you. God's most anointed are buried in splendor. How will you spend eternity? Will you rot in an ill kept cemetery? Or will you lie in state in a Lunar mausoleum? Consider the rich. They stink not. Neither do they rot. They are the Lord's most anointed. They die and they are not forgotten. They are buried in waterproof caskets and sealed in lead vaults in the peaceful Lunar Fields. Where will you be in those last days when the Lord gathers the wealthy unto his bosom?

MEDIUM SHOT. The Disciples, giggling uncontrollably, rise.

> DISCIPLES
> Let us drain the sewage and bury the garbage.

DISSOLVE:
INT. MEDIUM SHOT ELEMENTARY CLASSROOM DAY

Doug, Cindy and Willa Kay enter. All three look seriously at the students. The TEACHER enters. CLOSE SHOT of Willa Kay's torso and face. She squirms, delighted, and touches her full upper lip with the tip of her tongue. MEDIUM CLOSE SHOT *of Teacher introducing them.*

                TEACHER
These folks, children, are Representatives of the Church of the Lunar Being.

MEDIUM SHOT of Doug and Cindy setting up projector and lectern. Willa Kay poses and stares at the teacher.

                TEACHER
These kind folks are here to discuss the effect of mortality on children.

MEDIUM CLOSE SHOT. Doug approaches the lectern.

                DOUG
               (*smiling*)
I'm certain that in the innocence of childhood you think death is a joke. Grandma looks funny all made up and in a box. Hamburger tastes good. You've never thought about Bossy the cow, dead and cut to bits. But think if you will for a moment, about the time that you thought it would be a funny joke to shut your little dog Spot up in the garbage can. Remember how surprised you were when you realized for the first time how the garbage men managed to get so much garbage in that truck. I'm sure you can still hear little Spot's long, high pitched yelp of pain as the familiar sound of the compactor motor crushed his small body. Of course, you didn't expect Spot to be crushed to the size of your kitten when you put him in the garbage pail. Think how you felt when Daddy explained that Spot had gone to Doggy heaven.

    Remember when the garbage man handed you his bloody corpse and you, not wanting to believe that he was dead, tried to put him in the car to go to the Doctor. Remember Daddy saying, "Get that bloody beast out of this car!" And how you cried when Daddy grabbed him out of your hands and threw him over the back fence, saying, "The damn thing's dead! You killed him. You vicious little bastard!" And how you wished at that moment that Daddy would die and someone would throw *him* over the fence. Remember what Spot looked like a week later.

    What if Daddy forgot to look behind when he pulled the car

out of the driveway and it was you who was killed. Remember when you didn't move your skates from the top of the stairs and Mommy said, "You could have killed me. You little bastard." Maybe Mommy and Daddy didn't realize, like you often forget how just one little mistake can make them disappear forever.
(*long pause*)
Where would you put them? Where would they put you? Remember Spot?

CLOSE SHOTS of individual children crying. CLOSE TWO SHOT of Willa Kay and the Teacher, totally absorbed in each other. Willa Kay has one hand on his leg while, with her other hand, she is pushing his hand gradually up the inside of her thigh. Her short dress is up, revealing her soft inner thighs and crotch covered by thin white panties. MEDIUM CLOSE SHOT of Doug.

DOUG

Do you love Mommy and Daddy? How many times have you heard Daddy tell you, "If it weren't for you kids, I could live a decent life." How many times have you heard Mommy say, "I'm working myself to death for you."

Think about it. Where would you put Mommy if she died? How would you dress her?

Picture Mommy in the dress she calls a rag, no grave to lie in, saying, "What did I do to deserve this?"

MEDIUM CLOSE SHOT of children in classroom. They are wailing in hysteria. A fight breaks out. Two girls claw each other mercilessly. CLOSE SHOT of child vomiting. CLOSE SHOT of Willa Kay and Teacher involved in heavy petting. Willa Kay's legs are wrapped around him, revealing her bikini underwear. MEDIUM CLOSE SHOT of Cindy, drunk, passing out cigarettes and pills.

CINDY
(*staggering and slurring her words*)
You'll be okay. You'll be okay. My mommy died.
(*starts to bawl*)
I didn't want to bury her. Everybody just goes and dies.
CINDY joins the hysteria.

MEDIUM CLOSE SHOT of Doug who, with his usual sales persistence, continues. He walks over to the projector, turns it on and walks back to the lectern. BIG CLOSE SHOT of screen, showing disastrous consequences of dummies not wearing seat belts in consumer tests.

DOUG
Government studies show that two out of five of you will be mangled like these dummies. Do Mommy and Daddy drink? In that case, terrible accidents are sure to befall them. How will you patch them up and bury them? How many times have you heard Daddy say, "I need to go to the Doctor, but we can't afford it." How will you feel if you can't care for his corpse properly?

SOUND of song, "Will the Circle be Unbroken," playing in the background.

DOUG
Do you want your corpse to sleep with Mommy and Daddy?

BIG CLOSE SHOT of screen showing beautiful Lunar Family Plot. It is one hole, a mini mass grave.

MEDIUM CLOSE SHOT of Doug.

DOUG
Tell Mommy and Daddy that for eight thousand dollars, your entire family can sleep together safely.

MEDIUM SHOT of a BIKER entering with two MOTORCYCLE MAMAS.

BIKER
(*waving bomb*)
Cut the crap! Day after day, I watch this shit get worse and worse. The price of drugs is unbelievable. I can't eat. I can't sleep. And these little voices keep telling me that someone has got to fix this shit.

MEDIUM CLOSE SHOT of classroom reveals the previously depicted scene. All of the children, Doug, Willa and Cindy are not impressed by the Biker and his Mamas.

> BIKER
> (*breaking into tears*)
> Pay attention! You've been told and told! If you'd just listen, this sort of thing wouldn't happen.

CLOSE SHOT of Motorcycle Mama going into a seizure. MEDIUM CLOSE SHOT of Biker, looking at Mama with consternation on his face. Turns to the room.

> BIKER
> See!

BIKER prepares to throw the bomb.

> CHILDREN
> (*noticing bomb*)
> See! See! See! See! See!

MEDIUM SHOT of children rising, as if hypnotized, advancing on the Biker. They begin to chant in unison.

> CHILDREN
> See! See! See! See! See! See! See! See! See!

MEDIUM CLOSE SHOT of Biker. He is suddenly very frightened and begins to back away from the Children.

> BIKER
> (*putting his hands out as if to push them back*)
> Okay. Enough's enough. I'll go now.

> BIKER
> (*holds the bomb out*)
> See. It isn't even real. I'll go now. Just an innocent little joke. Just something to get me five or ten years in the joint.
> (*laughs hysterically*)

MEDIUM CLOSE SHOT of the Children pulling on him. SOUND of Children chanting SEE! louder and louder until the noise reaches one long screeching crescendo. Over the sound of the chant can be heard the horrifying screams of the tortured and dying Biker.

DISSOLVE:

INT. RURAL NEIGHBORHOOD BAR—DAY

MEDIUM LONG SHOT: Doug, Cindy and Willa Kay sit at a table in a small neighborhood bar. A television set behind and above the bar is the center of attention for the customers in the darkened room. CLOSE SHOT of Willa Kay. She looks about, smiling at an occasional customer. She is wearing a tight top and a short skirt that reveals her sensuous thighs. Doug seems depressed, concentrating on his bottle of beer. Cindy looks blank, drinking from her glass. It is a country bar. The patrons wear overalls, jeans, etc. They are mostly men.

CAMERA FEATURES the television. Then BIG CLOSE SHOT of television screen as normal programming cuts to newsman RICHARD GUNN. MEDIUM CLOSE SHOT of Richard Gunn in television studio.

> GUNN
> (*sitting behind desk*)
> We interrupt this program for a special report on today's events. As we reported earlier, Malcolm Redbridge, founder of Lunar Industries and powerful religious personality, was arrested today for fraud. When arrested, Mr. Redbridge would only respond to Officers' questions when addressed as "the Divine Lunar Being." Supposed Disciples with him at the time were involved in a drunken orgy when police burst into the Lunar Industries boardroom, referred to by Mr. Redbridge as the Lunar Toilet Facilities and Conference Room. They immediately scrambled and ran. Mr. Redbridge, looking after them as he was being read his rights, said, "Father forgive them. They know not what they do." And, as he was being shoved into the showers at the Jackson County Jail, he screamed, "Oh God, my God! Why hast thou forsaken me?" He then fell silent.

Newscaster Gunn turns to stage right. Another newsman, PETER EDWARDS, is about to be introduced.

> GUNN
> Peter Edwards was on the scene earlier today. Peter, we understand that there were some unusual events spurred by the demise of Lunar Industries.

CAMERA PANS to Newsman Edwards.

EDWARDS
Yes, Richard. There were indeed. As everyone knows by now, the Stock Market was devastated and violent incidents were sparked throughout the country by young Lunatic Capitalists who have been profoundly affected by drugs and the Lunar Industries theological position.

CAMERA FEATURES Gunn.

GUNN
Peter, I understand there was an even more unusual event in the city of Hickman Mills this afternoon, apparently instigated by certain sales representatives of Lunar Industries, or Lunar Disciples, as they're called.

CAMERA FEATURES Edwards.

EDWARDS
It apparently happened around three o'clock this afternoon. A Doug Winthrop and two accomplices, a Cindy Dubrowski and a Willa Kay went into an elementary school there and took the fifth grade, three civilians and the teacher hostage. There is speculation among experts in terrorist tactics that they took these people hostage in order to negotiate for Federal intervention in the impending bankruptcy of Lunar Industries. There is little information at present regarding whether or not this activity was sanctioned by Mr. Redbridge, Head of Lunar Industries, or Head Luney, as he calls himself. There is some indication that Mr. Redbridge may have known of the incident. However, when questioned in his cell at the Jackson County Jail, Mr. Redbridge responded by urinating in his pants.

Later, when Mr. Redbridge seemed capable of understanding that some kind of violence had been perpetrated, he did make a plea for non-violence and said that he had never been in favor of Militant Capitalism.

It seems, Richard, that Mr. Redbridge has always pretty much reflected the attitude of Senator Goldbladder in matters regarding the fight between Communists and Capitalists. He has always believed that Communism should be violently opposed. That is,

fought with foreign aid to puppet governments and, wherever possible, troops from the United States in foreign countries. But
CONTINUED:
EDWARDS (CONTINUED)
violence should not be used in American communities.

Richard, you apparently have some information regarding the elementary school where the students were taken hostage.

CAMERA FEATURES Gunn.

GUNN
Yes, Peter, there is some indication that two of the teachers there were being investigated by the FBI for Communistic behavior. The FBI would not elaborate, except to give us their names. Their names are Mabel Evans and Walter Crane. Our source with the FBI went ahead to say that they are alleged to be having an affair.

CAMERA FEATURES Edwards.

EDWARDS
Richard, does the immorality of these two teachers suggest that they may have been inculcating Communistic behavior into the students? Have not the Liberals always argued, Richard, that the views of the teachers, like everything else they do, have no effect on the student?

CAMERA FEATURES Gunn.

GUNN
Yes, Peter, there does appear to be a trend toward ignorance. The Liberals believe that American children who are well fed, healthy, selfish, etc., will continue to reflect these characteristics in later life. They believe that any hint of rebellious unselfishness is simply a meaningless psychological stage about which we should not be in the least concerned.

For more information regarding the fugitives, we have consulted our expert in the intelligence field, Mr. Jonathan Wainwright. Mr. Wainwright, for some years, until his retirement at the age of forty-five, was with the FBI. We hired Mr. Wainwright this morning because of his contacts with the FBI.

Mr. Wainwright will identify the fugitives for vigilantes. The

FBI hopes that vigilante groups, before proceeding with the elimination of these suspects, will not only possess weapons, but that they will also have a license to carry those weapons. If you kill the criminals, be certain that they were indeed dangerous. The dead suspects must have weapons when the police arrive.

We go now to Mr. Jonathan Wainwright, outside the Lunar Industries central office complex in Fargo, North Dakota. Mr. Wainwright.

DIRECT CUT TO:

EXT. LUNAR BUILDING—DAY

MEDIUM LONG SHOT: CAMERA FEATURES Wainwright standing on a deserted street in front of a nondescript utilitarian building constructed of cement blocks. He holds a microphone and a collection of pictures which he occasionally drops. MEDIUM CLOSE SHOT of Wainwright dropping pictures and chasing after them in the wind. CAMERA FOLLOWS ACTION. Wainwright turns and faces the camera, pushing back his thinning hair with the hand that holds the microphone. SOUND of static caused by microphone scraping against his head. Wainwright nervously attempts to gain composure. He will continue to fail.

WAINWRIGHT

Hello. Hi there. O.K. I'm Jonathan Wainwright, speaking to you from the hub of Lunar activity in downtown Fargo. As my good friend, Mr. Richard Gunn, has informed you, I am going to familiarize you with the fugitives of the FBI's most recent kidnapping incident.
(*He turns and looks at the building behind him*)
I would like to be inside this building.

Looks about himself for help, shrugs his shoulders, grins and proceeds.

WAINWRIGHT

I would like to present, first, a profile of what I consider the most dangerous member of the trio,
(*grins*)
Miss Willa Kay. Willa Kay grew up in Boise City, Oklahoma. She was elected Prom Queen of Boise City High School in 1974. There were rumors regarding her virtue and certain faculty

members, concerned with the sexual morality of the student body, objected to her assumption of the position. We recently discovered

CONTINUED:

WAINWRIGHT (CONTINUED)
this photograph of Willa Kay engaging in intramural sports with the football team.
(*holds up photo*)

BIG CLOSE SHOT of the photograph. Willa Kay is bent over, hiking the football between two well-developed thighs. She is wearing only bikini panties, which, of course, offer an excellent view of her body. Her blonde hair hangs along both sides of her flirtatious face and her firm breasts with large, dark nipples are visible. CLOSE SHOT of Wainwright, grinning lustily.

WAINWRIGHT
After graduation, Miss Kay moved to Amarillo, Texas to pursue a career as a secretary. She attempted to sleep her way to the top through a relationship with the Sales Manager of the company she worked for there in Amarillo. However, she made the mistake of sending her own picture for publication to the Sales Manager's favorite pornographic magazine, giving him credit for the excellent photography. His wife saw the photograph and Miss Kay was terminated without notice.

Miss Kay came to the attention of the FBI for the first time in Amarillo when an incident involving this photograph occurred.
(*holds up photo*)

BIG CLOSE SHOT of photograph. Willa Kay, hand-cuffed and under arrest, walks between two Texas Rangers toward a Texas Ranger patrol car. A third Ranger walks behind her. She is smiling and waving at the photographer. She proudly reveals her handcuffs. She wears a short skirt with a kick pleat that reveals most of her thigh as she walks. She is wearing a very low cut white blouse. The Rangers on each side of her are laughing with this very attractive prostitute. The one behind her is caught by the camera obviously enjoying her body.

WAINWRIGHT
This photograph, taken by an amateur photographer outside a truck-stop in Amarillo, became quite useful to the FBI in the case that followed.

These three Texas Rangers were discovered by a search party of

The Compound

fellow officers, walking back toward Amarillo from a point sixty miles from the city limits on the following day. When questioned regarding the location of their vehicle, they reported that they were transporting Miss Kay to the Amarillo City Jail when she expressed a need for the privacy of toilet facilities. Finding none for some time, they headed South out of Amarillo, strangely enough, and pulled off on a side road. Worried that Miss Kay might escape, having seen the movie *Cool Hand Luke*, the three officers said that they elected to surround her in the bushes. Whereupon Miss Kay did, in fact, escape with their vehicle.
(Holding up another photo)
Here is another photograph showing Miss Kay travelling to San Jacinto County, California where the patrol car was finally discovered. The FBI became interested in the case when she was discovered travelling with two illegal aliens disguised as Texas Rangers.

BIG CLOSE SHOT of photograph. Willa Kay stands with her arms around two large Indians. They are dressed as Texas Rangers, wearing long braids and grinning. They both have .357 magnum pistols playfully in their hands. Willa Kay, dressed as before, is laughing.
WAINWRIGHT

Here is the photograph of the car after its discovery by CHP officers, and upon it's delivery to the officers responsible for it's loss.

BIG CLOSE SHOT of two Texas Rangers getting into a patrol car that is decorated with garters hanging on rear and side view mirrors. Women's garter belts, hose, etc. hang from radio aerials. The California Highway Patrol officers, surrounding the car and opening the doors for their colleagues from Texas, are thoroughly enjoying the ceremony to which they have invited the press. CLOSE SHOT of Wainwright.

WAINWRIGHT
(*grinning*)
When the Attorney General of the state of Texas was asked why he had never pushed for extradition of Miss Kay to Austin for trial, he stated, "The dignity of the Court and the State of Texas could not bear the false and malicious publicity that would be inflicted on them by a hostile press." Then he added angrily, "But that Bitch had better *never* show her ass in the state of Texas!"

Later, Miss Kay drifted to Washington, D.C. where she procured work as a Congressional Whore.

(laughs. Holds up photograph)
Here she is outside the Broadmore Hotel and X-rated cinema with Senator Goldbladder.
BIG CLOSE SHOT of Willa Kay dressed in a low cut evening gown. She is bent over laughing, revealing even more than the ordinary revelation of bosom. Her blonde hair falls over her shoulders. The tall man with full head of white, wavy hair and dark rimmed glasses next to her is lecherously hugging her close and taking advantage of the opportunity to look down the front of her dress.

WAINWRIGHT

I would like to take advantage of this opportunity, on behalf of myself and my colleagues in the FBI, to apologize to Mrs. Goldbladder and any other family members who might be watching, for that photograph from our confidential files, and to wish Senator Goldbladder the best in the upcoming Congressional investigation of his affiliation with Mr. Redbridge.
(laughs uncontrollably)
As you can see, Miss Kay can definitely be hazardous to your reputation. Approach her with a great deal of caution if you have anything to lose.

Mr. Doug Winthrop, believed to be the Charles Manson of the trio,
(grins sarcastically)
was raised in Topeka, Kansas. He was at one time a promising student and athlete. This career, however, was nipped in the bud by his seventh grade teacher, Miss Rosemary Limpiss, who discovered him in the boy's bathroom recording the sound of his own excretions and promptly reported this behavior to the entire faculty. He was diagnosed schizophrenic by Mr. Harry Phillips, the school counselor and football coach, who held Mr. Winthrop up for ridicule to the football team and sent him to Eastern Missouri Mental Health Center. The diagnosis was found to be incorrect and Mr. Winthrop was sent home.

Mr. Winthrop had difficulties both with fellow students and with faculty in High School as a result of his Junior High School reputation. He also had frequent fights with his father who drank a great deal and was fond of saying that he did not raise a son to record the sound of his own excretions. His father left permanently during this period with Mrs. Harry Phillips.

The Compound

Holds up photograph. BIG CLOSE SHOT of Doug's father, drunk, attempting to disentangle himself from an overweight woman with tousled hair. Doug stands nearby laughing.

      WAINWRIGHT
Here you see Mr. Winthrop's father with Mrs. Phillips before their departure. Observe Mr. Winthrop's unorthodox point of view about the impending loss of his father.
 Mr. Winthrop dropped out of High School at the age of seventeen. He became a Color Tile salesman and, at first, did well. Then sales began to plummet. His manager pressured him. He threatened to rip out the manager's spinal cord and strangle him with it. The judge, considering his background and economic condition, sent him to Boy's Industrial School in North Topeka where he became a track star, honor student, and was nominated Prom King.
      (*holds up photo*)

BIG CLOSE SHOT of Doug, wearing long hair, dressed in gym shorts, being carried on the shoulders of several teenaged men.

      WAINWRIGHT
Mr. Winthrop later went to Kokomo Junior College where he majored in gourmet cooking. He was particularly interested in Folk preparations. His use of cocaine and his role as dealer to fellow cooks and stewards during his employment by the Hostel Tree Hotel, brought this interest to the attention of the Society for Prevention of Cruelty to Animals.

BIG CLOSE SHOTS of a series of pictures depicting cats in cages waiting to be boiled alive in cauldrons adjacent to the cages. Dog's hanging from makeshift scaffolds and barbecue pits in which whole animals lie, preparatory to their dissection for serving. A photograph of Doug reveals him with shaved head, particularly alert, holding a living chihuahua by the scruff of the neck as if it were prized game.

      WAINWRIGHT
Mr. Winthrop had influenced hotel management to finance this addition to their kitchen. Stewards and fellow cooks had been persuaded to procure animals and to remain silent regarding the nature of the delicacies served here. Management, aware of the low cost of supplies and attractiveness of preparations, had not

been particularly inquisitive. However, there had been some concern about disappearing pets and management suspected angry stewards of kidnapping them.

CONTINUED:
WAINWRIGHT (CONTINUED)
On Thanksgiving Day, 1978, a repentant steward, far too high on cocaine and alcohol, having recently been reborn, showed these photographs, particularly the one of Mr. Winthrop holding the Manager's little dog, to a feasting party of the Manager and his friends. Winthrop was dismissed immediately and the newly acquired food preparation facilities dismantled.

Mr. Winthrop then joined a rock band as a bassist and distributor of amphetamines.

(*holds up photo*)

BIG CLOSE SHOT of Doug with shaved head, wearing army fatigues and holding a Winchester rifle, staring directly into the camera, tense and alert.

WAINWRIGHT
His Neo-nazi beliefs, a party of which he was a member at that time, and unorthodox manner of dress drove him away from the other rock musicians.

Mr. Winthrop traveled about for some time, was arrested for possession of narcotics, dangerous weapons and vagrancy. He was hospitalized and released.

Some time later, he began to write romantic letters to Henrietta Ford, Great Granddaughter of Henry Ford. He was arrested and hospitalized again. This time detoxification was achieved, he acquired Christianity, and began what appeared to be a respectable sales career.

Cindy Dubrowski graduated from Kansas University School of Business where she was an average student, married her Computer Science Professor and divorced him a month later. She acquired a managerial position with Osco Drug. Security personnel discovered Miss Dubrowski drunk on more than one occasion and, noticing a shortage in the liquor department, were able to acquire the following photograph of her.

BIG CLOSE SHOT of photo of Cindy. She is looking anxiously to her left as the security camera catches her taking a bottle of Canadian Mist from the shelf.

> WAINWRIGHT
> The evidence gathered was overwhelming. Miss Dubrowski was arrested and prosecuted by the State of Kansas. With a felony on her record, Miss Dubrowski was unable to acquire another decent job. She attempted commission sales, but was unable to pay her own expenses. It was at this point that she began working as a model for fraudulent advertisers, advertising make-up and weight-loss programs. Here are some samples of before and after photos.

Wainwright holds up a photograph. BIG CLOSE SHOT of Cindy, disheveled, heavy black make-up under her eyes, wearing old fashioned, high necked dress. This is immediately followed by a BIG CLOSE SHOT of Cindy refreshed, wearing a low cut, short dress that emphasizes her attractive shoulders. Her brown eyes and dark hair shine.

> WAINWRIGHT
> It was during this period of time that she also began working at the Pink Garter as an exotic dancer. She called herself Letty Lovelace.
> (*holds up photo*)

BIG CLOSE SHOT of Cindy wearing a negligee, g-string and nothing else. She stands next to a gentleman at the bar. He is buying her a drink. CAMERA FEATURES Wainwright.

> WAINWRIGHT
> Unfortunately, this young man was a vice cop and Miss Dubrowski was hustling more than drinks.

Wainwright looks about, grinning, having finished his broadcast of the profiles. At first he is confused, then he talks into the camera.

> WAINWRIGHT
> As you can see, these fugitives range from crazy to drug addicted and should be considered quite dangerous. Attack with caution.
> (*laughs*)

CAMERA FEATURES Gunn.

                             GUNN
Thank you, Mr. Wainwright. The children involved in this thing are, perhaps, the most tragic victims. Dr. Amanda Klagstrip Skaggsworth, interning at Eastern Missouri Mental Health Facility, has been kind enough to consent to our intrusion into her work there at the center. Dr. Skaggsworth! Are you receiving me there!

MEDIUM SHOT of DR. AMANDA KLAGSTRIP SKAGGSWORTH. Her mid-length dishwater-blonde hair needs both washing and combing. She is dressed in a wrinkled cotton dress with a large floral pattern. She is wearing a white lab coat over the dress. Dr. Skaggsworth is being taped in a children's ward. The children are the victims of the apparent tragedy. CAMERA PANS AROUND the ward. The children are fighting, throwing food and screaming. MEDIUM CLOSE SHOT of two large orderlies moving into the group, throwing them about, throwing one on a bed to be strapped down, and stopping the physical violence. SOUNDS of crying, an occasional scream and plaintiff cries of, "I want my mama, you motherfucker!" can be heard. BIG CLOSE SHOT of Dr. Skaggsworth attempting to gain composure.

                       DR. SKAGGSWORTH
What was the question?

Dr. Skaggsworth looks about confused, then finds Gunn on the monitor.

                       DR. SKAGGSWORTH
I thought for a minute there was a voice from God.
                       (*giggles and wiggles*)
Silly me!

CAMERA FEATURES Gunn.

                             GUNN
Have you confirmed a diagnosis of these children who, at the time of the incident, apparently reflected the insanity of the terrorists to the point of, themselves, becoming murderers involved in the most malicious mutilation of their victim?

CAMERA FEATURES Dr. Skaggsworth.

                         SKAGGSWORTH
                          (*confused*)
What was the question?

CAMERA FEATURES Gunn.

                    GUNN
                  (*annoyed*)
    Have you confirmed a diagnosis of these children?
CAMERA FEATURES Dr. Skaggsworth.

                SKAGGSWORTH
Oh yes! Crazy! Lunatics! Unbelievable trauma! I shall not recover. I just begin my internship and would you believe it? Every other Doctor on the floor takes a motherfucking vacation! I pray to God to help me!
         (*looks up at ceiling in exasperation*)
Oh, Lord! Please look down on thy humble servant and grant me the courage to meet such adversity.

CAMERA FEATURES Gunn.

                    GUNN
                  (*patiently*)
    And the treatment?

CAMERA FEATURES Skaggsworth.

                SKAGGSWORTH
Of course! I take tranquilizers. I go home, take Demerol capsules for these terrible headaches and leave the blessed children to these wonderful aides.

SKAGGSWORTH motions to his aides.

MEDIUM CLOSE SHOT of aides strapping a young girl to a bed.

CAMERA FEATURES Gunn.

                    GUNN
                  (*annoyed*)
    We are concerned about the children!

CAMERA FEATURES Skaggsworth.

                SKAGGSWORTH

Aren't we all? Bless them!
> (*exaggerated gesture*)

Bless all God's children. Suffer the children if they come unto me.
> (*laughs*)

They'll never be the same! Horror of horrors!

POV SHOT of the aides working over a small girl. Dr. Skaggsworth turns to observe the aides who are busy tightening the straps on the struggling girl. SOUND of almost inhuman grunts and groans as the girl struggles.

CAMERA FEATURES Skaggsworth.

SKAGGSWORTH

Give her ten cc's of thorazine, intravenously!
> (*turns to camera*)

They'll never be the same. Bless them.

CAMERA FEATURES Gunn.

GUNN

You don't expect a cure?

CAMERA FEATURES Skaggsworth.

SKAGGSWORTH

Oh my Lord, no! The dental work itself will be amazing! Can you imagine! They chewed all the way to the bone! You should have seen their little mouths when the police brought them in.
> (*grimaces*)

God, I'd hate to be their parents. You know, none of them have dental insurance.

CAMERA FEATURES Gunn.

GUNN

Insurance?

CAMERA FEATURES Skaggsworth.

SKAGGSWORTH

Oh yes! They have hospitalization. Otherwise, we'd treat them the way we treat all difficult vagrants.

CAMERA FEATURES Gunn.

> GUNN
>
> How's that?

CAMERA FEATURES Skaggsworth.

> SKAGGSWORTH
>
> Send them to the terminal hospital for the cure!
> (*laughs*)
> God help us. We're awfully busy. Excuse me.

CLOSE TWO SHOT of Dr. Skaggsworth and NURSE. NURSE hands her some pills and a glass of water. Dr. Skaggsworth laughs and turns back to the camera.

> SKAGGSWORTH
>
> Physician, heal thyself!
> (*swallows pills, drinks water*)
> Jesus!
> (*shivers*)
> That hits the spot! I get so tired. Can't sleep. Can't eat. But the medicine I take gets me through these days.
> (*to nurse*)
> Hurry up with that thorazine!

CAMERA FEATURES Gunn.

> GUNN
>
> You said they'd never be the same?

CAMERA FEATURES Skaggsworth.

> SKAGGSWORTH
>
> The hell I did!
> (*pauses, then realizes*)
> Oh. Yes. You mean the children. I thought for a minute there you meant *my orderlies*.
> (*laughs*)
> It's only a minor social disease.
> (*rubs her eye*)

CAMERA FEATURES Gunn.

> GUNN
> (*angrily*)
> Yes, of course, the children. What is your treatment plan?

CAMERA FEATURES Skaggsworth.

> SKAGGSWORTH
> Shock treatments. Lots and lots of shock treatments. And then follow up with much thorazine.

Dr. Skaggsworth forgets that she's on camera. Goes over to the child that has now been given the intravenous thorazine. CAMERA FOLLOWS Dr. Skaggsworth. CLOSE TWO SHOT of Dr. Skaggsworth with the child.

> SKAGGSWORTH
> Nice little zombie. Mommy's good girl.
> (*turns back to camera*)
> Soon they'll all be this way. It's a miracle.
> (*laughs uncontrollably*)
> Shoot 'em up baby!

CAMERA FEATURES Gunn.

> GUNN
> Psychiatry has come a long way since the days of our grandparents. Has it not, Peter?

CAMERA FEATURES Edwards.

> EDWARDS
> Yes indeed, Richard. Large numbers of people that at one time were noticeably different can now only be distinguished by a certain thorazine manner of walking and talking.

CAMERA FEATURES Gunn.

> GUNN
> That reminds me, Peter, Dr. Jeremiah Lingstrom is standing by with his lab assistant to give us the benefit of his medical research in determining the reasons for the demise of Malcolm Redbridge. Dr. Lingstrom is a Full Professor at the University of Decatur School of Medicine. He is noted for his genetic research. His book, *The Origin of Difference*, is in widespread use throughout the

country. He was recently honored by our President for his work at the University of Alabama during the late fifties. Dr. Lingstrom! Can you hear me?

MEDIUM CLOSE SHOT of DR. JEREMIAH LINGSTROM in his laboratory with his Assistant, OSCO. There is one lab table with the usual accouterments. The water runs continuously throughout the scene. Dr. Lingstrom and Osco appear not to hear it. A large box with a lever sits on another table. There are two unmade half beds in the laboratory. It appears that the men live here. There are stuffed, mythological animals throughout the laboratory. Mannequins of the races of Homo Sapiens and mixtures of those races stand, fully costumed, around the room. Dr. Lingstrom is a very old man with tousled, long white hair and a long white beard. He is bent and quite thin. Osco is a very old white headed black man. He wears overalls, is stooped and walks with a limp. CLOSE TWO SHOT of Dr. Lingstrom and Osco. Dr. Lingstrom cups his hand to his ear, looks about the room for the source of the voice and talks loudly. Both men speak in high volume throughout the scene.

LINGSTROM

Huh? Wha'd you say?

OSCO
(*laughing*)
He say he's the Black Devil and he gonna git yore white ass.

Dr. Lingstrom falls to beating Osco about the head with a pillow. The pillow is a souvenir of one of the Wallace campaigns for Governor of Alabama. It bears his image.

CAMERA FEATURES Dr. Lingstrom.

LINGSTROM
(*out of breath*)

Goddamn animal!

Osco guards against the blows and laughs hysterically. Dr. Lingstrom throws the pillow at him and, regaining his composure, looks about for the source of the voice. He is breathing heavily. CAMERA FEATURES Dr. Lingstrom and Osco in a MEDIUM CLOSE SHOT.

LINGSTROM
(*looking about*)
Don't pay no attention to him. He's just a nigger.

OSCO

Who you callin' a nigger?
(*laughing*)
Go ahead. Ask the man. Ask him if he's got any more of them dirty pictures you was so interested in on the television.
(*winks at the camera*)

LINGSTROM

He don't get much company. He don't know how to act. You know how they are. They have to watch other people to know how to act and they can't remember very long.

OSCO
(*grinning*)
Shee-it! You don't even know that you on the same program you been watchin'.
(*points to the television*)
There's your picture. And there's the fellow you lookin' for.
(*to camera*)
He can't do nothin' by hisself.

LINGSTROM
(*still on the previous subject*)
Nobody comes here no more. The students used to come for experiments
(*laughs*)
until the University took the drugs away. Used to keep 'em in that box.

Dr. Lingstrom points to the black box with a lever.

LINGSTROM

I used to write down how much electric shock they'd endure to get 'em. We'd change the voltage all the time and me and Osco'd laugh our asses off watchin' those wise ass sons-a-bitches jerk and twitch when the current hit 'em. Just to get the drugs.

> OSCO
> (*laughing*)
> The white ones was the worst.

> LINGSTROM
> (*winking at the camera*)
> Aw, he don't know nothin'. He ain't even graduated from high school.

LINGSTROM grins affectionately at Osco.

CAMERA FEATURES Gunn now somewhat embarrassed.

> GUNN
> I understand you were recently honored by the President for your genetic research.

CAMERA FEATURES Dr. Lingstrom and Osco. Osco grins at Dr. Lingstrom.

> OSCO
> He says he understand yore bowels ain't regular.
> (*starts laughing*)

> LINGSTROM
> Can't get no prunes. He don't tell them people that bring the groceries to bring me prunes. I told him over and over to order prunes. But you know how *they* are. Stubborn, like mules. He don't like prunes.

CAMERA FEATURES Gunn. He raises his voice, horrified by the conversation.

> GUNN
> I *wish* to discuss the genetic reasons for the demise of Malcolm Redbridge, President of Lunar Industries.

CAMERA FEATURES Dr. Lingstrom and Osco.

> LINGSTROM
> You'll have to talk clearer than that. The boy . . .
> (*looks at Osco*)
> . . . can't even understand you.

OSCO
(*angry*)
Who you callin' boy? You that can't even order your own prunes. Who you callin' boy?

LINGSTROM
(*laughs*)
I don't see no other nigger.
(*looks around in mock search*)

GUNN
(*horrified*)
Men! Men! Think of your dignity! Now, let's talk about Redbridge.

OSCO
He white or black?

GUNN
For God's sake!

LINGSTROM
Huh? Wha'd he say?

OSCO
He say he Zombo.

LINGSTROM
(*suddenly very interested*)
Bring the Zombo model, Boy.

OSCO
Ain't gonna git nothin' 'til you say my name.

LINGSTROM
(*laughing*)
Name hell! You ain't got no name. What's your last name?

OSCO
(*serious*)
Lingstrom! Same as yores. You ought to know. Yore mother birthed me.

The Compound

LINGSTROM
(*grabs another pillow*)
You son-of-a-bitch.
(*beats Osco*)

OSCO
(laughing)
You hadn't ought to talk that way about our Ma.

GUNN
For God's sake! Get the damn model!

OSCO
Okay. Okay.
(*goes toward the mannequin, grumbling*)
Can't have no fun. Never get company and can't have no fun.

CLOSE TWO SHOT of Osco bringing back a large, gray mannequin with a large nose and a great deal of hair, dressed in Costa Rican costume. MEDIUM CLOSE SHOT of Osco, Dr. Lingstrom and the Mannequin. Osco looks across the mannequin at Dr. Lingstrom and says loudly:

OSCO
Zombo Lecture!

Suddenly, the two men assume their new roles with a dignity and awareness that belies their previous lack of awareness.

LINGSTROM
The Zombo, being of South American Indian and African descent, is given to emotional delinquency. He tends to be alcoholic, have a large penis and the Negroid desire for sex.

Osco points to the extra large crotch of the mannequin.

GUNN
(*interrupting*)
What does this have to do with Redbridge?

OSCO
(*indignant, eyes and face are hostile*)
He Zombo! Dr. Lingstrom talks! Shut up and listen!

                    LINGSTROM
                    (*grinning*)
Unlike the Caucasian newscaster, who, because of his extreme nervousness, is usually impotent and given to masturbation.

                      GUNN
You! Honored by the President?

                    LINGSTROM
The Caucasian newscaster is indeed quite clever. Caucasians have a good vocabulary, but, unfortunately, lack balls and the will to reproduce. The Zombo race will breed Mrs. Gunn!

                      GUNN
You crazy old fart!

                      OSCO
Shut up and listen! Afterwards, you can discuss. Don't you understand? This man's a scholar! He doesn't have to make sense. He's listened to by important white men!

CAMERA FEATURES Gunn. Gunn is visibly upset, staring in a hostile manner at the monitor. He immediately gains his composure, making no comment on the preceding interview.

                      GUNN
Perhaps the most important political personality to be affected by today's events, and the one in the best position to comment on the effect of the collapse of Lunar Industries on this nation's economy, is that powerful senator from the State of Missouri, Senator Michael J. Goldbladder.
  Derrick Livingston is standing by at Lackland Air Force Base and, I believe, is talking to Senator Goldbladder.

                                        DIRECT CUT TO:

EXT. LACKLAND AFB AIR SHOW IN PROGRESS—DAY

MEDIUM CLOSE SHOT: DERRICK LIVINGSTON is a young, well dressed Black reporter. Senator Goldbladder is drunk. He is accompanied by several AIDES. A young, dark complected woman is on his arm. She is very attractive, with long, dark hair and dark eyes. Her sun dress is both low cut and short. She is a high class prostitute. She watches Senator Goldbladder with infatuation, responding warmly to every comment that he makes. He is also accompanied by a young, tall, dark Air Force Major. SOUNDS of crowd in background and jet planes passing overhead. Livingston looks into the camera then turns to Goldbladder. CLOSE TWO SHOT of Goldbladder and his lady. Goldbladder is smiling. MEDIUM CLOSE SHOT.

LIVINGSTON
Sir, I'm sure you're aware of today's events.

GOLDBLADDER
Yes, indeed I am, Mr. Livingston. I'm here at Lackland Air Force Base watching them put the best airplanes in the world through their paces. And it is the good fortune of Congress to be in a position to choose from those airplanes.

LIVINGSTON
That wasn't exactly what I was referring to.

GOLDBLADDER
And why not young man?
(*smiles*)
Are you too liberal to be interested in the defense of your country?

The young lady with Goldbladder smiles at the joke and brushes her breast against his arm.

LIVINGSTON
No, Sir. But right now, my country seems to be undergoing an economic crisis due to the collapse of a group of companies headed by your friend and ally, Mr. Malcolm Redbridge.

GOLDBLADDER
(*waving to an acquaintance.*)
I wouldn't know about that. I was busy most of the night.

GOLDBLADDER smiles at the young lady.
CLOSE UP of the young lady. She is looking seductively up at Goldbladder. She blushes appropriately, as if she were reliving the experience.

                    LIVINGSTON
Sir, I think your voting public would view your comments as foolish and your display here as revolting.

                    GOLDBLADDER
                    (*sobering quickly*)
What?

                    LIVINGSTON
If you don't understand what's happening, Sir, I suggest you catch up on the news. You, personally, are in a very vulnerable spot right now.

                    GOLDBLADDER
                    (*furious*)
I don't care if you're the Son of God. To me, you are an impertinent son-of-a-bitch!

                    LIVINGSTON
I remind you, Sir,
                    (*points*)
that's a television camera.

                    GOLDBLADDER
And you're a Nigger. I'll have you terminated and you'll never get a job in this country again! I will not allow a nigger to talk to me this way.
                    (*turns to AIDES in background*)
For God's sake! Do something!

CAMERA FEATURES *Aides moving toward Livingston.*

                    LIVINGSTON
Just calm down, Sir. There is no reason to go to this extreme. I suppose you either can't or don't wish to discuss the upcoming Congressional investigation of your affiliation with Malcolm Redbridge.
                    (*the Aides grab him*)
Wait a minute!

CAMERA FOLLOWS ACTION. One of the Aides pops him quickly. SOUND of crack against his face. They hustle him off, beating him brutally. MEDIUM CLOSE SHOT of Goldbladder, stumbling drunk, grabbing the microphone. The camera crew does not stop him, knowing the network would not want to miss this opportunity.

> GOLDBLADDER
> (*muttering to himself*)
> Damn liberal press. How was I to know that motherfucker, Redbridge, was crazy? How was I to know he really believed that crap? This is America! Nobody ever says what they mean.

> AIDE
> (*to Goldbladder*)
> You better shit or get off the pot, Senator.

Goldbladder gets control quickly and brings the microphone up to speak.

> GOLDBLADDER
> People enjoy nothing so much as bringing down the mighty. I remember Richard Nixon, drunk, talking to portraits of dead presidents through those long, lonely nights in the White House. General Robert E. Lee paced the floor alone throughout the night, searching for guidance. And he returned from a lost war, alone, to find Union troops buried in his front lawn.

SOUND of song, "Nobody knows the sorrow I feel. Nobody knows, but Jesus." Goldbladder begins to feel the grandeur.

> GOLDBLADDER
> (*in a somber tone*)
> And in those last hours when great leaders lie in state, their bodies cold and hard, they have lived alone, and they die alone. When I am driven to my grave, when my body is cold and hard on that cold, cloudy day when I am carried to my final resting place, will I be alone? Then, as now, will there be no one to share my burden? And I have given all?
> No. I am not blameless. No man is blameless. But I say to you, with a heart that beats free from the burden of guilt, that I have never betrayed the trust of my countrymen. I can say with a clear conscience that from the halls of Montezuma to the shores of Tripoli, I have fought my country's battles.
> (*Pauses, bows his head, then gravely raises his eyes to look directly into the camera*)

MEDIUM LONG SHOT. A crowd has gathered. They are listening

intently to Goldbladder's speech. They cheer this last statement and begin to sing, as a chorus, "Onward Christian Soldiers." MEDIUM CLOSE SHOT of Goldbladder.

GOLDBLADDER

At the end of my long, lonely fight for liberty, justice and freedom, will I hear my Lord speak these words? Will my God say to me, "Michael J. Goldbladder, you have fought the good fight, you have run the good race. Come home?"

SOUND of song, "Come home, come home, it's supper time."

GOLDBLADDER

Oh, if I could only hear those words now as I stand before you, and I say to myself, "We Americans are not perfect. Far from it. We make mistakes. Humbly, we must repent. Admit those mistakes. They are part of our burden of freedom as God's chosen."

The CROWD chants, "Father forgive us!"

GOLDBLADDER
(*quietly*)

And we must forgive. You have no idea of the hurt I felt when I learned of our brother's betrayal.

CROWD sings, "Nobody knows the trouble I feel. Nobody knows, but Jesus."

GOLDBLADDER

In the stillness of the early morning hours, with troubled soul, I searched my heart for the guilt I knew I must share with Malcolm Redbridge. Is there not some of Malcolm Redbridge in all of us? Are not all of us in some way with Malcolm Redbridge when he takes the thirty pieces of silver?

CROWD begins to sing, "Were you there when they crucified my Lord? Were you there when they nailed Him to the tree?"

GOLDBLADDER

And when that great governing body of our nation, the Congress of the United States, is forced by a public that knows not what it does, to form a Congressional committee to investigate one of their own. What will they say? Will they not wash their hands of their matter as did Pontius Pilate, saying, "We find no fault with this just man?"

Sadly, I turned from the window in those darkest hours just

GOLDBLADDER (CONTINUED)

before the dawn. I looked out into the deserted street, and with a heavy heart, with tears streaming down my face, I looked out onto that land, that country of my people, the source of my wisdom and strength to fight my country's battles

(pauses and bows his head)

and I said, "Be with me now as you have in times past when I have not known where I would get the strength to fight."

And somehow, I could hear then, as now, the battle cry of all my fellow Americans, rallying behind me, giving me the strength to fight one more battle for my people.

The Liberals gather in their smoke filled rooms crying out, "Give us Barrabas! Crucify him!" But I know that the heart and soul of the American people is with me.

And in those last hours, when it was darkest, I saw what those who fight the Lord's battles see. I saw that first glimmer of light in the Eastern sky. And I knew that God and my people were with me.

CROWD begins to sing, in a mighty chorus, "Hallelujah! Hallelujah!"

GOLDBLADDER

Since that time, my brothers, I have felt faint and, perhaps, somewhat embarrassed. But I have girded my loins, taken up the banner and my faith is restored in myself and my people. We *will* be victorious!

CROWD cheers frantically.

GOLDBLADDER

We will go into the Valley of the Shadow of Death. Into those dark rooms where the Liberals, who do not have the strength of the Lord our God on their side, and we will root out the wicked!

CROWD cheers.

GOLDBLADDER

I, as all of us must, will root out the evil from my own heart. For, unlike the Liberals who, without God to guide them, have faith in their own perfection, I know that I am human. I *know* that my redeemer lives!

CROWD cheers wildly.

GOLDBLADDER

And my God asks of all of you what he asks of me. He asks that I feel no anger. He asks that I feel no hatred for those men, who with their unjust accusations, brought me down. And I say to you as I stand here before you with a pure heart, "I, as Jesus asks, LOVE MY ENEMIES!" It is for all of us, the just and the unjust, the righteous and the unrighteous, the weak and the strong, that our forefathers brought forth on this continent a new nation, conceived in liberty, with freedom and justice for all. And we *will* have justice for all!

CROWD cheers hysterically. They continue to cheer as Goldbladder raises his hand, attempting to quiet them. They will have none of it until he bows his head as if to pray. Then a hush falls over the crowd. There is almost complete silence for a moment. Then Goldbladder prays.

GOLDBLADDER

Father, in these last days, these days when brother rises against brother, daughter against mother, father against son; be with me and with my people as we, as did King David, gird our loins to do battle, not against men, but against the evil that lurks in the hearts of all men. Let the blood of the Lamb, that from his wounded side did flow, wash and make us pure. Let us go forth to fight our country's battles, both here and throughout the world, with the knowledge that thou art with us. We call on you as did our forefathers in those early days, those days when the land was fraught with evil, and freedom was threatened. We call on you to bind up the wounds that threaten us and to heal the wounds that divide us. AMEN.

The CROWD begins to sing "Blest Be the Tie that Binds." Goldbladder, through the miracle of television, has become a hero. CAMERA PANS to sky. SOUND and sight of Air Force jets flying in formation overhead. A brass band strikes up the National Anthem.

DISSOLVE:

INT. NEWS STUDIO—DAY

BIG CLOSE SHOT of Gunn looking into the camera with emotion that creates tears in his eyes. Then MEDIUM CLOSE SHOT.

> GUNN
> We have just witnessed one of those rare moments in American history that bind a nations wounds. Senator Goldbladder has just made a most moving appeal to the nation to cast aside our political differences in this moment of great crisis and unite with one accord to insure freedom, justice and tranquility for all in these troubled times. What are your feelings in regard to this, Peter?

MEDIUM CLOSE SHOT of Edwards.

> EDWARDS
> It was indeed moving, Richard. I can't help reflecting, as I sit here, on the past great moments in history when our statesmen have risen to the occasion of other crises that have threatened to divide our nation and deprive us of our liberty.

CAMERA FEATURES Gunn.

> GUNN
> I have just been informed by a Congressional spokesman that the malicious rumor regarding the possibility of a Congressional investigation of the Distinguished Senator from the State of Missouri is deplorable. Congress asks that, in this moment of great crisis, we all pull together in support of those who blaze a path for all of us.
> (*holding earpiece*)
> I have also just been informed by our network president that there will be a special presentation at 8 o'clock central time this evening. "The Life and Times of Senator Michael J. Goldbladder: A Profile in Courage" will be presented at that time.
> (*smiles*)

DISSOLVE:

INT. THE BAR SCENE—DAY

MEDIUM SHOT: The people in the bar are dressed as in the previous scene. WINSTON, the local postman, thinker and political authority, sits at the bar with JACK, a local farmer, MATTHEW, a local store owner and CLAUDE, who drives into town to work at Remington Arms. Other characters sit throughout the bar and will join in the action later. Willa, Doug and Cindy are rapidly exiting the bar. A STRANGE YOUNG MAN with very short, bleached hair, wearing an earring, and two YOUNG LADIES, wearing jeans and army fatigue shirts, sit at a table in approximately the center of the room. They are very congenial and make some attempts to join the conversation. MEDIUM CLOSE SHOT of Jack.

JACK
That man has done more for farmers than any politician of this century.

MEDIUM CLOSE SHOT of YOUNG MAN, smiling, attempting to be friendly.

YOUNG MAN
It's true that this country has not been particularly supportive of farmers.

CLOSE TWO SHOT of Jack and MATTHEW, both grinning, both giving each other a knowing look of disapproval for this young man's lack of patriotism.

MATTHEW
I think most of our problems come from folks who don't know what they're talkin' about.

Matthew, NADINE and WINSTON laugh, looking at each other and at the three strangers.

WINSTON
I think if a man's got God on his side, he can't keep from doin' what's best for everybody.

NADINE
'Course, some folks don't feel that way.

Nadine looks at the strange young man. He mistakes it for a friendly overture. MEDIUM CLOSE SHOT of Matthew.

> MATTHEW
> The Lord helps them that helps themselves.

CLOSE UP of Jack.

> JACK
> (*angrily*)
> Are you sayin' that farmers don't help themselves?

MEDIUM CLOSE SHOT of Young Man.

> YOUNG MAN
> That's right. I agree with the man.

CLOSE TWO SHOT of Jack and Winston.

> WINSTON
> I don't think Matt's statin' his own. He's statin' what you believe, punk.

CLOSE UP of Nadine.

> NADINE
> Yeah, Jack, the punk's sayin' the Lord don't intervene; and yeah, Winston, you'd think he didn't see Senator Goldbladder.

Winston speaks with gravity, studying his beer.

> WINSTON
> Well, I think that Senator Goldbladder put it real well. This country was founded with the help of God and folks had better keep that in mind.

Winston looks at the strange young man with suspicious hostility. The strange young man looks at Nadine with a smile on his face and is playing to her as if to an audience.

                        YOUNG MAN
Some politicians don't live like that was true.

YOUNG MAN grins in triumph.

Winston looks at the young man in angry surprise.

                         WINSTON
Humph! Some liberal politicians. But I believe you'll find that all of them profess belief.

                        YOUNG MAN
                         (*grinning*)
Profess!

CLOSE TWO SHOT of Nadine and Winston looking meaningfully at each other.

                         NADINE
                    (*smiles at strangers*)
You don't?

                        YOUNG MAN
I don't pay attention to it one way or the other. I would like another beer, though.

Young man smiles at Nadine. Nadine looks at Jack. She draws a beer and goes over to the table. She sets the beer down.

                         NADINE
                         (*smiling*)
Where are you all from?

                     1st STRANGE GIRL
Around.

                     2ND STRANGE GIRL
Yeah, we've been everywhere.
                         (*laughs*)

The Compound

                    YOUNG MAN
                     (*grinning*)
  Profess!

CLOSE UP of Matthew.

                    MATTHEW
  I'll bet you have.

The strange young man looks at Matthew, a bit worried about the connotations of that remark.

                     JACK
             (*looks knowingly at Matthew*)
  Amarillo, perhaps.

The girls laugh.

                    YOUNG MAN
  What did you mean by that?

                     JACK
  Oh, nothin'.

Jack gives Nadine and Winston a meaningful look. By now the whole bar is listening.

                    YOUNG MAN
  Look, mister, you don't talk to a lady like that.

                    MATTHEW
         (*looks with hostility at the young man*)
  I don't see no lady.

Jack and Winston laugh loudly.

                    YOUNG MAN
  What's going on here?

                    JACK
                  (*sobers*)
Why don't you *tell* us?

                 YOUNG MAN
Look, mister, I just came in here to drink a beer, I'm trying to be friendly. Shit! I don't want this kind of trouble.

                   NADINE
              (*suddenly hostile*)
Maybe them school children didn't want no trouble either.

                 YOUNG MAN
What?

                  MATTHEW
I think crazy people ought to be killed.

                 YOUNG MAN
Hey! Wait a minute! I don't know who you're talking about, but I guess I came at a bad time.

The young man and the two girls start toward the door.

                    JACK
                  (*laughs*)
You folks ought not to leave so soon.

Two PATRONS block the door.

                 YOUNG MAN
Hey! Now! Wait! This joke's gone far enough. I think maybe everything would be better if you just let us leave.

MEDIUM CLOSE SHOT of Jack.

                    JACK
                 (*knowingly*)
You do, do you?

NADINE
Maybe that's what them children thought.

1ST STRANGE GIRL
(*looking around, near panic*)
Look ma'am, I'm scared. Please don't do this.
(*starts to cry, shaking convulsively*)

YOUNG MAN
Look, people. What is happening? Wake up!

MATTHEW
Looks to me like you should'a waked up a long time ago.

JACK
Freedom's precious.

YOUNG MAN
Are you all crazy?

NADINE
(*meaningfully*)
Are you?

YOUNG MAN
Good God, lady! I'm not doing this! For Christ's sake! What's happening to us?

MATTHEW
If I was you I wouldn't be usin' the Lord's name in vain right now.

Second strange girl becomes hysterical, falling down to a sitting position on the floor, making loud noises that are half crying and half yelling.

YOUNG MAN
Look! Don't you folks have any feelings?

NADINE
We're not the ones that don't believe in God.

                           YOUNG MAN
             Good God! What's that got to do with anything?
Matthew and Jack advance on the three. The young man starts trying to
drag the girl sitting down. He inches, hopelessly, toward the back door.

                            MATTHEW
             Do unto others as you would have them do unto you.

                           YOUNG MAN
                            (*desperately*)
                    Please! Yes! Think about that!

                              JACK
             We ain't no killers!

                                                        DISSOLVE:

INT. RURAL COURTROOM MID-SUMMER—DAY

MEDIUM CLOSE SHOT of Jack, Winston and Nadine sitting behind the defendant's table in the courtroom. Jack and Winston are dressed in cheap, black wool suits. Nadine is dressed in a black cotton dress. Their lawyer, LINCOLN COMSTOCK (nicknamed "Linc") is dressed in an expensive, out of style, dark purple sharkskin suit. Nadine's face is puffy from crying and she occasionally resumes crying. Winston and Jack look in any direction rather than look at the jury or the audience. And they are particularly careful to avoid looking at the witness. The witness is elderly MRS. JOHN BENSON "MAUDE" CLINE, grandmother of the deceased young people (Marshal, Claudia and Georgia Cline) killed in the last scene. Maude is crying, sometimes hysterical, as QUENTIN RAMBAUD, the prosecuting attorney, an older man with thinning gray hair, questions her. She rambles in her grief. MEDIUM CLOSE SHOT of Rambaud.

                            RAMBAUD
             Maude. When did you first discover that the defendants had
             murdered your three loving, young grandchildren at Nadine's tavern?

                              LINC
             Objection, Your Honor!
                            GALLERY
             Shut up!

JUDGE

In this case, Linc, I think we can assume the defendants are murderers. Proceed Mr. Rambaud.

RAMBAUD

Let me rephrase the question.

Maude, when were you first informed that the defendants, at the time engaging in a drunken brawl, illicit sexual activity, and other disgusting and profane acts only to be imagined in a Clyde Pornographia movie, had mutilated, dissected and played in the gore of your sainted, forever lost-to-you, grandchildren.

The young defense lawyer shakes his head in disbelief. The judge laughs. The jury expresses unbelievable anger, revulsion, horror and contempt for the defendants. Nadine screams and falls, sobbing, on the table in front of her. Winston and Jack both begin to cry openly like whimps. Maude Cline straightens up, still crying through the anger, hatred and desire for revenge that shows on her face as she looks at the three defendants.

MAUDE

Your Honor, Wade Forsyte, you know Wade, always such a kind man.
(breaks down crying, regains composure)
He used to give little Marshal, Claudia and Georgia candy when they'd come to his store. Their parents were killed by Claude Thompson in a car wreck, you know. And I, although John was dead and I didn't have no money, took the little things to raise. I can see 'em now, Marshal speakin' for little Claudia and Georgia, tears runnin' down their little faces and their little clothes hangin' wrong on their bodies, sayin' "mamma where's mommy and daddy."
(breaks into uncontrollable grief)

LINC
(in exasperation)

Judge!

GALLERY

Beasts! Bastards!

JUDGE
(*laughing*)
Just tell the story, Maude.
(*sobering*)

JUDGE
Please don't cry, Maude. We all love you and we did so love the little ones.

Maude goes further into hysteria, then, shaking and sobbing, gets control of herself.

MAUDE
As I was sayin', he used to give 'em candy even though he knew we didn't have no money. When he came to the house to tell me about these awful murderers,

MAUDE looks at the defendants —if looks could kill . . .

CAMERA PANS defendants, the gallery and the jury. Linc is shaking his head.

MAUDE
He said how poor little Marshal would stand there in front of the two little girls. He always used to take care of 'em you know. And they'd be lookin' with their pitiful little faces at the purty candy . . .
(*breaks down crying, then gains control*)
How Marshal would speak for the other two, sayin' "Mr. Forsyte, that sure is purty candy." And the other two would be noddin' their little heads. Too proud to beg, you know. I taught 'em . . .
(*breaks down again*)

MEDIUM CLOSE SHOT of jury.

JURY
Electrocution is too good for 'em! Burn 'em! Kill 'em with hot pokers! Torture 'em with cigarettes.

The three defendants break into uncontrolled bawling.

The Compound

NADINE
(*screaming*)
No! No! Oh, please! No!

GALLERY
Shut up! Whore!

JUDGE
(*laughing*)
Now quiet down, or I'll clear the courtroom!

LINC
(*exasperated*)
Judge!

The judge grins.

JUDGE
(*sympathetically*)
Go ahead now, Maude. We know it's hard. Just remember they're in a better place with their mommy and daddy.

Maude straightens up and glares at the defendants.

MAUDE
He told me that whore!

Maude points at Nadine, who falls to the floor writhing and making loud noises in terrible pain.

GALLERY PERSON
(*interrupting*)
Jesus, Judge! She's pissing all over herself!

MAUDE
(*smiling bitterly*)
He told me that whore, and
(*sarcastically*)
her gentleman callers . . . Ain't they a threesome?
(*starts breaking down*)
murdered them three babies what never done a mean thing to nobody.
(*breaks into uncontrollable crying*)

                    JURY
Hang 'em. Burn 'em! Butcher 'em!

                    JUDGE
                   (*laughing*)
Now, now folks. Let's have a small recess 'til you get better control.

                                              DIRECT CUT TO:

EXT. COMPOUND OF NATION OF GOD—NIGHT

LONG SHOT: CAMERA PANS lighted compound. Area flood lights light the compound, complimented by bonfires. CAMERA HOLDS on the flag of the five state Nation of God flapping in the wind, lighted by a flood light. It is a bright yellow Lion of the Tribe of Judah, below five white stars, on a green background. CAMERA PANS the compound, viewing men and women dressed in fatigues, carrying weapons in various states of readiness. SOUND of brass band playing Sousa marches. A large crowd is gathered around a lighted stage. His Highness, Prince of the Aryan Nations, EMANUEL STONE, in full dress gray military uniform, a collection of military medals on his chest, stands in the middle of what appears to be a boxing ring. He is middle aged, overweight and has an impressively handsome face. He holds a microphone in his hand. Willa Kay, scantily clad in what appears to be the pugilistic attire of a female wrestler. Cindy, dressed as a Roman soldier in armor, etc. with bare legs, and Doug, clad only in tights, are in one corner. Jack, Nadine and Winston, dressed in Halloween costumes and wearing masks, are waiting in the other corner. Both groups hold weapons reminiscent of ancient gladiatorial combat and are guarded by men dressed in gray uniforms, carrying submachine guns. CAMERA FEATURES Prince Stone.

                    STONE
In this corner
         (*points with baton to Willa, Doug and Cindy*)
we have the degenerate Jews of militant capitalism.

The CROWD cheers and chants.

                    CROWD
Kill the Jews! Destroy Christ-killers! Bring down the bank!

STONE
In the other corner we have the representatives of faggots, niggers and the corrupt Federal Bureau of Investigation.

CROWD
Dance, Niggers! Cake walk, Faggots! The Lord will bring down the FBI.

STONE
We found these traitors to our people, asleep in the Royal forest, not ten furlongs from each other. They were poaching the King's Royal space. What is their punishment?

CROWD
Let them entertain us!

STONE
We will pit them one against the other. The slave that pleases us most might live. The slave that pleases us least will be delivered like a roast pig to his brothers!

CROWD's low murmurs turn to wild cheers.

STONE
Come, Nigger!
    (*points to Willa, who is in black face*)
Let's dance!

Willa Kay does not move. One of the armed men pushes her into the center of the ring. SOUND of band playing jazz. Willa begins to tap dance.

CROWD
Better! Faster!

STONE
If you value your life, you will please us!

Willa begins to dance erotically as music changes to appropriate tune. Stone points to Winston with the baton.

                    STONE
Come, Jew! On your knees and worship your nigger mistress.
Offer her your jewels!

CROWD laughs and cheers. Winston shakes his head, trying to refuse until one of the guards strikes him in the back with the butt of a weapon. Winston stumbles toward center ring, falling on his knees, his face down, whimpering. CROWD begins to boo this performance. Willa struggles to be more sensuous.

                    STONE
Look up, Jew! To the nigger mama from whence comes thy strength.

CROWD begins to throw garbage, hitting Winston. Winston looks up, tears on his face.

                    STONE
You're not doing well, Jew! How do you expect to survive with this kind of performance?

                    CROWD
Crucify him! Crucify him!

Winston, bawling, puts his hands in prayer under his chin.

                    STONE
Pray to her for your salvation, Jew.

                   WINSTON
Help me! Help me!
CROWD laughs. Stone paces about the ring pointing to them with his baton. CROWD laughs and cheers then, becoming bored, begins to throw garbage.

                    STONE
                (pointing to Nadine)
The FBI must investigate this. What? The Jew wants the Nigger mama to have his children!

A guard pushes Nadine into the ring. She sprawls full length, crying, face down, beside Winston.
CROWD laughs.

Nadine doesn't move. The crowd begins to throw garbage into the ring, hitting Nadine and Winston. Winston grabs her and begins kissing her.

CROWD
More! More!

STONE
Alas! Babylon! Is this the best you can do?

Stone puts up his arms, shrugging in dismay. The audience makes noises of discontent. Stone points to the other two corners of the ring.

STONE
A battle royal before it is too late!

The guards in both corners push Jack, Doug and Cindy into the ring.

STONE
Fight! For the night cometh wherein no man can fight!

CROWD
Deliver them up to us! We will show the FBI Fight! We will show the Jew Fight! We will mutilate the Nigger!

Stone laughs derisively.

STONE
Come you ugly Jews, Faggots and Traitors, strike one another!

He strikes Jack with his baton. Jack strikes Doug, at first hesitantly, then full force. Doug, angered, strikes back furiously.

STONE
Look at the brave communist bastard! Get him, woman!

He strikes Nadine. Nadine attacks Doug from behind.

STONE
What? The FBI is afraid to move?

One of the guards gooses Winston, threateningly, with a gun barrel. Winston, in fear, plunges awkwardly into the melee, flailing at Doug. Willa, seeing Doug attacked by all three, jumps like a tiger onto Winston's back, pounding him on the head. Winston begins to stumble about the ring wailing. The CROWD cheers and starts to throw all kinds of refuse. SOUND of band striking up a march. Cindy tries to run. The crowd grabs her, throwing her back into the ring, jeering: "Coward."

> STONE
>
> An FBI agent has been recognized.
> *(he laughs, the crowd jeers)*
> The scum of the earth is collapsing.

As the band plays, the crowd cheers, the prisoners fight and Stone harangues.

> STONE
>
> Enemies of the people!
> *(he points to the battle royal)*
> Despicable men who are traitors to God's chosen. Niggers and Jews who wish to corrupt the purity of men made in God's image.
> *(points with his baton)*
> Look at the scum of Sodom and Gomorrah! Jew, where is thy money? FBI, where are thy masters?

Stone points to Winston who is still being ridden about by Willa and laughs. The CROWD cheers wildly.

> STONE
>
> The nigger wench is the bravest! See her ride the Jew!

The CROWD cheers and throws things. Stone points to Jack, who is fighting Cindy.

> STONE
>
> See the brave FBI. In the last days they will fight women.

Suddenly a voice, speaking over a loud speaker, breaks up the frenzy.

> VOICE
>
> Oh, brave men made in God's image, lay down your weapons. Give yourselves and the fugitives that you're harboring up. This is your FBI!

The Compound

                    STONE

Never!

A large shell explodes in the compound. The crowd makes a noise of surprise.

                    STONE

Show us your warrants!

A round strikes one of the guards near Stone. They all scramble from the lighted ring, including Stone. Another large shell explodes, flashing, in the compound.

                    CROWD

Oh, my God!

                VOICE OF STONE
              (*coming from the crowd*)

O.K.!

The guards and crowd begin to throw down their weapons.

                 VOICE OF FBI

This is your FBI. We can't hear you.

Another large round explodes, near the crowd, sending some of them sprawling.

                VOICE OF STONE
        (*this time coming from further back in the crowd*)

Please! Let us live!

Another huge round explodes. The crowd, tossed about violently, begins to disperse, panicked, in all directions. They only think of themselves. SOUND of shrieks, cries of terror, women calling out for men, children calling out for their mothers.

                 VOICE OF FBI

We can't hear you!

Another huge round explodes, fires break out. People are being blown up everywhere. The shrieks intensify. People are screaming in pain and terror.

                    VOICE OF FBI
    We can't hear you.

Another shell explodes. Then another, until there is complete silence.

                    VOICE OF FBI
    We can't hear you.

                                                    DISSOLVE:

            THE END

Biographical Note

Robert Reid is a short story writer, an essayist and a playwright. He has published in *The Literary Journal of Long Island University, Eratica, Poems and Plays, International Third World Studies Journal and Review, American Culture and Literature, The Prague Revue, the Southern Quarterly, the CLA Journal, The Literary Journal of The National Cheng Kung,* and the *Potomac Review.* His short fiction has been published in two former releases by Red Hen Press including *The Crucifix is Down* and *Fake City Symptom: American Cultural Essays*. Over the course of his career Reid has taught at Tennessee Wesleyan College, Bilkent University in Turkey, King Saud University in Saudi Arabia, The University of Guam and the University of Kentucky. He lives in Al-Ain and works at the United Arab Emirates University. Through his extensive experience, working with many types of people throughout the world, Reid believes that "the conflict in the human heart" is the means to rise above divisive anger, hatred and denial to the realization of a living world community.